Praise for the Book

"The warts and wackiness of Corona's litscapes mirrored masterfully through the lens of subtle satire and wit in Chetna Keer's book. Prose, that is poignant and part prayer, threaded as much with a vocabulary of invincible hope as *ibaadat*. The perfect tonic to drive away the Pandemic's blues."

—Commander R.K. Sharma (Retd)

"Chetna's sharp observation and wit delight and tickle the readers. Her creative use of language and expressions lend her a unique writing voice that is scarcely seen in the Indian literary circuit. With a host of interesting and relatable characters, she creates a world that entertains, informs and reflects the modern-day society. The body of work she has created has firmly established her as a recognisable name in Indian humour writing."

—Sajita Nair, *Author*

"Reminiscent of Miguel de Cervante's *Don Quixote,* this is a racy literary saga that tickles one no end. A comic tale of the misadventures of fab fortyish, small-town writer Lollita, dreaming of making it big to the elusive B-List, and her lit agent Lamba ji, as they navigate the cataclysmic Corona-scape. A message of humour and hope in these dark times. Chetna Keer does a great job."

—Lippi Parida, *Author & Artist*

"Brilliantly poetic in its prose, the book captures one's imagination and paints a picture of life in India as it is today (very different to what it was in 1987, when I left India). It is as sad as it is funny and goes into the psyche of anyone who wants to make it big as a writer. A brilliant read that keeps one on edge to hear what happens next!"

—Parminder Irvine, aka 'Pari' ma'am,
Former English teacher, Carmel Convent, Chandigarh

"A riotous parade of Litfest luminaries lace the rollicking narrative. Best not to dip into Lollita & Lamba ji's antics publicly, guffaws could invite stares!"

—**Indu Balachandran,** *Author*

Happy meeting
PANDEMIC's PEOPLE
like you & me!
Chetna K.

Giddha On My Gulmohar

CHETNA KEER

Readomania

Readomania
An imprint of Kurious Kind Media Private Limited
readomania.com
email: contact@readomania.com
Facebook: facebook.com/iamreadomania
Twitter: twitter.com/iamreadomania
Instagram: iamreadomania

First Published in 2022 by Readomania

This book is a work of fiction. Any resemblance to real persons, living or dead, or actual events or locations, is purely coincidental.

ISBN: 978-93-91800-21-5

Typeset in Palatino Linotype by Shine Graphics
Printed in Delhi

To the eternal Ittar in my Rose

GURUJI

The 'Maha Shiva'

whose

LIGHT Unlimited & Unfiltered

in these darkest of times

tosses Life

Sunny Side Up

Foreword

No other incident has impacted mankind in the last five millennia as the outbreak of the Covid19 pandemic. Chetna Keer is a writer who, in her own characteristic style, paints a literary portrait of this lockdown and eventual unlockdown. The result is this riveting book of fiction that keeps the reader in her firm grip right from the word go to the last word.

Satire is not the cup of tea for most writers. Chetna has that innate ability to make the reader smile, if not laugh, as she rummages through her words that flow like the mighty Ganga in spate. She achieves this without in any way making the serious flippant or the profound profane.

I have known Chetna since the day I joined *The Tribune* in 2003 where she had already established a reputation as the best headline or caption giver. In my heart of hearts, I knew that she had the mettle to strike off on her own in the wondrous world of fiction. I was not disappointed or saddened when she left the comforts of *The Tribune,* for I knew that it signified a new innings as a full-time writer.

Her column 'Witerati' in the Chandigarh edition of the *Hindustan Times* is an eye-opener, for it reveals how effortlessly but effectively she lampoons the big and the beautiful, the mighty and the meek, to emerge as one of the top humourists of the country. What makes a writer great is her ability to observe and learn, and to use these observations to give a realistic content while not letting down her imagination. It is not just Katrina Kaif's tempting waistline or (Shashi's) Tharoorisms that attract her attention.

She is able to present a totally imaginative Peacock Lane where Lollita arrives in style.

It is said that everyone can write one novel, culled from their own life experiences. I am sure that anyone who starts reading this book will find it unputdownable for the sheer beauty of her words and thoughts.

Chetna can find satisfaction in the thought that she has written a book that not only promises but also fulfils.

A.J. Philip

Former Senior Associate Editor of *The Tribune*;
former Chief Executive of leading NGO, Deepalaya

"The wound

is the place where

LIGHT

enters you."

—RUMI

1

The Curious Case of a Pink Jacket

Somewhere in the suburbs of Gurugram

Lollita let out a long, soulful sigh that unsettled and tickled her Trishul nose-stud into opening its Eye. Lollita's kohl-smudged eyes looked through the lens that was her fettered French window. Arresting her gaze was the grand Gulmohar, frilled in full-blooded feistiness, a blood-thirsty redness, as Spring gasped for breath and sighed its last in the blazing arms of this harshest and hungriest of summer.

Lollita was hard put to fathom what it was that the contact lenses of her mind's eye were staring at. Was this the most unforgiving of Summer swallowing the most unsuspecting and unarmed Spring of hope? Was this the uncommonest of times for the commonest of dreams?

The asymmetrical attractiveness of Lollita's face was plastered with the pallor of a peculiar paste. The smallness of her elfin ears was suffering a sensory overload from an orchestra of shrillness emanating from the heart of the house. The unmanicured unkemptness of her tapering fingers toiled away at her Work In Progress on the ThinkPad, between bouts of her battery recharging she basked in through the sheer curtains of day dreaminess.

Driving her daydreaming in these digital times, defined by Bucket Lists, Big Basket Lists, or Big Bazaar Lists to Swiggy-Zomato wishlists and such sundry business-of-living inanities, were more of surreal lists.

The elusive B-Lists.

Perched near Lollita, upon the condo's caged windowsill, her queen cat, 'Bholi Punjabban', aka Iraa Singh, peered curiously at a creature, resplendent in royal plumage, prancing on the Gulmohar. This solitary summer tree's bejewelled boughs, brimming forth crimson couture from between their condo's concrete high-rises, looked like Tabasco oozing out of a Subway sandwich.

Bholi Punjabban's cocked calico ears and piercing pear-green pupils were all agog at who was this majestic migrant gambolling upon the Gulmohar. Her snooty nose sniffed the air as if to ascertain why no neighbourhood folks were trooping out to toss the customary grains under the gigantic Gulmohar, why there were scarcely any pigeons promenading near their patio for her to long and lust after.

Wafting towards the windowpane, filtering the ferocity of fear outside and the sun, was a decibel-ism that made Lollita reflect at the peculiar paradox. What was it that the feather-fragile filters of her senses and sensibilities were finding more unsettling—the squeaking on the small screen or the silently stifling stranglehold of this unprecedented season?

A voice on the Idiot Box dripped swag as much as swagger. It caterwauled with war-like emergency on one of the channels which made up the Theatre of the Absurd that was *tamasha* TV.

"Black Friday...Black Friday...We have a new enemy... Black Fungus!" the bloke babbled out the Breaking News.

On another channel, another voice prattled. Much in the manner of a rapper Himesh Reshammiya or Honey Singh ululating to higher octaves, stuck and stranded there, unable to lull the lungs to a lower pitch. The only difference, this particular piercing vocal cord was not rapping, it was rasping.

"The Nation wants to know... Will we flatten the curve? The Nation wants to know...when can we flatten the curve?"

Unsettled by this 'Flatten the Curve' telly narrative, she shifted self-consciously on the EMI-funded extravagance that was her chic chaise lounge. Lollita's right hand unwittingly inched guiltily to an alarming curve. It strayed and stayed for a second, subconsciously stroking this curve's convexity.

The mid-anatomical curve as convex as an idli fluffing up to bloatedness. Disquieted and disconcerted, Lollita's hand hastily twitched back towards her ThinkPad.

"Fatten the Curve, sounds more like it," she mumbled, sinking into the cushiness of the chaise lounge. Her hand, too, plunged, dipping into her comfort food—Aloo Bhujia—an excess of which could partly be blamed for the protuberance popping above her pyjamas.

"Enough of this jibber-jabber about 'Flatten the Curve', better treat myself to the newest on Netflix!" Lollita pledged purposefully as she patted her plastered face that was now pricking. The pale paste had dried up and resembled a parched Mother Earth whose skin, in a horribly harsh summer, creases into a crowdedness of cracks. The oxidised, 'Trishul' nose-stud, the flag-bearer on the landscape that was her asymmetrically alluring face, was bestirred by this air of determination bouncing out of her nostrils. It quivered into the 'Chali' dance mudra.

Lollita reached out for the television remote on her mantlepiece. The sudden sweep of her hand unsettled a piece of her framed Past. It crashed into the encroaching paraphernalia from the Present.

A mahogany mantlepiece. An intricate ivory inlay-work antique chest of drawers, a Hoshiarpur-crafted heirloom of haveli living from her great-grandmother. A solid legacy, but heavy to shoulder. An asymmetrical ornate oddity, tottering on its last legs with one wobbly taped-up limb, in an apartment dressed in the minimalism of modern condo living.

A mantlepiece that was a monument to gilt-edged milestones, filtered through memory's maple leaves mapping faded seasons, making up the four decades of her lifetime. Portraits from a golden childhood with parents long since gone, a giggly girlhood of them three siblings in polka-dotted and pig-tailed chubbiness long since outgrown. Frames that clocked the growing up from girlhood to a yummy mummy-hood. Of cradling her son to adulthood. Frames that were Canon chroniclers of loves lost. Of happier times with her former spouse.

A mantlepiece that was a miniature museum crowded with curios and collectibles culled from crafts fairs.

With one sweeping stroke, the face of the mantlepiece had metamorphosed when an uninvited guest had knocked on their doors.

Move over, memorabilia. Move in, new must-haves.

Standing as sentinels on the frontiers of the mantlepiece now were New Normal's impersonal safeguard souvenirs—sanitiser bottles and safety masks.

A mantlepiece makeover emblematic of the times.

Lollita snapped shut the negativity on *tamasha* TV and called up her Netflix Encyclopaedia 1. Her goddaughter-niece Kaavya, the teenaged offspring of her younger sister, Radhyaa.

"Hey sweetie pie, wassup?" Lollita's voice dripped saccharine sweetness like syrup pouring over a perfectly done pancake. "What was that new flick of the Holmes chap you were watching last week?

"Awww, Maasi, it's not a chap, it's a chick," Kaavya chirruped.

"Chick?" Lollita sounded at sea.

"Enola Holmes!" pat came Kaavya's reply. "Maasi, can I chat up later, please? I'm in the middle of watching the *F.R.I.E.N.D.S.* reunion." Kaavya signed off, as Radhyaa then took over the conversation and chatted a bit.

Next, Lollita called her Netflixing Encyclopaedia 2, elder sister Meera Di, aka Meeraya (named after Meera Bai for being besotted from babyhood with the blue-skinned God, Krishna).

"Di, how's that latest Kangana flick just released on OTT?" Lollita asked, all agog for the Netflixing 'breaking news' from her IIM-A alumnus sister.

"*Thalaivii*," Meera Di said and delivered her verdict, "A must-watch!"

Lollita's carpal tendons twiddled to migrate, from Netflix to YouTube, to first browse *Thalaivii* curtain-raiser clips.

Only to stumble not on a reel political diva, but a real B-town diva.

Bholi Punjabban purred at the plumed pageantry beyond the window. Lollita was all agog and awestruck at the plumage of B-town socialite birds unfolding on Windows. For, what had popped up instead of *Thalaivii* teasers was a clip of a bygone Bollywood bash.

The video clip unveiled that amid all the commotion and cacophony of B-town's glitterati rubbing shoulders in shimmery gowns, to pose 'n' preen for the Paps, taking centrestage was an object of desire. It made this event look a shade apart from the regular red-carpet galas—the Show Stopper.

Ms Purple Pout, with her bulbous bumble-bee lips reminding of an oversized pea pod, popped her streaked scalp bang next to the object of desire for the Paps so selfie-consciously that she treaded on the touchy ego as much as toes, boasting brand new pink socks, of Mr Chai Chai Chatshow. Mr Pink Pants, bright like a beetroot that's just come out squeaky clean from a fruity facial, craned his long arms to touch the object of desire. In doing so, he almost dislodged the dapper black hat of Mr Wardrobe Malfunction. The latter's green, printed jumpsuit, imbuing him a poetic resemblance to an elongated jackfruit mistakenly sporting a brinjal crown, almost did a detachment at the derriere seams as he darted down to retrieve his dismantled headgear. Mr Brattish Bachelor Boy, looking like a Chocolate Brownie meets Bavarian Cream Donut, kept clinging less to the object of desire centrestage and more to the latest among his arm candies, who far outnumbered the number of his hits at the box office.

Ms Socialite Stylista struck such a pose that half the Paps got diverted, thinking it was her red carpet event. . .until. . .a million Paparazzi flashbulbs popped to catch the solitaire-ringed manicured hands caressingly circling round the object of desire, showcasing up close and personal a breath-taking, blow-dried Bollywood diva—the Mademoiselle of the Moment. Bholi Punjabban erupted into a pronounced purring of delight. The parade of other plumed visitors had flapped away. The majestic migrant, lording it on the lap of the Gulmohar, unveiled its face towards the fettered French window. Ballerina of a Bird!

Lollita's eyeballs danced with bated breath upon her Windows screen.

Amid the popping of a zillion zooms, pouting of a trillion tinsel town teeth whose polished enamel and gold-studded molar pockets had enriched the pockets of a million orthodontists, and the preening of a billion botoxed pouts that had made the gold pile of cosmetologists look as big as an inverted beehive, there was launched the Show Stopper—the Pink Paper Jacket.

Lollita goggled and gasped: "Wow, what a Bollywood-esque way to be born—for a 'Bestseller'!"

This Botoxed Bibliophile-ism Meets Bollywood razzmatazz was the rainbow-tinted lens refracting and reigniting Small Town India's Big Dream driving Lollita—making it to the Million Copies' Club powered by a Bollywood-esque ride down the red carpet with her *Wannabe Bestseller*.

This was the gilt-edged gossamer grandeur framing and feeding middle-class Lollita's day dreaming— the commonest aspiration of arriving in A-list Author-hood riding the B-list.

Until uninvited along came the uncommonest Party Pooper or Game Changer—Lockdown 1.0.

2

The Curious Case of Not Too Late to be a Late Bloomer

"Uff, why did life have to dish out its lemons just now? Why did Lockdown have to bolt life's doors...just when it was time for my 'baby'...?" sighed Lollita.

The star-studded spectacle of the birth of the Pink Book Jacket over wine and cheese presided over by the crème de la crème, had bestirred in Lollita's bosom befuddled emotions about those very life's lemons and lemonades we spoke of, dear discerning reader, lest you think all that was piffle.

Ironically, it had bestirred mixed feelings. Conflicting emotions that embodied a paradox. As Lollita's eyeballs had soaked in the star-studded spectacle, one part of her had been dazed, while another part of her had gazed, in wonderment: what would her iconic Poster Girls of Prose—Dames Agatha, Austen or Du Maurier—have said if their books had been born in times of these literati glitterati galas?

For Lollita, Lockdown life broadly translated into two things. Firstly, that Lollita couldn't go for her weekend trips to her favourite book café where she caught up with her BFF (Best Friends Forever) bunch back home, or to her #ThankGodItsFriday meetings of their comedy club, or, most importantly, to her kitschy oases of cultural exotica—Dilli Haat or Saturday Night Bazaar.

Secondly, Lockdown meant she was caged in the claustrophobic confines of the concrete jungle called condo life, somewhere in the suburbs of cyber city Gurugram. Where she was a bit like fish out of water, as it was a metropolis where she didn't really belong and where she shuttled to and fro for the sake of her son.

Where the one thing as fancy as the sky-rocketing cost of living was the faddish nomenclature bestowed upon the housing skyrises.

Orchid Isles.

This fancily named suburb boasted everything from Ashokas to Amaltas and Gulmohars to Gerberas in the name of fauna, but nary a sign of Orchids. Nor was this slice of suburbia positioned on a picturesque Lonely Planet-listed island, to lay claims to the latter half of its nomenclature.

More of Lollita's laments later, dear reader, first it would be but befitting to give a glimpse of the *dream* that had lately been consuming her, the *dream* that she had been living... breathing...or feeding upon.

Lollita, aka Laasyanga Mansingh (dear reader, if you could but stay possessed with patience, the story of how she earned the moniker 'Lollita' shall reveal itself a tad later in the book), the columnist-cum-content writer, Obsessive OTT and Online Shopping Surfer, Netflix-aholic, Saree-aholic, part-time poet and devotee of Rumi poetry, and single yummy mummy to a college-going brat, dreamt of doing at least one of these two things before she dropped dead (a fear magnified manifold by the new killer called Corona, considering her life policies were taken out at a time when dropping dead from a malignant microbe was considered as remote as Tuscany is from Timbuktu).

Dream One: Upon foraying into the Fab Forties, to churn out that one million-copy selling masterpiece—*The Wannabe Bestseller*—whose dream Bollywood-like star-studded launch would further be her ticket to navigating the red carpet of big-league author-hood—Bestseller-hood. Or if Dame Luck was in terribly high spirits and even a tad tipsy to dish out largesse, then it was Lollita's secret dream to hit that ultimate literary jackpot—the Booker—which, even at the height of Lollita's wishful day-dreaming, tinged with realism, translated into bagging not the Booker, but at least booking a berth in the Booker Long List.

The only B-lists that were thus surreal enough to be on Lollita's Wishlist. Bestseller List. Booker List.

Or a Consolation Wishlist. Made up of their Long List, Short List or Mid List. That was the Long and Short of her day dreaming.

Dream Two: Talking of jackpots, Lollita's second secret dream entailed winning the jackpot on game show *Kaun Banega Crorepati*. Her dream to make it to its hot seat was driven not so much by that selfie moment with Big B, aka Amitabh Bachchan, but by a burning desire to unveil a bit of Bollywood in her, by breaking into copious histrionics (oops, hysterics) the way many a Miss India Universe or Miss World were wont to erupt into the moment, amid a zillion bated breaths and a million facial muscles itching to contort, the winner was announced.

This dream was driven essentially by a bit of pragmatism. If Dame Luck indeed happened to be in high spirits and propelled her to pocket the seven-crore *KBC* jackpot, other than it bestowing upon her the luxury of paying her bills without plodding at a penny's worth of work for many, many months, Lollita would be able to kill two birds with a stone—she could not only upgrade her couture collection of sarees by adding coveted Chanderis, Kanthas, and Banarsis from her Wishlist Longlist to her already crowded closet, but also drive her Dream One. Ah well, it didn't take rocket science or a PhD in Maths to figure out the numbers game—that if only Lollita could bag that more than a million bucks, on *KBC*, she could jolly well herself buy a million copies of her *Wannabe Bestseller* and propel it to top of the bestseller charts!

(Alas, Dream Two had trundled not towards the hot seat but had taken a temporary backseat, since tidings trickled in of the Big B coming in the clutches of the Corona virus.)

Coming back to Dream One, it came with a catch, there was a timeline to it—5 Bestsellers before 50.

At least.

Blame Dream One on many a bestselling Dame—Toni Morrison, Mary Wesley, JK Rowling and others. If late bloomers Toni, Rowling & Co, or closer home, mid-life or post-midlife writing's poster girls Shobhaa De & Co, could churn out award-winning works or bestsellers in middlescence, cocking a snook at ageism, why couldn't Lollita?

At her age (which we must reveal at this point of time, dear discerning reader, as her having forayed into the forties), you weren't really spoilt for choices as far as the Fifteen Minutes of Fame from writing went. The forties were the crossroads between making it big in one of the two 'Bs'.

If one did not make it to the league of 'Bestselling' Writers even in middle age, then perhaps the only other fate that awaited one was to die unsung as the other kind of 'B' writer—Blog Writer.

If you didn't write books that everyone reads because they adorn the bestseller shelves or trolleys at big bookstore brands, your fate as a full-time writer was shelved and you were destined to die having had a dalliance only with author-hood's poor country cousin, the other B—Blogging. This usually meant that you penned blogs that no one really read or even heard of, except perhaps BFFs bullied into reading you or poor pets bored into listening when you ended up reading aloud your blogs, to who else but yourself.

Now a bit about the death of some of her dreams—#DashedDreams.

#DashedDreams 1: Dream Three that was dealt a death blow by Dame Luck was writing a lifestyle column as fabled as the fictitious one by Carrie Bradshaw (*Sex and the City*, essayed by Sarah Jessica Parker) or a satire column that would become as irreverent and immortal as Khushwant Singh's 'Malice Towards One And All' such that it would be syndicated in dailies across the country (secretly she had dreamt of even bigger breaks than 'KS' by making it to global syndicated columns).

Alas, the only closeness she had achieved to KS's 'Malice…' was inviting the malice of many an Editor or Op-ed page Pasha who'd treated her submissions less suitable for syndication, more suitable for spam.

#DashedDreams 2: Dream Four that Dame Luck had brushed under the carpet was that there had thus far been no literary red carpet for Lollita by the time she trundled into the fab forties, simply because she had been lending a hand to other writers for putting their best foot forward on the literary red carpet. And how!

What this translated into was that Dame Luck had thus far assigned her writing roles that brought name or fame to others more than her—roles such as using her writing skills more to churn out content for web magazines and websites (content writer); writing forewords for the books of BFFs and buddies who were the ones racing towards bestseller lists, not her; and to top it all, rewriting or ghost writing the book of a European author (in her role as a manuscript re-writer) so that he could hopefully make it to the Man Booker while all she got in the process was to earn enough Euros to make both ends meet or maybe also travel in the future. (It's another story, that one of the other factors that had propelled her to plod in her precious time on the script of this Irish professor-turned-author was his surname, which carried a ring of resonance with Lollita's own maiden suffix in the light of the fact that her Naani Maa had once spilled the beans that they had an Irish descent on the maternal side.)

Thus, it was carrying on her middle-aged, exotic saree-swathed shoulders the first two dreams, despite Dame Fate's decided disfavour towards her, that Lollita had lunged her 5′5″, wheatish-bronze skinned, and pleasantly plump frame into the fab forties. (Ah, but befitting to mention here, dear reader, that Lollita quite upset the 'gori Punjabban' stereotype by not boasting a peaches 'n' cream complexion like most of her siblings and cousins, and the blame for this went to an unsuspecting, unseasonal fruit. For, Lollita's Ammi ji (paternal grandmother), in keeping with the robust diet of regressive folk myths she'd been fed upon, never let Lollita's dad forget nor forgave him for pandering to and pampering her pregnant mother with generous helpings, through all trimesters, of that purplish-blackish monsoon season fruit—jamuns!)

Lollita thus manifested herself to be manoeuvring middlescence not by straddling six-inch stilettoes but Bata floaters for a bad back, which in a way was a grim reminder that you can't turn the clock back.

As a writer-in-waiting-for-a-bestseller, when she was not writing, she was twiddling on touchscreens for a twin exercise, doing a double workout for her carpal tendons on the two hottest digital stages—OTT and Online Shopping.

The way most writers of the old school collect pens, Lollita had this pen-chant for collecting ethnic exotica—as symbolised by six yards of wondrous weaves from nooks and crannies of the country. This fascination, fuelled as well as fulfilled online, fashioned her into that incorrigible species—Saree e-Shopaholic.

It was a matter of speculation, what did her shelves have more of—Wodehouse or Weaves of India. Between themselves, the shelves of her late parents' cosy cottage in the Kansal suburbs of her hometown Chandigarh (from where she travelled back and forth in between her work projects to be with her son in the national Capital) had a border dispute over making space for her wonders. Wodehousian versus Weaves.

"Hey love, I'm gonna beg, borrow or steal your Kasavus for my next Onam hashtag," Sabrina, the leading saree blogger from the South, often alerted her.

Seconding her was Jyothy Misra, an intelligence officer and saree connoisseur, "Watch out, dear, intelligence reports tell me you house an undisclosed wealth of Kanjees and Kanthas!"

"Darling, are you aspiring to be the Imelda Marcos of saree shopaholic-ism?" Rasikaa Singh, the corporate czarina chum had once gushed and goggled awestruck at her choc-a-bloc closet showcasing sarees.

"Awww, if only I had half the storage space gobbled by your sarees for my Punjabi juttis and mojris," Raagini Singh Chandel (or 'Rags'), the erstwhile royalty among her BFF bunch, often teased her enviously.

"Hey sweetie, before the *Limca Book of Records* gets to your collection, I better steal your Banarsis for our Bollywood nights back home, in Melbourne," her childhood chum, Amaiyraa Sharma Khanna, had jested, winking at her daughter Azraa, on one of their India trips.

Lollita's quirkiness didn't end with collecting weaves from all corners of the country, off the shelf or online.

She showcased some piece of her six yards daily, such that even if she was not stepping out of the house, she would still pull out of the closet for airing, a saree of the day—#sotd.

How she longed to leg it to her favourite saree stores, to feel the featheriness of fabrics between her fingers, before splurging on the showstopper among them. Alas, with Lockdown bolting life's doors, it would be long before she would be able to gallivant off for her saree travels.

Instead, that morning, she found herself in the throes of travel of another type. For, even in Quarantine's time of zero travel, the YouTube clip about the Bollywood-like birth of the Pink Book Jacket had propelled her on a different trip—guilt trip.

Gnawing guilt at letting her Work In Progress—*Wannabe Bestseller*—lie around unattended and unfinished. She had been given three months to complete her manuscript, yet she had been sitting over it. Simply because she was spending most of her time doing the other sort of sitting—New Normal's Netflixing Couch Potato.

But now she had been bestirred by that Show Stopper of a Pink Jacket. It had suddenly lifted the mist of writer's block that had for days been shrouding her grey cells. Her 'baby' was waiting to be born....

Nothing was going to stop her baby from being born. Never mind if she was huffing and puffing to attain literary puberty at an age when her biological clock was ticking and tearing towards speed-breakers like mid-life blues, pre-menopause and all that.

Nothing was going to stop her ride down Lit-scape's red carpet, neither unpredictable hormones, nor an uninvited virus.

#LifesLemonsIntoLemonade. As Lollita set about that morning, to turn Lockdown into the proverbial Lemonade, a blessing in disguise, to plod at and propel her literary Work In Progress to completion, Life smiled mischievously at her window.

Would Lollita be able to squeeze up Life's lemons into Lemonade or was Life eyeing even her Lemonade to toss in more lemons?

BEFORE CORONA

"What you seek,

is seeking you."

—RUMI

3

The Curious Case of Malba on My Manuscript

Somewhere in NCR

Lollita disgorged daintily from a middle-aged Ola cab, wrapped in her crisp Kasavu saree. Its gaily emblazoned Kuthampully pallu floated about like a prayer flag at Mount Kailash sniffing the air in uncertain climate, of geo-polity or ground reality. The pallu's painted parade of palanquins and caparisoned elephants perhaps the only resplendent cavalcade on this landscape.

A landscape where other than this stray Ola, there popped up another stray element. A stray creature synonymous with the bylanes and backyards of Incredible India and its Photoshop-packaged Oriental totemhood. A stray cow.

Lollita's Bata-encased feet skirted the stray elements to plunge forth into the mouth of a clogged and cramped alley. A blithe and bubbly stream being discharged into the subterranean sleepiness of a narrow canal nestling in the back of beyond.

The cab had navigated a maze of miniscule bylanes, to lapse into cliché-ism, slimmer than Katrina or Kareena's waist, to deposit Lollita at this narrowest of narrow alley.

Heck, maybe even a Katrina or Kareena's waist wasn't this narrow!

The resemblance ended there, with only its narrowness akin to tiny tinsel town waists. The face of this literary landscape was far removed from the peaches-and-cream complexions of beatific babes. It bore more resemblance to the freckled face of a teeny-bopper, where pimples popping from every pore present an eyesore.

Lollita's legging it into this landscape had been paved by a common friend who had connected her to a commissioning editor of a traditional establishment. The editor, out of deference for the common friend, had acquiesced for an audience. Not a favour easily granted, being as rare as the blue moon.

At the mouth of the alley tentatively tottered this Wannabe Bestselling Author, armed with a folder that was a repository of relics from a published past as much as pennings for her hopeful future—the *Wannabe Bestseller*. Lollita stared ahead at what was the backyard of one of Delhi's plush neighbourhoods. Panchsheel Park.

"Gosh!"

Lollita's legs had skirted the stray cow only to land now in a pothole.

A pedigreed presence ploughing through the potholes of the publishing world.

What on the face of it looked like the back of beyond was, in reality, the new hot and happening home to many of publishing's Movers and Shakers.

Shahpur Jat.

The relocated pocket of the publishing industry camouflaged in the backyard by the sheer-curtained sophistication or snobbery of plush Panchsheel Park. The way avenues of Amaltas or Aparajita, with their frilly façade of flora, may veil from view not only sprouting shrubbery but also the unkemptness of undergrowth.

Lollita inched ahead into this emerging publishing and fashion hub, now popularly known as the 'poor man's Hauz Khas Village' (HKV). A lower-cost version of that elitist artistic haven where, one by one, fashion designers, artisans, design studios, publishers, and book cafes had been relocating. She had arrived at *THE* destination.

Peacock Lane.

Where pockets of e-pub or self-pub may fast be swallowing chunks of the conventional publishing pie, like a quicker, ready-to-make MTR poha or upma munching into the traditional snack's market share.

Where stray, staid-looking country cousins of publishing biggies stand studded in the part residential concrete-scape. Their signboards peeping out of the grey façade like stray advertisement hoardings unexpectedly popping up on a deserted terrain. Their faces resembling those of de-glam models strewn far from the Showstoppers, at the fag-end of a fashion catwalk.

On a weekday morning, Peacock Lane bespeaks a strange silence.

A resounding silence.

A restless silence.

A deceptive silence.

A silence akin to that of a cat, like that of Lollita's own queen cat, Bholi Punjabban, ostensibly in siesta mode. Come the footfall of a pigeon or a sparrow, and the slumbering cat cocks its ears into alertness. Poised to pounce into action. So does sluggish Peacock Lane spring to bustling busyness, come the footfalls of its parade of publishing gentry or visiting citizenry.

It was through the Peacock Lane of this new publishing address on the country's literary radar that Lollita threaded her way, legging it gingerly on Bata wedges that were proving misfits in this crammed and clogged back lane. Clogged not just with low-budget DDA housing, packed into constricted space like a Maharaja Mac burger stuffed into a micro cheese puff carton, but choked also by the cartful of *malba* (boulders) at its mouth that made ploughing through it an uphill task.

It was a landscape into which many a dream script of a Wannabe Author had travelled, only to either never have made it to the table or eyeballs of a book editor or to have breathed its last upon the first sentence itself, being perused by a prospective publisher whose eyeballs at that moment may have been more engaged in tweeting titles trudging up bestseller charts or in scanning social media to see how many rival publishing house authors had made it to the recent JLF.

Peacock Lane. The path that, Lollita hoped, could pave her ride down the red carpet to bestsellerhood.

The lane where seats of conventional publishing collided with the new blood of digital publishing and self-publishing.

Oops!

Lollita found her middle-class Bata footwear colliding into the mound of *malba*. Before she knew, this collision saw the folder with the manuscript flying out of her hands and landing face down on the *malba*. This bore an uncanny resemblance to a prostration the pious end up doing when they're knocked unceremoniously down in all the shoving at a shrine.

The stray cow pottering closeby peered up and mooed with empathy. As if it knew what it meant not to be enshrined, to be straying hither-thither.

Lollita pronto plucked up her script, lest it breathe its last in the gargantuan grazing arms of a heapful of boulders.

Was this perchance an omen?

Gingerly gambolling forward, she spotted signboards punctuating the crammed housing, peeping out to proclaim that therein lay tucked a party that still made traditional publishing its business. In these challenging times of e-books and digital publishing, when profits from printed books may have been plummeting though, paradoxically, Lit Agents and Litfests looked to be mushrooming. As fast and furious as measles mapping out on a vulnerable visage.

It was through the cantankerous, narrowly ajar grilled door of one such establishment that Lollita's pleasantly plump, fortyish frame squeezed forth around mid-morning in the mid-week of the winter Before Corona.

Stepping into the dark and dingy stairway that dispelled all images of publishers presiding over plush grandeur, her foremost feeling was of foraying into the fortress of a moneylender or a stock broker, who subsisted on selling dreams of turning the middle class into multi-millionaires overnight.

As she plodded up the publishing den, the initial impression was immediately overshadowed. A niggling familiar feeling crept up behind her. The same edginess, which swallowed her whenever she scrambled up the stairway to that dreaded destination—the dental clinic.

She trundled up to the reception desk and asked to meet the commissioning editor with whom she had an appointment. She was ushered into the conference room and as she waited—dabbing her brow with Kleenex wet wipes, to get her breath back as much as her morale—she noticed stacks and stacks standing in a corner of the hall. These were brand new piles of bundled books, issuing forth the fresh smell of ink on paper that gave the conference chamber the look of doubling up as a sort of glamorous godown.

"Good morning," breezed in the voice of Commissioning Editor, Chaitali Sengupta, "Hmmm...so tell me?"

"Hi, thanks for your time. Some great titles you've come out with...," Lollita dished out an ice-breaker.

'Ya, we just launched Ashwamedh Sanghi's latest mythology title last month which is already topping the Amazon bestseller list," Chaitali reeled off some fancy figures of how the book was already close to selling half a million copies.

Lollita lapsed into a reverie, day dreaming about such fancy figures being cited one day for her *Wannabe Bestseller*.

If you can, dear reader, picture a novice cricketer, prior to perambulating into the pavilion, day dreaming about seeing his maiden runs flashing and flickering on the scoreboard in king-size neon iridescence, powered by mega brands and mega bucks, you'll sort of sense the sentiments suffusing Lollita's bounteous bosom at that moment.

"So, about your script...," Chaitali said knitting her brow in contemplation.

Every time Chaitali's brow knitted in thought, it sent her thin arched eyebrows on a mountaineering expedition to salute the sindoor emblazoning the parting of her dark hair, knotted into a casual bun. Eyebrows as arched as the doorways dotting and defining the forts of Mughal architecture.

"Yes, yes, have you seen it?" Lollita snapped out of her reverie, back to ground reality, trepidation dripping from her face as much as voice, much the way a wannabe starlet aspiring to make it big in Bollywood sounds post an audition.

"Well..." Chaitali left the word hanging in the air, as her brows knitted and plunged in pensive perusal of the manuscript before her. Pencilled outlines of Mughal archways in danger of dilapidation.

Lollita was consumed by the feeling that she was in the clinic of her dentist.

Now, the thing with 'well' when it prefixes a statement is that it comes loaded with lots of possibilities that may be conveyed through the intonation with which the prefix 'well' is delivered.

If the 'well' is delivered with a dilation of pupils that sends the brow un-knitting itself into a beaming, with eyebrows darting off on an excursion northwards, in a curious combination of convexity and circularity, like an idli puffing up in the idli-maker, then it may augur that pleasant tidings are on their way to dissemination.

If the prefix 'well' is uttered to the accompaniment of a deeper knitting of the said brows that scurry on a southward expedition this time, the eyebrows collapsing into a concavity, flattening like an idli batter gone wrong, and the lips are pursed in a tautness like a cling film being tightened over packed goodies, then it heralds the delivery of not too delightful tidings.

The thing with Chaitali's 'well' was that it was sending out mixed signals, which was borne out in the course of the conversation.

"Well...we've gone through your sample chapters. Your style is good...it's racy like our bestselling Bollywood author Taarika Khambatta's..."

These words made Lollita puff up much like a robust idli herself. Lollita's nostrils, too, responded to the air of anticipation, with her Trishul nosestud perking up into a 'Chaalibada' jollification mudra.

"Really, you think so!" she beamed from side to side, like a dental patient who, for a fraction of a minute, forgets the future flossing or fleecing at the hands of the orthodontist. And beams beatifically into the mirror at the mere prospect of getting a new smile.

"But...," Chaitali paused again.

Lollita again noticed Chaitali's eyebrows travel afresh in salutation towards the sindoor mapping the partition of her knotted hair. The pencilled imitations of Mughal archways on an annexation of the North.

She waited with bated breath for what was coming next.

"The thing is, when we publish Taarika, given her Bollywood celebrity quotient, we're sure she'll sell a million copies," Chaitali dropped the magic figures making up the numbers game. "But, the thing is, the million mark is unreachable by small-town or non-celebrity writers, like *you....*"

Lollita shuffled in the seat, sending it to swivel sharply on its spine. The same disquietude again stole up her spine. As if she were seated before her dentist, hearing him spout severe orthodontic judgements. How she was deficient in a robust dental heritage or hygiene.

"We would love to publish your script...the style is good..." Chaitali's words had just begun reviving Lollita's hopes, when up popped a rider. "But, the thing is...," Chaitali continued.

"What?" Lollita asked all agog, her eyebrows poised for take-off to a northward trek, even as her Trishul nosepin froze into statue, manifesting a 'Mana' mudra.

"The theme..." Chaitali pronounced judgement.

"Theme?" Lollita was trying to get the drift of the conversation.

"Look at the bestseller lists, which are the titles topping the charts?" Chaitali rambled on matter of fact, then noticing the look of hesitation hanging over Lollita's visage, she spelt it out.

"Mythological fiction," Lollita volunteered, whilst she racked her grey cells to grasp where the conversation was going.

"Exactly!" Chaitali gently pounded her fist on the table. "That's the stuff that sells a million copies! Not humour... not humour from a non-celeb author...like *you....*"

A couple of moments later, as Lollita trundled out of Peacock Lane, with her saree pallu limply trailing like a flag in a state of un-hoisting, she bore a poetic resemblance to a peacock bouncing out with plumage downcast and downsized.

Her body language bore an uncanny likeness to that of an IPL player packed off to the pavilion even without opening his innings, who misses the chance of even seeing his score on a scoreboard, that simply screams two tell-all words—RUN OUT.

What had transformed Lollita's manner and mien were Chaitali's parting shot: "If you want to sell the proverbial million copies...why not switch to...?"

When Lollita had gaped as blank as a zero-charged smartphone screen, Chaitali had dropped the bombshell.

It had sounded the sort of prescription the dentist pronounced that meant only one cure could save her—root extraction.

The sort of prescription that made the Trident on Lollita's nasal landscape plunge into 'Orayaka' mudra.

"Why not try 'revisiting'..." Chaitali had egged on, eyebrows knitted in a togetherness of profound pondering that precedes the postulation of literary enlightenment.

"Revisiting?" Lollita had babbled in befuddlement.

Pencilled gateways of Mughal architecture puckered up to dwell fondly upon familiar terrain.

"Revisiting...of *Mythology*!"

4

The Curious Case of Sundry 'Isms' Over Sarson da Saag-a

Somewhere in the centrestage of 'City Beautiful'

Revisiting. What Lollita ended up revisiting soon after was surely not Mythology, but her comfort zone.

She breezed in through a frosted glass door, etched with the signature 'Pen' insignia. If breezing about is what one does when one is straddling the Fickle Forties, a time of life when, as far as body bile, hormonal flows or creative juices go, one can scarcely be sure which way the breeze is blowing.

"Hi darling, so good to see my Sounding Board!"

These breezy greetings were being mouthed by Lollita to none other than a revered Arrived Author—Lollita's old philosopher-writer friend, Nazaakat Dutt. A much published poet, author, and senior scribe who had witnessed the literary landscape up close and personal.

Lollita had landed back in her hometown, 'City Beautiful' Chandigarh, and was meeting up her Lit gang for a weekend of makki di roti-saag, mocktails, and mock tales.

At the Press Club.

The media fraternity's India Coffee House.

The hub of hospitality feeding not only the Fourth Estate's waistlines, but also the nation's news headlines.

Where free-flowing Patiala pegs of Bacardi Breezers and Blender's Pride were to this media fraternity's watering hole what endless rounds of filter coffee were to the India Coffee House culture.

Where when the Fourth Estate's Pashas of Primetime and kingmaker editors stabbed decisively into a mutton lollipop or chicken tandoori, it spelt Doomsday not only for many a poor rooster, but also for many a power-hungry alliance or minister.

Where higher than the bills from chicken malai tikka and fish Amritsari was the fish market decibel-ism that the former stoked among the Badshahs of Breaking News. The only place where the lungs of the Pashas of Primetime News, Arnab Goswami, Rajdeep Sardesai & Co, met more than their match. The one place where both the lungs and mouths of the Fourth Estate vied to be second to none. Where the mouths more often than not won the battle, by temporarily silencing the Nation's Newsmakers' garrulous gabs, thanks to butter chicken legs coming in the way of their lungs.

It was over the cacophony of this collective lung power that Lollita and Nazaakat tried to make themselves heard.

"Hey dearie, how lovely to have our Humourista back!" Nazaakat lipped loudly to Lollita over the din.

Nazaakat and Lollita first headed towards the corner dotted with bar stools.

The bar stools of the Press Club were hosting the new narrative of a Fourth Estate, caught on the cusp of a cataclysmic shift. The high stools were perhaps the only thing tall in the hall, for perched atop their long legs were less of renowned faces and towering stalwarts from a print media tottering on its last legs. And, more of the nameless new crop of cub correspondents from digital dailies and news portals.

Nazaakat tried parking herself on one of the bar stools. When it wobbled under her weight, of extra kilos as much as of experience that mid-life piles up, she, with Lollita in tow, then gravitated towards her comfort zone in the metamorphosing milieu—the constant that were the good ol' leather sofas.

Sprawled now on the leather upholstery, sprinkled against the backdrop of the mammoth 'Pen' insignia emblazoning the club interiors, upholstery weathered by press conferences that oftentimes attracted footfalls more for the freebie fish pakoras or mutton seekh kebabs than for meaty sound-bytes, the fifty-plus Nazaakat, aka Naaz, took out her cigarette case.

"Darling, why don't you give a shot to this bright breed budding all over the place?" Nazaakat dished out this friendly advice, as she took a pensive puff at her Marlboro.

A revered embodiment of the old school of writers and journos. A tribe whose writerly words were propelled by the puffs of smoke curling up from cigarettes. The signature stamp of an entire generation of scribes who, with one hand, puffed away and, with the other, had pounded away on that antiquity called the typewriter. A generation of writers whose ideas and ideals were loftier than the curls of smoke pumped up into the air. A generation that had almost faded like that relic of a typewriter.

Nazaakat's cost of cigarettes consumed in the course of a day may have exceeded the paltry earnings from poetic or prose pennings. But, since her literary oeuvre enjoyed a merit taller than the rising curls of smoke from her Marlboro, she was a name to reckon with at most leading litfests and in literary circles.

Nazaakat's was the wiser and weathered face of a generation whose standing in author-hood was scripted more by acclaim at Sahitya Akademis, less by ascent on Amazon bestseller charts. A generation whose best bet at book marketing were scripts with more of 'meat' meets word of mouth, less of Who's Who 'meets' mouthfuls of wine and cheese over cheesy smiles.

"The new 'Middle Class'," Nazaakat said, racking her brains for suitable names.

"Middle Class?" Lollita sounded at sea.

This species being alluded to here by both friends was none other than the publishing industry's mushrooming 'Middle Class'.

The bright young things who were the bridge between the Wannabe Writer and the Wanted Publisher. The breed burgeoning all over the literary landscape like lettuce leaves sprouting as a secondary layer in a flower bed full of copiously cultivated cabbages and cauliflowers.

Nazaakat rummaged into her purse for a scribbled slip.

"Rejection slip *pe* rejection slip," Lollita spouted another sort of slip, striving to sound as dramatic as Sunny Deol had in delivering his dialogue *"tareekh pe taareekh"* in *Damini.*

"Haha...that's one sure-shot sign of future fame... Remember Rowling & Co and their fabled rejection slips?" Nazaakat teased.

"Could it be that Ageism is coming in the way?" Lollita voiced her secret dread.

A mid-life dread as daunting as switching tracks in any sphere, be it having to experiment with loud streaks of Garnier on the tresses, neon hues of Royale on the walls or a 'Rebel Red' on the lips.

Lipping a lyrical 'hello', a rich and resonant voice butted in, as another fellow author friend joined the two.

Prettiness meets pedigree. Documentary filmmaker and poet-writer, Rehmat Anand. A rare breed of authors embodying a confluence of hard-boiled reportage in her role as a filmmaker of documentaries on drug abuse corroding the innards of Punjab and of a fragile Sufi soulfulness in the pursuit of her passion for poetry. Among the latter pursuits, a soulful evening prayer penned in collaboration with late legendary writer, Khushwant Singh.

"Ageism? Hope you girls weren't bitching about me?" Rehmat teased as she plonked her Fab India-clothed frame into the leather upholstery.

A gurgle of greetings and giggles rent the air.

"Not about you, darling," Lollita bantered. "I was wondering if the speed-breaker impeding my bestsellerhood could be that dreadful 'ism'—Ageism!"

Nazaakat tried to sound a note of optimism. "Well, younger debutantes may enjoy a definite advantage, in publishing as elsewhere. But older debutantes, too, can have their day out!"

"Haha, Naaz, it's all fine to sport optimism, but on a note of realism—does one even have a chance in a book biz driven by Million-ism and Millennial-ism?" Lollita bantered.

"Million-ism?" Nazaakat raised her thin eyebrows behind puffs of smoke.

"Hey girls, are you talking of Wannabe Millionaires," butting in was a teasing voice belonging to another fellow author who joined them at the table.

Happiness Guru and Spirituality Coach, Krrish Sathe. A forty-something, author-scholar who dabbled in a decidedly different genre. A researcher and raconteur of real rebirth stories.

"Haha, Krrish, you'll never be a millionaire unless you switch to mythological retellings," teased Lollita.

Another round of greetings ensued, more makki ki roti and sarson da saag thaalis, with drinks, were called for.

"We're talking of Millennial-ism, my coinage for the multitudes of Millennials making it to the bestseller lists," Lollita continued.

"And what's with 'Million-ism'?" Krrish asked on a serious note.

"Ah, that's to describe authors making it to the Million Copies' Club!" Lollita offered enlightenment, her large, kohl-lined eyes lighting up at the secret hope of one day belonging to the Million-selling club.

"So, what does it take to make it to this million copies' mark?" Krrish said as his eyes twinkled.

"Instead of being a raconteur of rebirth tales, you need to be reborn...," Lollita teased back. "Reborn as a self-help author penning titles like *How To Be A Millionaire In 40 Days After 40, How Not To Lose Your Mind & Job Day-Dreaming of Millions...*"

Then, on a sombre note, Lollita added, "Seriously, being told to switch my genre, *at this age,* in order to sell the proverbial million copies, is like being asked to change from my staple Maybelline matte nude palette of Constant Toast, that I've been using most of my adult life, to a 'glossy' pop fuchsia lip liner!"

In middlescence, switching to storylines or genres with more Marketability Quotient is not as easily mechanical as switching a Ford or Ferrari's gears. A sentiment that was echoed by Krrish.

"True that. It's like being asked to switch from the Bullet bike one has been riding all along...to a racier brand," Krrish, the biker, articulated his own analogy. Then grinning at Lollita, he added, "Maybe, I should switch to writing self-helps like *The Monk Who Sold His Sawaari*!"

Munching on her makki di roti, Rehmat couldn't help but see it from a foodie's point of view, "Umm, it's like having to switch from my paranthas to pita bread."

"Huh, this author-hood's Ageism versus Millennialism narrative smacks so much like heirloom salwar-suits having to compete with micro mini-skirts on the red carpet," Naaz aired her own take, as her salwar kurta-swathed ample frame sunk further into the comfort zone that was the Press Club's weathered upholstery.

Rehmat, who could find no publisher for her new poetry collection, was niggled by her own concerns and voiced her own take on 'isms'.

"Darlings, if my poor dear poetry doesn't find a publisher soon, you may find me suffering from an attack of 'pessimism'!"

"Ah, and as if Ageism wasn't enough, there's another new 'ism' haunting all creative domains now," Lollita said as she sighed.

"And, what would that be?" Rehmat looked all agog.

"Nepotism!" Lollita said, dramatically. All of them burst out laughing.

"Haha! Credit it on Kangana!" Nazaakat twaddled teasingly, stubbing her cigarette butts. Then on a serious note, she wondered, "Hmm...Nepotism in the book biz, is it?"

"Ah, I don't really want to get into the 'writes' and wrongs of all these fancy 'isms'," Lollita laughingly skirted the raging debate that had been besieging Bollywood of late.

"You think 'nepotism' has struck the 'write' chord, too?" Rehmat poked and prodded her teasingly.

Nazaakat spelt the last word on the 'isms', "When we started out as authors, there was only one 'ism'—Idealism!"

"I don't know if this spells one of these fancy 'isms'—Nepotism, Ageism, and all that...," Lollita said, steering the chat towards specific speed-breakers she'd been encountering. "But, I was told very politely by one book editor that though I write as well as bestselling Taarika, unlike her, poor non-starry me wouldn't sell a million...," Lollita grimaced at the recent rejection.

"Drop the 'isms'...," Nazaakat dropped her punchline with a wise smile. "What you need is a Shock Absorber!"

By then, Nazaakat had fished out a soiled slip from her handbag.

"Here's the number of this Lit Agent who had met me at a litfest and told me he runs an agency called something something '... Ink'?"

That indeed was the signature stamp of this new 'Middle Class' mapping the lit-scape. The trademark term 'Ink' screaming aloud as an occupational prefix or suffix. Never mind if the ink that a Lit Agency's fashionable name dripped was hardly ever blue, but mostly purple, peach or pink.

All four scrambled up to exit after their weekend tête-à-tête and ambled out to the parking lot. An arena which, in bygone days, had housed mostly Lambrettas, Bajaj Priyas or Fiats, almost as extinct as the dying breed of veteran print journalists. Lambrettas that had boasted baritones as boisterous as the cigar-hoarsened croaking of the scribes of yore they had ferried. Priya scooters as pot-belied as some puffed or pompous newsroom gentry that came bouncing upon them. This arena, with time, had graduated to hosting more of Maruti 800s and Altos to grander Audis and Accords, as fancy as the nomenclatures of new-age electronic media executives or news portal barons.

Into this bustling bastion gingerly glided in that ubiquity, an Uber. A Maruti Wagon R or Tata Indigo reborn. Every man's car. No one man's car. As Lollita was about to troop in, Nazaakat's now nourished grey cells suddenly belched to awakening.

"Oh, I recalled the Lit Agency's name," Naaz exclaimed with enlightenment.

"Aubergine Ink."

5

The Curious Case of 'Musk' Ado About Middle Men

Shock Absorbers.

It indeed defined an important supporting role of this species making up the book biz's 'Middle Class' —Lit Agents.

Desperately seeking Mr Shock Absorber, Lollita connected to him soon after to deal with her book rejection blues, even if his agency name spelt more things purple.

"Hullo," the voice at the other end dripped swag as if it were ink from a prolific pen. "Yeah, tell me...?" said Mr Shock Absorber.

Lollita gave the reference of her writer friend, Nazaakat, and came straight to the point.

"Can I send you the synopsis and sample chapters of my manuscript? And...what are your terms for taking on a script?"

"Sure, you can mail me...," came the voice from the other end.

"Uhh...ummm...by when would you be able to revert?" Lollita twaddled on tenterhooks, uncertainty dripping from her voice like a class 10 or 12 Boards student enquiring when the marksheet will be out.

"We'll revert soon... There's a pile of proposals we have to go through," the voice cut in, then continued, "Here's my email... *Uthha lo...*"

"Uthha lo?" Lollita mumbled more to herself than aloud, wondering that this was a strange way to pass on an email.

"Utthaa lo...uttha lo," the voice signed off, ostensibly sounding busy on another line.

The perkiness, with which she had embarked upon the conversation, fizzled out like the froth flattening on a frappuccino.

While she waited to hear from Mr Shock Absorber, Lollita tried to connect to some other names in the book biz that fellow authors had suggested.

This entailed a revisit to Peacock Lane—a revisit that was breezy, both in terms of entry and exit.

She breezed in more confidently this time, for she was now treading on familiar terrain. Her Bata footwear now practised in skirting potholes that a Wannabe was wont to encounter.

She found herself stepping into a younger e-pub establishment, younger both in terms of presence in the publishing industry and in terms of proprietorship.

Soon she was seated before a thirty something, third generation scion of a publishing house that had refashioned itself into the e-publishing format.

What assailed her nostrils was not the signature smell of ink from freshly printed paperbacks, but the odour of oodles of eau de cologne.

"Hullo," a slick voice rose over an overpowering fog of fragrance. The surroundings stood bathed in the scent of juicy juniper berry mingled with musk.

Ketan Mitra, the scion of the e-pub establishment, greeted her. The fashionable face of the GenNext of publishing. Nattily attired in Allen Solly, he exuded a briskness of dialogue as much of deportment.

Any visions that Lollita harboured of publishing houses exuding odours that had to do with books, paper, and publishing paraphernalia were submerged the very next moment. Ketan briskly reached out for a spray parked on his desktop. And he deluged the cubicle in the lemongrass scents of room freshener.

Calvin Klein meets Forest Essentials.

As the small talk got rolling and led to the usual shop talk about scripts, Lollita tried to get her senses attuned to the swagger as much as the scents of the man.

Her Trishul nose-stud wriggled and squiggled in a chain of emotions sparked by the tickled nostrils, staging its Srinkhala. She was hard put to figure out what was stronger on her senses, the eau de cologne or the voice that did drone.

"E-pub is where the action is... You're at the right place, lovely lady!" Mitra spouted his swag.

"True that. So, would you like to look at...?" Lollita sounded sceptical, having tasted rejection previously. With her characteristic delicacy of demeanour, she thrust forward her manuscript folder.

"Cool... Cool... We love to give a chance to new writerly voices..." His male gaze scanned her as though magnified through a pair of pince nez, giving her the feel of being in an X-ray lab. "And new faces!"

The mists of eau de cologne began to defog.

"Great! So, you'd like to look at my script?" she said, hope bursting through the fogs of fragrance.

"Cool...cool. Why don't we look at your script over a glass of wine or vodka?" he said, subtly.

All that Lollita smelt now was something fishy.

Before she knew, she was breathlessly breezing out. If breezing out is what feet dressed in Bata flats do in middle age, a time of life when one never does know which way the wind will blow.

It was in a multiplex, while Lollita was in the throes of watching the latest entertainer—*Chhichhore*—that *the* crucial call came.

"Application daal do...if your luck is good you may make it...," the silver screen crackled with a dialogue on these lines as the clerk in the flick disinterestedly doled out this advice to the wannabe engineer, essayed by late actor, Sushant Singh Rajput.

Lollita's hello tunes bleated off bang in the middle of this dialogue. Her smartphone almost squiggled and slipped out of Lollita's fingers as she groped for it in the darkness of the cineplex.

There, the face of the hero froze at the clerk's words on the silver screen.

Here, as her phone trilled to pierce the pin-drop silence of the spectators. The neighbouring faces off-screen darted frosty glares in Lollita's direction that could have put even the super-chilled cineplex's air-conditioning to shame.

'Hullo! Sample chapters *bhej do...,"* boomed Mr Shock Absorber's voice at the other end, shattering the silence further as Lollita groped to lower the volume.

"Agar accept naa hua toh...," the on-screen hero sounded all jumpy and jittery.

Lollita jumped off her seat. "Just gimme a moment...," she whispered into the phone, threading her way through the aisle. But not before treading on a couple of touchy toes while squeezing herself out of her row, only to invite another round of frost-laden looks.

"Phir kya...phir tum losers mein...," the big screen's doomsayer was dripping forth dampers to dull the spirits of the hero.

Her heart was pounding as she scurried out of Audi 3 into the lounge, like a kitten scampering out of a dark and dingy attic, where it had been locked inadvertently, into the iridescence of a sunlit room.

"Yes, now I can hear you better, what were you saying?" she asked with the same sense of jumpiness with which the film's hero had faced the chit of a clerk.

"I said I've been through your synopsis and... Ohh, I have a call coming on my other phone, can we meet and discuss this later?"

"Where?" Lollita's breath was bated as one whose fate is hanging in the balance.

Mr Shock Absorber signed off with, "Let's meet the week after next at Dilli Haat."

6

The Curious Case of KBC Clones

Somewhere in 'City Beautiful'

The week before the tryst with Mr Shock Absorber saw Lollita making a quick dash to her hometown for the weekend.

She was dying to catch up with fellow author friends, all agog to hear their tales of trysts with Messrs Middle Men and more.

The weekend outing thus turned into a stage for Lollita's Lit game show. The Wannabe Writers' unabashed, unofficial clone of *Kaun Banega Crorepati* (*KBC*).

In the 'hot seat' would be an Aspiring Author or Arrived Author from among Lollita's literary circle, who would be subjected to grilling about Lit Agents and publishing procedures while being treated to steaming idlis and piping hot filter coffee at the India Coffee House. Hence, the sobriquet 'hot seat'.

The perfect stage for this *KBC* clone of a game. India Coffee House.

The humble seat that had hosted authors of all shapes and sizes. Failed writers who had a script but didn't get to meet a publisher to well-wired writers who had a publisher but not scripts with meat. Retired professors and retired sarkari sahebs aspiring to be authors, to bombastic Brigadiers and Majors not so retiring by nature also wanting majorly to make it to author-hood. The Coffee House had harboured such sundry struggling authors in times when fortunes were clinched not so much on Amazon, as in the city's landmark bookstores—Capital Book Depot, The Browser, and English Book Shop—hemming in this relic of coffee culture.

The hallowed seat for the hobnobbing of intelligentsia. No-frills editors, who didn't mind holding morning meetings here, outside of air-conditioned studios. Bureaucrats, who descended here from their rarefied stratosphere in ancient or ageing Ambassadors, boasting blinking ruby crowns, as self-importantly bloated as the officialdom they ferried. Well-lettered scholars from the university academia, who, over infinite rounds of vadai and sambar, ventilated views on the Vedas' stature or Vice-Chancellor candidature.

A 'hot seat' that was struggling to survive as much on vadai loyalists as on ventilator support. That is, the falling footfalls of gentry who hadn't yet migrated to the CCDs, Baristas & Co, out of choice or compulsion of pockets.

It was this busy and bustling hangout that the KBC clone of Lollita and her literati gang unfolded.

Round One.

"Darlings, how long do Lit Agents take?" Lollita popped the million-dollar question to her literati gang. "The options are:

A. A year
B. A lifetime
C. If Tomorrow Comes
D. Till Dearth Do Us Part."

"Option A... Three months or more... some Lit Agents deliver fast," averred the Arrived Author, her bestselling buddy Bindu Balachandran, aka BinduBee, as assuredly as a contender for the *KBC* crown.

She was, anyway, a pro at being a contestant, having won practically every sundry contest worth its weight in gold under the sun—from magazine contests to supermarket lucky draws, which was why Lollita had anointed her the 'Contest Queen' of their lit gang.

"Option C...," ululated Aspiring Author Sudha Priya as she spouted a smattering of Sunny Deol-esque Hindi in her Chennai accent. A TamBrahm poet and author-doodler whose genre had suffered unceremonious rejections like Lollita's, propelling her towards self-publishing poetry as quirky as the kitschy spectacles she sported. One with a square frame, the other a round one.

"Option B...it can be a wait of a lifetime. My Lit Agent never ever got back," spilling the beans was Arriving Author Two, debutant Advaitya Kant, who after being disappointed with Lit Agents, had had to go in for self-publishing of his thriller, which was now inching up Amazon's hot new release lists.

"Option D. My Lit Agent told me there was a *dearth* of publishers doing my genre of non-fiction," blurted Self-Published Author, Rita Kamra, who had circumvented all the birthing pangs to be suffered in the cubicles of commissioning editors or Lit Agents by simply e-publishing her book of middles.

Round Two.

"Who's the best ticket to Bestsellerhood? Your time starts now and the options are:

A. Lit Agent
B. Publisher
C. Dame Luck
D. None of the Above."

"Lady Luck," Advaitya declared, sporting some new gemstones to woo this elusive Dame.

"Kala Ghoda," Just Arrived Author, Sujatha Nair, unveiled her trade secret.

"Kala Ghoda?" all literati lounging around for this *KBC* clone of a game show were agog.

"What an unusual name for a Lit Agency. I thought their names dripped 'Ink'!" Lollita sounded surprised as she dipped into her ICH favourite 'Jelly with Cream', inquisitive as much as intrigued.

"Haha," Sujatha burst into mirth. "That's a writing contest where I pitched my script and before I knew they'd lapped it up!" she showered enlightenment on lesser literary mortals. "Kala Ghoda."

"I got a 'Shorts' cut to Fifteen Minutes of Fame," disclosed Sudha Priya.

"'Shorts' cut to fame?" Lollita was intrigued, as were the others.

"Haha…a blink-and-miss unveiling of my poetry at JLF 'shorts'," Sudha Priya showered literary enlightenment.

"Frankfurt!" blurted BinduBee.

This was the million-dollar answer that clinched it for BinduBee. And made her the unofficial, uncrowned winner of Lollita's lit game show.

BinduBee flashed her cheesiest smile on the 'hot seat', unlocking her secret ticket to bestsellerhood.

The magic formula unveiled by BinduBee was how her first book first made it to the Frankfurt Book Fair, where it fell into the randomly browsing hands of a Brit publisher looking for a subcontinental script. (The kind of random pick for which writers would die to give their right hand, even if it's their 'write' hand.)

Voila! BinduBee had landed, if not a million dollars, at least a mega-pound contract, without lifting even a fraction pore of a finger of her famous copy writer's hand.

No Lit Agent. No Parakeet Ink or Pink Ink. Simply an enviable unwritten contract with Lady Luck did it for BinduBee. Scripted in Indelible Ink.

This was thus the prelude to her upcoming tryst at Dilli Haat that signalled curtains down on this round of Lollita's literary *KBC* clone called, *"Kiska Bestseller Crown"*.

7

The Curious Case of Rang De Basanti on My Rumaal

Somewhere in the heart of Dilli Haat

"*Sau ke do…sau ke do.*"

This tittle-tattle of trinket-sellers greeted Lollita as she forayed into the forecourt of Dilli Haat.

This culturescape was where she not only picked wondrous weaves to feed her saree-a-holicism, but where she also loved to air her saree wardrobe. Being aired that day in the dappled luminescence of its aisles and alleys was her Pochampally Ikat teamed with a mustard 'Saraswati' Kalamkari print blouse.

Her handwoven meenakari motif pallu caressed Spring's balmy breeze with the flair of a Basant Panchami kite kissing the streamer-studded skyline of Dilli Haat. The Patola pallu's palette of poppy yellow burst out of its black canvas. Like saffron suffusing the air at the Somnath 'dhwajarohan'. Like golden flames leaping out of the lap of charcoal, restless to blaze their path.

A cobbled path took Lollita up this kitschy craft bazaar. The Haat that was her only haven in this city of cramped living and congested roads, where her heart and soul didn't really reside, where only her son's studies, sundry work, and her small-town literary dream brought her.

Lollita blithely pottered about in the patio of Dilli Haat.

Its confluence of cuisine and culture and throngs of *firang* tourists in so many ways resonated the global feel of the flea markets and Saturday Night Bazaars of Goa that Lollita loved legging to on her trips to the state of sand 'n' surf.

Yet, Dilli Haat stood not as a sum of parts, but with its own trademark throbbing cultural soul.

A culture-scape that hosts the crème de la crème as much as commoners.

Where well-heeled culture connoisseurs are driven less by #VocalForLocal and driven to more by Mercs, BMWs or Fords, the chauffeurs of which do double duty of also ferrying forth the contents of craft-a-holicism.

Where social butterflies splurge on pricey peacock-embellished Kanthas or Kanjeevarams for socialite evenings.

Where booty-full memsahibs bring better halves or Bahadurs to bear the burden of breath-taking Banarasis to Begumpuris, bought less for boosting the #Vocal4Handmade self-reliance narrative and more for powering their Selfie-ism.

Where heavyweights from the corridors of power perambulate to pick khadi kurtas or Nehru jackets for sporting #AtmaNirbharBharat hashtag-ism on their sleeves.

It was into this pulsating stage of culture meets crafts that Lollita came scurrying on that crucial day.

Today, all that twaddle of rustic women at the entrance peddling trinkets and other trivia didn't much catch her fancy, as the fate of her script and fancy dreams of the *Wannabe Bestseller* were uppermost on her mind. All else took a backseat, somewhat like ordinary apples and oranges get pushed to the back of a Big Bazaar shelf to make way for exotic kiwis or passion fruit at the forefront.

Just as she was navigating the cobbled path towards the entrance, two vendors caught her eye.

They were selling cheap imitations of some bestselling books, at obviously even less than half the market price. This was the parallel economy of pirated editions pandering to booklovers on the move—metro commuters, office goers, college chicks—whose reading habit was dependent and directly proportional to the time spent commuting on the Metro. It were these folks who were the primary customers snapping up these cheap versions of bestselling authors, more for demonstration effect aboard a Metro than maybe for any love for that author or for reading.

Her eyes fell on some names of the biggies of bestseller-hood vying for eyeballs perched in neat rows on that crumpled musty sheet that was the poor man's bookshelf or mall window. Imagine! As she bent down to finger through some of these bestselling titles, Lollita wondered how these authors would have felt to see cheap versions of their bestsellers being peddled here, as if they were anklets or artefacts being sold by their neighbouring vendors.

"Sau ke do," peddled a plump, bronze-skinned vendor woman on Lollita's right.

Two cheap white metal versions of *raani haars* or *kundan jhumkaas* going for Rs 100, thus croaked this component of the micro economy.

"Teen sau ke do... Teen sau ke do," peddled the man on her left, selling cheap unofficial versions of Shashi Tharoor's *The Battle of Belonging* to Michelle Obama's *Becoming*.

Two books going for Rs 300 at the hands of this squeaking specimen of the parallel economy.

Many an author's day out in the Culture-scape.

Many an author's magnum opus meets here its poor pirated country cousin.

Many an author's months of toil crying for takers accoutred in faux, shoddily tailored jackets.

Many an author's slickly packaged paperback attired here in cheap, clingfilm-thin paper.

Many an author's Amazon bestseller vying for eyeballs here in the company of cheap, white metal jhumkas and jhaalars.

Many an author's height of literary accomplishment rubbing shoulders with the pits of writerly trash that is pulp fiction.

The irony inherent in this parallel book biz did not escape Lollita. Nor her own role as a micro consumer powering the parallel economy's macro narrative.

Lollita picked up Michelle's bestseller blithely, delighted at the bargain she was getting. Imagine, having to shell out just Rs 150 for a bestselling book that was priced at Rs 800 or so. That, too, with the unofficial edition looking almost as squeaky clean as the original.

As she navigated the narrow pathway past the security check, what should she bump into but laden shopping bags. From behind which peeped her shopaholic *sakhis*, Sabrina, Shirley, Jyothy Misra, Indu Chithra, Letha, Leena Sidhu, and Pragya Lulla.

In the backdrop, Lollita spotted a famous face strutting from stall to stall in her mustard and fuchsia 'Gollabhama' saree depicting the folksy milkmaid motifs and sporting her signature bindi. Handloom's beautiful brand ambassador, Chiinaar Di.

An exotic Bani Thani portrait on the Basant-scape.

"OMG, is there any stall you ladies have not raided!" Lollita gushed at her friends' treasure trove of handlooms —Mangalgiri cottons to Moga silks—peeping out of their paper bags.

"Look at what we raided," Pragya, the fusion fashionista, flaunted the flared haldi yellow Kutch-work, while art curator Leena unveiled bandhani stoles and gemstone nosepins from the Rajasthan stall.

Jyothy dug into her shopping bags to flaunt her new buys, Balucharis and Venkatgiris, while Letha exhibited her exorbitant Jamdani with the fabled zoomorphic doodles of Rabindranath Tagore woven by award-winning weaver, late Ramananda Basak.

"How're these looking?" Indu gave a peek into the Peddapuram silks and Kasavus she had picked up. She unveiled her pièce de résistance, a gold tissue Kasavu painted with a tapestry of Theyyam.

"Sweetie, we had to rush in and grab all this before you arrived to raid these woven bestsellers!" Sabrina teased her, strutting to showcase her stack of Sungudis.

Some banter and bag-unveiling later, Lollita moved on, her mind more on the other kind of bestsellers.

Hunger was now nibbling at her innards and just as well that Lollita was meeting up some friends to quickly snatch sumptuous bites before the tryst with sound bytes from Mr Shock Absorber.

Hasty steps encased in the famous Patiala juttis, picked on a previous visit from the Haat itself, took Lollita towards the food court.

The alley leading to the food court was a riot of colours. Puppeteer Vicky Bhat and his troupe of folk dancers from Rajasthan were putting their best foot forward.

Gargantuan ghaagras flung forth their arms to groove the Ghoomar. To the Lehariya heartbeats of a Mother Earth with Basant folk lyrics on her lips.

"Odh Nu Rangii De Lalariya..."

Lollita couldn't help but groove the Giddha meets Ghoomar to the symphonies of spring, before turning towards the Kashmir stall.

A chorus of chitter-chatter greeted her as she joined her soul sisters Sangeet, Reena, Resham Ambika, Nutan, Anju, Aradhnaa Sardhana, Ritaa and daughter Simrann. All of them a pretty picture in Panchami palettes.

"Where in the world have you been, darling? We're starved waiting for you?" Simrann squealed, affectionately.

The chitter-chatter got more boisterous as they all settled down to a repast of Kashmiri biryanis and kehwaa.

Post the biryanis, Sangeet, Reena, and Ritaa fished out packets from their handbags.

"Guess what we have here?' Ritaa and Nutan first thrust a boxful of crunchy homemade kachoris under their alerted and aroused nostrils.

"How could I not bring my signature dish!" Reena unveiled her treat. "Sindhi Kadhi."

"And, how can Basant season be complete without saffron *gur wale chawal*!" Sangeet said, striking the sweet note to their revelry.

"I picked this for you from the Nathdwara craftsmen. Your lucky charm!" Aradhnaa sweetly slipped something into Lollita's palm.

A meenakari Ganesha pendant. From Laxmi Lal's Rajasthan stall.

Resham rummaged into the subterranean layers of her brocade potli purse to tug out something. The intoxicating fragrance of a thousand rose gardens rent the air.

"How could I not showcase my special scarlet silk rumaal...a souvenir from my Guruji!" Resham went gush-gush, riding the rose rush.

Red gulaal resplendent on resham.

A dozen hands dashed forth to finger the surrealness of the silken moment.

Lollita felt fond fingers placing a potli in her hands.

"This one's for you, dear... A Basant token from me," Reena thrust an exotic rumaal, bought from the Haat, into Lollita's hands, springing a surprise.

Golden yellow butterflies crafted with silk skeins on a mehndi green stole-scarf. The mellow goldenness of a million sarson fields blooming on a Basant-scape.

"I couldn't have wished for sweeter Soul Sisters," Lollita exclaimed, touched by their warmth.

The warmth of the Spring day was waning and she looked at the time on her smartphone.

Lollita hurriedly threaded her way through the Haat's cobbled alleys, the corners of her corneas only half skimming over the sights and sounds. Like a film strip only half watched on that antiquity of a Bioscope being paraded on the portico of the Haat.

Lollita legged it past the Bioscope-wallah to scurry towards the far end of the food court, where she strategically seated herself between the Naga and Bengal stalls, as if to tread the 'middle' path. If Mr Shock Absorber was a Bong (it wasn't yet clear from his first name), they would be strategically placed for a taste of 'bhetki patturi' or 'gur sandesh'. If his affiliation to cultures or cuisines was more pan-Indian, they could still savour snacks at the sprinkling of stalls from Punjab, Nagaland, Tamil Nadu or sundry states.

The ambivalence as to the cultural profile of the Lit Agent could be attributed to the fact that the communications with him had so far been purely on a first-name basis. Nor did his email ID in any way betray his surname or cultural roots.

Talking of roots, thus far not only had his cultural roots been shrouded in a sort of intangibility, but when he did trundle in bearing a scalp shorn of vegetation, it became apparent that his follicular roots, too, smacked of a sort of invisibility.

"Hello, I'm Lamba," is how Mr Shock Absorber introduced himself.

The skyline suddenly saw a sea of Basant Panchami kites swarming the horizon. A meteor shower of reds, greens, indigos, and what have you. Into this celestial canvas came bursting a butterpaper-fragile fragment of fluorescent flamboyance. A new kind of kite. A kite full of air.

Aubergine Ink meets Canary tie-dye.

8

The Curious Case of Myriad Ink & Mid-Life Inc

Breezing into the culture-scape with a self-important air was its proprietor, sporting over a pair of jeans the Rajasthani tie-dye kurta, as loud as his contrived accent.

Lollita reeled under the surprise of his appearance being at such odds with the image she had conjured in her mind. Goggling at this tall and middle-aged specimen of the book biz's noveau Middle Class, who also boasted a bulbous middle anatomy that could be blamed upon his partiality to beer, barbecues, and blueberry cheesecakes, she was still trying to figure him out when he himself laid all her conjectures to rest.

"Keshavaa Lamba," Mr Shock Absorber dropped his full nomenclature with as much nonchalance as he dropped his towering frame into the chit of a chair near the Naga stall. This plonking caused the cellulite of his lower anatomy to spill out of the seat's rim like extra cheese oozing out of a Maharaja Mac burger.

"Hi, how you doing?" Lollita started to small talk. "Good to meet you at last!"

"Nice place, this," said Lamba ji, casting a glance about the crowd, scanning it perhaps for any known faces.

"Do you come here often?" she carried on with all this small talk but her mind was on what was coming next, causing her heart to be aflutter with anticipation. "Uhh, what would you like to have?" she asked politely, as if buying time for any unpalatable tidings that might be on their way.

They spent the next couple of minutes ordering snacks. Lamba ji ordered palak pakoras from the Punjab stall plus fruit beer and fried momos from the Naga counter.

"Hmm…so I've been seeing your synopsis and sample chapters," he finally came to the point as he munched on his fried momos.

"The thing is…," his voice trailed off as the momos dripping with schezwan sauce demanded more attention in his oral cavity and his double chin, dripping from the jawline, contorted in concentrated consumption. Much in the manner of the layered skin of a pug performing a hip-hop when chomping on a mutton chop.

"The thing is…," he started off again, this time the preamble stumbled upon a speed-breaker of the pakora kind that was breathing its last between his molars, the upkeep of which in the form of root canal treatments was eating into a thick slice of his earnings from the book biz. Molars which had witnessed better days of chomping upon barbecued or tandoori treats at the Gymkhana Club and IIC—chicken malai tikka to fish tandoori to shami kebabs—than this apology of an Oriental fare they were at present partaking.

As the pakoras had their obsequies performed, he resumed.

"Hmm, so on the face of it, the synopsis and chapters read good and I'll pitch them but…" Lamba ji's voice trailed off again, leaving the 'but' hanging with suspense in the air. As a ball spun by a Bhajji or Bumrah. This time, the pause was to be attributed not to distractions of the gobble kind, but goggle kind.

His sunglasses, perched so far on his balding pate, did a southward skid 'n' slide and came crashing on to his nasal bridge, like a rafter tearing downstream finds his descent arrested by a protuberant boulder.

Having stubbornly re-parked his Ray Bans on his balding cranium, Lamba ji resumed his speech. "But...let's see if any publishers are interested in your genre. Now coming to our package... We have the Chhota Package or Bada Package..."

"Chhota and Bada? What's that?" Lollita goggled and gasped over her honey chilli potatoes, as if it was some new exotic menu that was being reeled off.

Just then, Lamba ji's iPhone decided to trill and he boomed into it, *"Haan, haan, toh uthha lo...bada maal uthha lo...*2010 *pe* 500 *uthha lo."*

From what Lollita could make out, Lamba ji was making neat packets even elsewhere, packets riding his '*maal*' in the share market.

Being a fledgling in the book biz, it sounded as if he had his fingers in many pies. Bulls and bears to books.

Returning to the conversation at hand, Lamba ji rambled off about the 'Chhota' and 'Bada' of his other *maal*. "Hmm, so as I was saying, the Chhota Package entails just our commission for landing you a publisher. That's about 20k to 25k, no hidden costs..."

The conversation was again interrupted as Lamba ji's phone squirmed and squiggled on the marble table top. *"Arre bhai,* why play *chhota khel...seedha* 500 *uthha lo...*wait wait...*bada uthhao...*make it 1,000," he spouted instructions about the day's trading.

Lollita listened all agog, while doing mental arithmetic about what the *chhota* and *bada* meant when translated into the book biz.

"But, if you want the bada dhamaka, then the premium package would fit you better. It takes care of the editing plus post-production, from book reviews, promos, and TV footage to social media campaigning and all that. It would cost Rs 50k onwards. Think it over and let me know," he signed off, sounding more like a real estate agent handling a couple of prime properties and enumerating their potential benefits to the client—vaastu vibes, sun facing, park facing, and such sundry face value.

"But be mentally ready, in case the script is rejected, it is better to have...," Lamba ji said, sounding less of a Mr Shock Absorber and more of a Mr Shock Giver, as his voice trailed off into his smartphone again to spout some specific instructions.

"Reliance...Reliance," Lamba ji gabbled to the voice at the other end, *"Uthhao...bada uthhao*. Best to have Reliance," he carried on with gusto.

Lollita couldn't make head or tail of the drift of Lamba ji's speech. "Reliance, on what?" she deigned to ask.

"Err...aah that," Lamba ji was jolted out of his cross-conversation about the *Reliance* stock talk on the phone. "Well, well, what I meant was..."

He absent-mindedly returned to the conversation at hand and tried to cover up as he stood up, dropping advice as deftly as his Ray Bans dropped from the slippery scalp for the umpteenth time.

"What I meant was, an author should have *reliance... err...self-reliance!"* he signed off with a boisterous boom, like a Punjab Roadways bus about to roar off to Garhshankar or Gidderbaha.

Lamba ji scrambled up to sail away in the opposite direction. Lollita, too, scurried away, looking totally at sea.

The skyline was now a sea of a million micro specks. Panchami *patanggs* staging their beat the retreat. On dusk's dimming canvas, a flashy kite flapped far away like a parakeet. Out of the blue, a *patangbaaz* tugged at his desi kite from the opposite side. Zoom, it came crashing and colliding into the kitschy kite. Ripping and robbing it of air.

Bang!

In the distance, Lollita suddenly heard a sound. The sound of skidding. The sort of sound the receding owner of a pair of Ray Bans emits when he finds his glares diving off his slippery scalp to the ground. In diving to retrieve them, he also finds flying off his smartphone, all that 'Reliance' or 'self-reliance' going for a toss, and he finds himself tumbling, too. Lock, stock, and apparel.

As Lollita beat a retreat, she saw a chit of a curious child peer into the eye of the empty box that was the Bioscope, to find the Past's pop cinema stare back. The Bioscope-wallah stared glassily into the fading day, into an empty Future. The sun had started to set on this pop-art projector, as it had been setting on the Bioscope-wallah. As the sun was soon to set also upon this kaleidoscope, of sights, sounds, and smells, of an era unsuspecting of an un-imagined turn in the alleys of Time.

Lollita passed the man on the accordion near the circular centre-court as she headed out of the heart of the Haat. The Bollywood Asha Bhosle song that he was playing on the accordion struck a soulful chord with Lollita.

"Aage bhi jaane naa tu..."

A yesteryear score resonating her restlessness for tomorrow. A haunting melody foreshadowing a Curse upon a cityscape, a Curse foretold by Resham Ambika and Sangeet's Guruji, a Curse tiptoeing to tumble out of the layered folds of the Present like that scarlet silk rumaal.

An antique accordion lipping a self-fulfilling prophesy, potli-wrapped, lurking in the labyrinths of the Haat.

9

The Curious Case of the Dervish and 'Darcy'

Somewhere in a side-stage of 'City Beautiful'

"Hey sweetie, what're you up to on Saturday night?" Ibaadat Thapar, her social crusader-poetess-philosopher family friend and Rehmat's younger sibling, had tossed this casual poser at Lollita when she'd called up to catch up back in her hometown.

"Umm...I don't know...," Lollita trilled, tentatively.

The thing about Saturday night is that it suffuses one with sentiments similar to those governing the spectacles we select. The Terrific Twenties are all about not only gazing at life through rose-tinted glasses, but also sporting rainbow-hued glasses. Funky and flashy glasses, oftentimes in the hope of some cool dude or damsel making passes. Frames radiating the psychedelic fluorescence synonymous with Saturday night stages. Sported not out of concerns of vision, but out of compulsions of fashion.

The Throbbing Thirties are when one is almost done with rose-tinted glasses, literal and metaphorical, and veering more towards realism-tinted glasses. It is a decade wherein it is not so much the frill or thrill of the lens that matters, but its comfort quotient.

The Furious Forties are when one starts sporting or befriending the bifocals. For a nearer vision. Or for an inner vision. Of life. As much as for the big picture. Of one's life narrative.

"Anything specific lined up for Saturday or you're sort of free," persisted Ibaadat, the art and culture connoisseur, who always had something up her sleeve on weekends.

"Nothing much as of now, dear. I just don't know what to do with myself on weekends," sighed Lollita. The soulful sigh of a mother grappling with a near-empty nest, her teenaged son away, spending more time chilling with chums or chicks, while she ended up spending most weekends consolidating her status as an OTT Obsessed Couch Potato or hyperventilating over her WIP—*Wannabe Bestseller*—as if it were an exam sheet for making it to the coveted Civil Services.

"Hey, well I know what's to be done with you. You get yourself out of the place and we're having a Saturday night out," Ibaadat, who was a single yummy mummy to two grown up kids studying abroad, sounded mysterious.

"But where in the world are we going?" Lollita was all wonderment.

The thing about Saturday night is that the rose tinted-ness of the lens through which one gazes at it is defined by the decade one is navigating. The stage for Saturday Nights also shifts with the ticking of the biological clock.

In the Hormonally Heightened Throbbing Twenties, Saturday night may be gazed at through a 3-D lens—amorousness, adrenalin-pumping action or alcoholism's allures. The Throbbing Twenties is when the hormones plus peer pressure see one gravitating towards Saturday night dens that are high on decibel and demonstration levels.

By the time one trundles into the Hormonally Happy Thumping Thirties, Saturday night is seen more through the lens of Pragmatic Prudence, as a stage for settling into steadiness—be it partners, peers or personal wealth. By this age, culinary or cultural attractions assert themselves more and the Saturday night stage may shift more to hubs of fine dining or fine music, suitably subdued on the sounds of shrillness.

Ah, but by the time, the Fast and Furious Forties kick in—fast, because they arrive way too fast before one can co-opt or coo 'mid-life' into the vocabulary; furious, because one's hormones are peaking before they peter off in the Fading Fifties to follow—the lens becomes tinged with those speed-breakers parading about as sundry 'isms'—Realism, Cynicism or Ageism.

Foraying into the Fab Forties, one thus least expects life to spring surprises about the sort of Saturday night setting it rolls out. Least expecting it to be as unpredictable as the mid-life hormones or hairlines hopping off scalps with nary a warning.

Or so Lollita thought.

"You just come over and we'll let you know where we're taking you," Ibaadat said with a finality, lending more suspense to the stage where Saturday night would unfold.

When Lollita did land up at sisters' Ibaadat and Rehmat's place, on Saturday night, she felt like a half bedecked Christmas tree which doesn't know where it's going—a hallowed hall, a nook or cranny of a corridor or a plush patio to serenade the spotlight. Since she wasn't sure if it was an exotic eatery or a night club they were going to, she'd sported a semi-formal look—a blingy black chiffon Anarkali kurta and black sequinned sharaara. As an afterthought, she had tossed on a silver stole with an Amrita Pritam poetess pose etched upon it in black.

Soon after, they were driving out into the crisp spring evening with Ibaadat and Rehmat and two of their friends who qualified as social butterflies and looked not only over-aged but also overdressed.

They rolled down promenades hemmed in on both sides by a profusion of radiant redness like an inverted red carpet canopying the sky-scape. Enrapturing the eyes was that fully accoutred Show Stopper of Spring-Summer—the Gulmohar.

This looked like a fashion show of ensemble excess. Boulevards and boulevards boasting the grand Gulmohar clothed the sprawling avenues of Lollita's Le Corbusier-esque hometown—'City Beautiful' Chandigarh.

Theirs was not the crimson coyness of a diffident debutante fashionista, but the bold and brazen sassiness of a Show Stopper that, season after season, rules the runways resplendent in its royal red regalia.

The rouge redness of a blushing Spring.

The blood red throbbing through the arteries of a smiling Mother Earth.

The crimson canvas of Mother Nature that revalidated the sobriquets of 'clean and green' earned by this young city, designed by the French architect.

A few miles yonder, like a bedecked bride-to-be suddenly lifting away her velvety veil, the expansive boulevards of this blooming beauty, the grand Gulmohar, gave way to a narrow bylane bereft of blooms.

Lollita found the road leading not to the plush high street housing the city's best pubs or fine dining restaurants. Meandering mysteriously off the beaten path, the car slipped into a back-of-beyond, Ashoka-lined alley of the forests framing the Sukhna Lake.

"Is something happening at the Lake tonight?" Lollita was all agog.

"You just wait, darling..." Ibaadat sounded more mysterious moment by moment.

Now, dear discerning reader, when you're straddling the spectrum spanning mid-life, then driving along dusty deserted alleys away from all roads leading to throbbing Saturday night action—DJs and dance floors or tequila shots and tandoori hotspots—towards silence and seclusion, that too minus a man on your arms, well that truly tells that not only have you arrived in the middle of nowhere, but also that your mid-life has truly arrived.

As the car grinded to a halt somewhere in the middle of the forest, the gaily upholstered inmates of the plush Ford spilled out, like the cookie contents of assorted curves 'n' colours popping out of a fancy looking cookie jar, into a clearing that now began to show signs of members of arty type accoutred civilisation. Faint notes of some instruments drumming in the background wafted to the ears as the eye's pupils pierced the dim lighting to make sense of the destination they'd arrived at.

"Hey, darling, welcome to the Sufi Saturday Night Bazaar," chorused Ibaadat and Rehmat, as if reading Lollita's thoughts and answering the question uppermost in her mind.

"OMG! I didn't know we had anything like a Sufi craft bazaar happening in the city… Just shows how cut off I'm from civilisation," gasped Lollita.

At this stage, dear discerning reader, the dilemma is whether to go heavy on detail to recreate for you the nitty-gritty of the scene unfolding before the eyes of the protagonists or to skimpily give a feel of the sights and sounds of the evening so as not to lose sight of our protagonists.

The minimalist approach to imagery asserts itself, dear reader, for we must not get too lost in the scenery to miss the moves of the protagonists, who'd already started meandering the maze of lantern-lit crafts stalls dotting the forest-scape, shimmering in the night like the sequins on the inky gown of a diva. The crowds milling around the scattered stalls had now started converging in the centre of the courtyard, which now served as a stage where some *firang* looking artists sat stringing and strumming their instruments into a state of readiness.

"Hey sweetie, is this some rock concert or what? You know I'm not much into western music and all that," Lollita whispered to Ibaadat. "What are they going to perform?" she sceptically scanned the instruments as she didn't really recognise any of them, like a cautious consumer on a gluten-free diet eyes the list of contents on the back of a food packet she's never tried.

"Watch on, babe," Ibaadat wasn't in any mood to let up the suspense.

As the night's cloak of darkness deepened, the stage sprang to action with surreal Sufism. Curious instruments came to life to belt out a silky softness that had nothing of the decibel or deafness of the DJ nights synonymous with Saturdays.

The heartbeat of the night started to sync itself to the Sufi rhythms in readiness to exhale into the exotica.

The auditorium of Lollita's five senses unbolted its doors. To usher into the aisles of her being the silkiness of the new sound of music.

The kettledrum, the reed flute, and the oud stirred and strummed in the greenroom of the abyss-black night.

A hundred heads hemming the stage started swaying and nodding to the beats beginning to breathe into the lakeside stillness. The instrumental newness whispered its mid-eastern mellifluousness into Lollita's eardrums.

Some slight movement in the forecourt caught Lollita's eye.

A black robed form started swirling subtly and slowly in the centre. Its arms stretched to touch the throbbing silence of the night. Its robe swirled faster and faster, propelled by the orchestra of the kettledrum, oud, and all that.

"OMG! A Whirling Dervish!" Lollita gasped open mouthed with incredulity. She had heard of the fabled dervishes of the Turkish Persian tradition, who danced to the accompaniment of Sufi poetry. To catch the action live was something Lollita hadn't imagined she'd get to see.

"Yeah dear, a dervish...that too all the way from Istanbul!" Ibaadat said with a wink.

Just then the voice of the bard on the centre of the stage resonated louder and clearer.

"OMG...and they're reciting Rumi!" Lollita's gaping mouth could have been invitation for any of the insects buzzing about in the forest air to come and do a detour of her oral region.

At that very moment, a bumble bee indeed was doing some aerial sight-seeing of all the action and when Lollita made some grand gesticulations to register her awe and amazement, the bee's attention was distracted to her.

From doing a general aerial survey, it decided to a specific aerial mapping of the gesticulating and gaping mouth. And so, it started its own whirl over Lollita's head. Now, as Lollita's gaze was distracted from the whirl on centrestage to the whirl over her skull, she started doing a sort of whirl herself to shoo away the intrusive insect.

The more the bee buzzed overhead, the more Lollita whirled to chase it away.

Her black Anarkali flared into frilled action. It started to stage its parallel concert. Swirling to the Raag Shoo-Shoo the bumblebee evoked, whirling like the robes of the dervish.

Before Lollita knew it, half the crowd, that was thus far engaged by the dervish, now stood encircling her, diverted by the side scene and shouting out all kinds of advice. Much like a congregation that gathers in the stands of a stadium when a cricket ball that's just delivered a six lands on the cranium of an unsuspecting spectator in the audience.

The bee was quite relishing her performance and the eyeballs it had attracted, hence was not much in a mood to relent.

The kettledrums throbbed higher.

The recitation of Rumi resounded louder and louder in the loud stillness of the Saturday night.

"I am only the house of your beloved,

Not the beloved herself…"

Lollita's black sequinned stole etched with the Amrita Pritam face, tossed casually around her shoulders, was ruffled into a state of detachment. A sartorial souvenir she had picked at one of the craft fairs to commemorate hundred years of the poetess, whose 'Ambar Ki Ek Paak Surahi' was an all-time favourite with Lollita.

The folds of the Anarkali stretched out their hands higher and higher as if folding in prayer at a Kashi or Kaaba.

Its whirling was that of the ripples of a random pebble in the sea of darkness. Its swirling was that of blood coursing feverishly through the capillaries.

The strains of soulful Sufism straddled a crescendo powered by the kettledrums.

"The real Beloved is that one who is unique,

Who is your beginning and your end…"

The buzzing bee was in no mood to end its aerial concert.

The Anarkali frenziedly flung forth its arms wider to embrace and envelop the surreal silkiness of the night within its folds.

The silk stole flew away into the folds of the charcoal dark night.

Amrita Pritam in the air as much as Rumi. Poetry in motion.

"When you find that one,

You'll no longer expect anything else,

That one is both the Manifest and the Mystery."

Just then a sinewy hand stretched out from among the audience. *Swoosh swoosh,* the hand directed a repellent spray at the bee, unceremoniously cutting short its whirling.

A sigh of relief rent the air and the spectators trickled back to the main Whirling Dervish on centrestage. The owner of the hand that had sprayed surged out of the crowd to step forward.

"What a whirl, must say!" grinningly said an impish face fringed by a wavy mop as a twinkling pair of eyes peered down at her.

"I…err…hah, thank you so much for saving me from the Whirling Devil!" Lollita bantered between getting her breath back, gratitude oozing from every pore.

"Ruhaan," the voice introduced itself.

"Hi! You a shutterbug?" Lollita asked, noticing the swank camera swinging from his neck.

"Photographer…Poet…Rumi lover," the silken vocal cords continued.

"Wow!" Lollita sounded impressed, as much by his professional profile as his facial profile.

With his curly mop swept up into a ponytail and his dimpled grin creasing his deep dancing eyes into a million crinkles, he smacked of a Darcy-esque rakishness and impishness.

"My camera caught all your impressive whirling dervish performance," the handsome hunk of a shutterbug started showing her the clicks and video footage incidentally captured by his Canon whilst it was recording the evening's show. "I can send it to you…if you'd like to share your number?"

"Gosh, he's hitting pretty fast!" was Lollita's first thought, but she didn't seem to mind the attention from such a dapper dude of a fellow poet-writer. Aloud she said teasingly, "Sure, how can I say no to the Prince Charming who saved me!"

He, too, went on impishly, "Maybe the video should be uploaded on YouTube to tell the world what hidden whirling talent your city has!"

They exchanged numbers and chatted a bit before he went back to his camera. Barely had he diverted the lens back to the performance on centre court when there was some commotion near the stage.

The organisers could be seen huddling near the stage to confer as one or two cops hovered in the backdrop. The organisers seemed to be trying to convince the cops about something, but the latter kept shaking their head more than their bellies shook. There looked to be an impasse and before the spectators could make sense of what was happening, the Sufi artistes had slackened their performance.

The recital of Rumi sighing to a slowness.

"The minute I heard my first love story, I started looking for you..."

The scene was suddenly plunged into darkness.

"What happened?"

"They've cut the electricity as someone complained to the cops that the organisers hadn't obtained a licence for the show...," a chorus of conferring voices could be heard piercing the darkness.

Rumi's verse hanging in the air. A half taken breath.

"Not knowing how blind that was..."

Lollita was blinded by the pitch black darkness the place was plunged into.

Suddenly, the stillness turned to a sea of surging and stampeding. The chaos and confusion of an exodus. As Lollita strained to spot Ibaadat and her bunch, who looked nowhere near, the chaos started to suck Lollita into its arms.

The recitation of Rumi running out of breath. Its resonance breathing its last on the leggy laps of the army of Ashokas.

"Lovers don't finally meet somewhere,
They're in each other all along."

Just then, firm fingers reached out and tightened their manly grip over her hand. Propelling her to safety, protecting her from being pummelled by the pushing populace.

Ruhaan to the rescue again, threading her through the throng to safely shepherd her towards the parking alley.

"Thanks much!" Lollita said, gazing into the molten-ness of his liquid, toffee brown eyes gratefully.

"Sorry, I didn't catch your full name," Lollita couldn't help asking, as after ages, she felt her hormones and the blood coursing in her capillaries whirl faster than the dervish.

The nonchalant answer that came riding his impish grin jounced and jogged Lollita's fleeting memory of last month's *TIME* magazine cover, featuring the world's 'Top 10 Upcoming Shutterbugs'.

Her Trishul nosepin cocked its ears, all agog, essaying the 'Ladhi' mudra. Her heartbeat hobbled to do a spin like the Whirling Dervish.

"Ruhaan Rai."

10

The Curious Case of Clouds over My Cappuccino

Somewhere in the centrestage of 'City Beautiful'

Cupid's narratives can be like cars. They may trundle forward gently and gingerly, with nary a hurry to switch from first gear to fourth gear. Ambling along like those good ol' Ambassadors. Or they may zip forward fast and furious as velocity on wheels, like an Audi.

The challenge for the raconteur is that the bibliophiles straddling the age of the digital natives may not much relish a slow and steady Cupid's narrative, ambling ahead as an Amby. A raconteur reeling off the racy narrative, speeding fast and furious much in the velocity of an Audi in fourth gear, may be more their thing.

In deferment of your wish, dear discerning reader, since Cupid's narratives taking a cocktail interlude or a coffee break is not what you wish, here's fast forwarding you to precisely the stage where Cupid flits into further action over (what else) coffee.

As is wont to be the logical drift in Cupid's narratives that propels the protagonists to share names, numbers and all that, the travel writer-photographer Ruhaan had soon after connected to Lollita, sending her pictures of her impromptu whirling performance at the Saturday Night Bazaar to get things rolling. The text chats led to phone conversations that then led to the next logical thing—coffee.

Copywriters churning creative catchphrases out of cubicles often imbue coffee with immense possibilities, romantic or otherwise, with advertising taglines that read, "A lot can happen over coffee. . . ."

When coffee comes riding such inherent possibilities, it is but natural to bestir the basic curiosity—does Life imitate Art or does Art imitate Life? Thus, dear reader, as our Cupid's narrative propels our protagonists towards a happening café, the air is pregnant with possible scenarios that the same chit of a copywriter stirred into a cuppa coffee.

Lollita was running late for the date, due to dashing off mails to the Lit Agent, so by the time she breezed into this cute café tucked away into one of the city's lesser quaint alleys, Ruhaan was already there.

Café Tortoise.

The country cousin-cum-clone of Café Turtle, the national Capital's hot hangout and book lovers' beloved destination.

What Café Turtle was to Cosmopolitan India, Café Tortoise was to this face of small-town India—a hot and happening hub of bibliophilism meets café culture.

The richer man's India Coffee House.

The crème de la crème's new-age stage for intellectual or pseudo-intellectual hobnobbing over coffee with cream.

Where *haut monde* book lovers or pseudo-book buffs spent more on a bruschetta than on a book.

Where the bygone coffee culture staples like filter coffee had been edged out by elitist brews like a Ristretto or Macchiato or Gazpacho.

Where conversations were fuelled not by vadai-sambar but by the Victorian vibes of pricey pancakes and penne arrabiatas or the European elitism of quiches and quesadillas.

Where the musty smells of old covers and animated book conversations now came attired in these aromas of big brand botoxed bibliophilism.

Dotting Café Tortoise's funky fuchsia and light lilac tables, curated in contemporary café décor, was a sprinkling of literati and pseudo literati, for whom hanging out in its intellectual ambience was a habit born more out of status symbolism than from a serious love of books.

In the heart of the hallway was a crowd of cool college chicks craning their pretty necks over Chic Lit, be it *Runaway Writers* or *The Devil Wears Prada* to appear 'with it'. Whilst waiting for their Mochas or Frappes, they felt it fashionable to finger Booker-nominated or bestselling titles, even if the prized paperbacks were to be, post coffee, dumped as unceremoniously as they discarded their outdated hair colours, used lip liners or out-fashioned boyfriends.

Beyond them was a suited-booted, sixty-something gentleman, waiting perhaps for his coffee cronies. Resembling a retired relic from the India Coffee House (ICH) era, he embodied the migrating population, perhaps. The breed that had been fed on a lifetime of lounging on ICH creaking chairs, but was now migrating to these snobbish stages of café culture to keep up with the times.

Café Tortoise was as much a happening hub where, over date cake with toffee sauce, bibliophiles found light or enlightenment, as much as it was a dim lit den for a date.

It was into this neon-emblazoned haven of cosmopolitan café culture that Lollita had arrived for this first date.

Lollita had barely taken the first few gingerly steps into Café Tortoise when she spotted Ruhaan at a table close to the entrance. So far so good. But what she spotted beyond his table was another table at the rear end, where she saw the back of a head and a T-shirt that looked vaguely familiar. Then the vague familiarity turned to a decided jolt of recognition.

Her first impulse was to start. In the sense of startled. Then, to again start, this time in the nature of retracing her steps towards the door. Alas, it was tad too late.

The face seated in front of the head that had in Lollita's bosom bestirred a wave of warm recognition had already seen her. It was Sakoon, a classmate of her young son. The skull that had so sent her spinning into startlement belonged to none other than that of her said offspring. He had rushed down from his corporate internship in Gurugram for the weekend, ostensibly to catch up with friends. But, as was clear now, more to catch up with his girlfriend.

The thing is when a single mom well into her forties is experimenting to inject some spice into her love life, by singling out some obscure café for her first date with a hunk of a poet-photographer, the sight that she least expects to befall her middle-aged vision is to find that her progeny has also chosen the same café. For the same season, for the same reason—obscurity and privacy for his own date.

Lollita slipped into the chair opposite Ruhaan, as skittish as a cat who has espied a rat but curiously doesn't want the rat to awaken to her presence.

"Hey, so how would you like your coffee, hot or cold?" Ruhaan grinned, scanning her appreciatively in her flowing black top and palazzo.

Ruhaan crinkled his eyes in an Antonio Banderas-esque way, which made him look even more rakish. His unruly locks, swept into discipline in a ponytail, made his irregular features even more pronounced—a nose that was a tad crooked on the ridge, thick lips that puckered mischievously ever so often, eyebrows that were bushy as a Tropical forest. A build that was lean, but made to look almost skinny by the six feet-plus frame.

The sparkling solitaire stud in one oversized ear was the only thing that outrivalled the glint in his toffee brown eyes.

On the whole, a package that spelt alluring asymmetry.

That's what did it for Lollita. Perfection, be it of countenance or of manner, put off Lollita. It was imperfection that worked better for her.

It was asymmetry that appealed to her. For, she herself spelt asymmetry. In looks as much as in life narrative.

Ah, but it was the other sort of imperfections that were bothering her right now. This imperfect start to her first date.

Lollita buried her head in the menu card as if it were the script of a film she had been invited to study, pausing and poring over its contents in the hope that the longer her face stood screened by it, the less the chances of her being sighted by her son. When she showed scanty signs of surfacing from behind the menu card, it was Ruhaan's pleasant voice that pierced the barrier she had erected between him and conversation.

"Is anything the matter, dear?" Ruhaan sounded concerned.

His hand reached out to comfort her.

Ruhaan's reassuring touch.

Ruhaan, a bridge between her teenaged son and forty-plus motherhood.

A befitting bridge between the Millennial mushiness being staged on her son's table yonder and the maturer romance unfolding on their table.

"So, a Frappe for you or a Cappuccino...and how about some croissants or cheesecake?" he asked, charmingly.

That did the trick and it was the mention of cheesecake that startled her swan-like neck shoot up from behind the menu. Like a gazelle deigning to dart up from behind dense shrubbery on hearing a hare in hospitality mode.

"Oh yes, their blueberry cheesecake is sinfully delectable," she cast an eye on neighbouring tables to eye the goodies going strong. As she was eyeing the goodies on tables hither-thither, her eyes wandered down the tables and caught Sakoon's eye just for a fraction of a second.

Has she mentioned my presence to him? Maybe she has scribbled an alert on a paper napkin to him? Lollita's mind had switched to sleuthing mode, imagining Sakoon in Dr Watson mode. Wondering that if this 'Dr Watson' had to draw the attention of Sherlock Holmes to an unexpected presence or apparition, how would he do it.

"So, how's our Whirling Dervish been?" Ruhaan's teasing voice snapped her out of her reverie. "Have you been making the world go round to your tunes?"

"Hah, it's me who's been doing the rounds," she slipped from sleuthing into banter mode, "Of publishers, that is!" She sipped absent-mindedly at her cold coffee, fresh and frothy.

"That sounds like Whirling Devilish than Dervish," he teased further.

"Yup, this looks more a case of things Devilish than the Dervish," she rambled a repartee. "So many cuts and chops in my script, I'm being cut to size!"

"As long as it's not Size Zero, it shouldn't bother you!" teased Ruhaan.

"Haha, enough about me, tell me more about you," laughed Lollita at his witty repartee. "How come you're into Dervishes, Sufi, and Rumi?"

"Haha, as I did mention earlier, too, I have nothing more to do with Dervishes other than that I'm collaborating for a coffee-table book on Rumi, the role and rituals of Dervishes and all that. I've been reading Rumi since ages." Ruhaan got into the mood for Rumi.

"So, how did Rumi happen?" Lollita shot the obvious question to set the conversation rolling.

"Ah that!" Ruhaan grinned, referring to the Sufi night and subsequent conversations. "My Amma was a poet deeply influenced by Sufi poetry...so it's sort of in my DNA."

"And, photography?"

"That, too, is in my DNA," Ruhaan beamed his bewitching smile that made the toffee brownness of his eyes crinkle, making him so irresistible.

"DNA again?" Lollita's brow puckered with puzzlement.

"Yup, that I get from my dad. He was a photographer covering a Baithak where my mom was reciting Rumi. That's how they met... She a Mallu, he a Punjabi... Love at first sight!"

"Awww... What old-world romance... So Georgette Heyer or M&B-ish!" gushed Lollita.

The romance on the table yonder, in contrast, was progressing at a pace fast and furious.

The Hip-Hop haste of the Pre-Millennials and Millennials.

The next time Lollita looked up tentatively beyond Ruhaan's shoulder at the spring romance, the scene in the script had suitably advanced.

Sakoon was no longer facing her. Instead, she had turned her back on Lollita, so to say. For, she had moved to Sidak's side of the table, ostensibly to watch some video on Reels, Instagram's answer to the now banned China video app, TikTok.

Sakoon and Sidak's heads would brush each other's as they giggled or gushed at the video.

Cupid staging a Salsa-paced spin at Sid's table versus its Waltz-slow trot at Lollita's table.

Spring mush versus the Summer-Spring gush.

"That was quick," Lollita rued to herself a tad enviously, as her conversation was still navigating the ice-breakers called small talk.

"And you a Punju, right? What got you to the Sufi night... you a Rumi lover, too, is it?" Ruhaan was as curious.

"Haha...full-blooded Punjabban," Lollita laughed. "We Punjabis love to be seen at all such arty Baithaks, that's what got me there. Anyway, if I'd known it was a recital of Rumi, I would have gone anyway. As much hooked to Rumi in poetry as to Wodehouse in prose."

"What have you read in Rumi...your favourite?" Ruhaan was all ears. It's not every day he met people with whom he could share Rumi with as much passion.

"I'm reading *The Forty Rules of Love* right now...," Lollita happily shared, warming up more and more to this fellow Rumi lover. Like an electric kettle blinking to its button start.

Forties' Rules of Love versus Twenties' Rules of Love.

In between peering into the molten-ness of Ruhaan's eyes, Lollita's gaze kept darting to and fro, to keep track of the new rules of love unfolding on the table inhabited by her offspring and his giggly girlfriend.

There, Sidak and Sakoon were done with their head-to-head engagement, riding on the raving over Reels videos. Sidak was now softly stroking Sakoon's tresses. Here, Ruhaan and Lollita hadn't even yet progressed beyond biographical guesses.

Pre-Millennials' Rules of Love versus Pre-Menopausal's Rules of Love.

"And the *TIME* honour? How did that happen at such a young age?" Lollita couldn't resist asking.

Ruhaan had trended on Twitter and on 'breaking news' as the youngest Indian photographer to feature on the *TIME* cover among the world's Top 10 upcoming shutterbugs. From among his published portraits of celebrated names, in particular seers and saints like Mother Teresa, Guruji and others, it was his unusual clicks of the Dalai Lama that had earned him a place in the *TIME* Hall of Fame.

"Ah, that was a stroke of luck. That was a photo series I had done for a leading newspaper and it was tough to get that interview with the Dalai Lama. There was that one unguarded candid moment of him in repose that I'd clicked in the zillions of clicks when he had invited me to his spring boulevard in bloom...."

"Ah, so the cosmos conspired! As Rumi says, 'what you seek is seeking you'!" Lollita gushed, and even as she uttered it, it was time for her to duck, behind the menu card again.

It looked as if her inner Dalai Lama had been unleashed, as she sat eyes closed, in contemplative silence. But, a silence born of inner chaos, not enlightenment or meditation.

Ruhaan peered at her rather curiously.

The next minute, the scene before her eyes cut into the conversation. Her son turned his head to gesture to the waiter and Lollita was certain now he would spot her, for there was that split second of a gap between the sideways swivelling of his neck to beckon the bloke and her ducking again behind the menu card, as if in search of more blueberry and black currant delights.

So sharply did she execute the ducking of her torso behind the menu card that she unsettled her tumbler of coffee. Its contents didn't quite relish this unceremonious eviction from their place of existence, hence meandered menacingly towards the edge of the table to do a dripping act of protest upon the trousering of Ruhaan.

In between mopping the caffeine contents staining his branded jeans and arresting the further downfall of caffeine from its heights, Ruhaan cast a concerned eye upon Lollita, watching her crouched like a gazelle behind shrubbery.

"Is all well? Are you suffering some stomach disorder or what?"

"No, err...I...ah...just having this queasy feeling... maybe the cheesecake wasn't fresh and didn't really agree with my system," she fumbled for explanations fashionable for actions farcical.

The thing with first dates is that looking constipated or gastronomically maladjusted doesn't quite augur well—meaning, that constipation or belly disorders aren't the best of excuses to flag for ducking actions on a first date.

Even those relationship gurus in *Cosmo* would enumerate it as topping a Not-to-Do Dating List.

"You don't seem to be in form…so let's just move from here," Ruhaan declared, mopping the last remnants of the caffeine calamity from his branded clothes.

Lollita heaved a sigh of relief so heavy that had she been positioned on the Thar desert, it might have bestirred the sand-dunes into shimmying helter-skelter, in anticipation of a blizzard.

As Lollita sprang up and spun around, sidestepping the spilt contents of the cappuccino and still ducking her face behind the upside down menu card, which she absentmindedly carried out, before she could be spotted by sonny dearest, the speed with which she swung out, with Ruhaan in tow, made her again resemble a whirling dervish.

This time, a whirling dervish in fast forward mode.

11

The Curious Case of Dosai Diplomacy

Somewhere in NCR

It looked as one of those days when life is in a mood to serve a delicious dessert, the way a *chef sous de cuisine* in a sunny disposition dishes a double dose of cherries atop a decadent chocolate cherry torte.

Lollita landed back in the Capital for the crucial meeting, her heart was all hop-skip-jump, much like when her kittens did a jump and jive on sighting a coveted pigeon on the patio.

At long last, the *Wannabe Bestseller's* birthing process was getting rolling.

Lollita and Lamba ji navigated the narrow back alleys in a cab, which deposited them at Peacock Lane. At another of Peacock Lane's nondescript-looking façades, gaping open with a grilled entrance leading to a cantankerous stairway that croaked like a frog suffering from laryngitis.

Revisiting Part 3.

That this traditional establishment did not exude any of the cool clinicality or the faux fogginess of fragrances of the previous establishments, that had left Lollita overwhelmed, had to do with a curious confluence of odours wafting down the stairs.

When Lollita stepped in through the brightly painted door, she was grappling with balances of two types. The first being the balancing act she was trying hard to achieve on her middle-class Sarojini Nagar bargains, faux Jimmy Choo platforms, whose sole was threatening to give away.

The sole reason she'd fished them out, despite knowing it was a precarious walk down Peacock Lane, was so as to put her best foot forward for her meeting with the Managing Director. The other sort of balance had to do with her bank account, as she juggled with some mental arithmetic, wondering what would be the royalty and what would be the balance she would be left with after paying the full and final commission to Lamba ji.

As Lollita almost tottered and tripped on the very first step with her sole threatening a complete break-up, it looked to her that she was totally out of balance, on both fronts—balancing act and balance sheet.

As they sallied past the reception, the peculiar odours tickling their nostrils became pronounced and announced that this indeed was a seat of traditional publishing. The ink-fresh odour of books mingled with the signature smell of filter coffee as well as the jasmine and sandalwood fragrance emanating from an assortment of pujai incense sticks.

Kanhaiyaa Publishing.

A traditional seat of the book biz that banked heavily on being in the good books of the Hindu galaxy of gods.

A conventional edifice of the industry wreathed not just in the iridescence of incense but also in a time warp.

A fading fortress where the fogs and fumes from filter coffee and incense were perhaps its fortification against the fast changing world outside.

A publishing signpost struggling to survive, swathed in its signature odours, in a world where the new kids on the block had smelt something better—a golden opportunity in e-publishing.

"Hi, have a seat. Mr Menon will be here any moment," a cheerful looking commissioning editor met them in the brightly lit meeting hall. "We're just getting copies of the contract ready," she sallied out with a sheaf of papers in her hands as her crisp Kasavu saree crackled like an over-bloated and over-crunchy Lijjat poppadum.

"Good afternoon," Managing Director Lasith Menon chirruped cheerfully as he joined them in the meeting room. "Good...good...good to have you on board... We always like to give a chance to bright new authors," he continued, thrusting a sheaf of papers in her direction with his ringed fingers that flaunted precious stones on almost all of them, from the topaz to emerald to ruby. As if to complement his over-ornamented neck, which boasted of gold-plated Krishna pendants as emblems of his allegiance to the blue-skinned God.

In terms of ornamentation, he bore an uncanny poetic resemblance to a miniature, downsized version of that legendary musician—Badshah of Bejewelled Excess, Bappi Lahiri—fabled for sporting gold chains on his neck weightier than his body cellulite and for flaunting yellow metal that came in all shapes, sizes, and surprises.

"Oh yes, I'm so grateful to you for taking on my script," Lollita gushed.

Paroma, the Commissioning Editor, bustled about getting all the signing and counter-signing and other formalities of the contract completed.

Lasith ji made polite talk while the formalities were under way. Now, in the publishing industry's scheme of things, Lasith ji may not have been among the top heavyweights, but he had his niche network and standing that begot him big names among authors and also sales. Such that though his books may not be flying off the counter or rocketing up bestseller lists on Amazon & Co, but they slowly and surely kept the cash register ringing at bookstores, thanks to a well-established distribution network as much as his well-cultivated networking.

Lasith ji, as an astute relic of the old school of publishing, had watched the recent rise and rise of digital publishing platforms with mixed emotions. Curiosity mingled with clever calculations and cool competitiveness.

When a leading publisher relocated from HKV bang next door in Peacock Lane to reinvent its business model and refashion itself as the newest kid on the e-pub block, Lasith ji knew deep inside that their Lit Landscape was never going to look the same again.

There was something brazen and brave in this new way of doing the book biz and the name of Lasith ji's new neighbour in Peacock Lane had a ring to it that said it all—JACKPOTT.

The jittery undertone to his jaunty jollifications at his Mallu Club weekend outing with intelligentsia perhaps echoed and embodied the apprehensions of this old school of publishing.

"All these digital books look great, but tell me, *whaaat* good is a book that you can't hold in your hands, eh?" he caterwauled to his cronies over piping hot filter kaapi and Alleppey curry with appams.

Thus it was an unsuspecting appam that bore the brunt of his embedded fidgetiness, at surveying this transforming lit landscape, as he jabbed a shaky fork into its spongy softness.

Not only was Lasith ji a revered relic of traditional publishing, but also a mascot for the old school of book marketing.

In this digital-driven marketing age, while for the e-pub titans Twitterverse was where the action was, for Lasith ji it was his three Cs—Clubbing, Calicut Cronyism, and Chettinad Dosai Diplomacy—where the promos were. While hashtag-ism did it for the young blood of e-pub, for old-world Lasith ji the marketing blueprint that worked had more to do with oral action—word of mouth and well-fed mouth.

Word of mouth at the Malayali Book Lovers' Club on the first Fridays every month.

Well-fed mouth at the capital's Malayali Cultural Club luncheons every third Sunday of the month.

The third Sunday luncheons with his Malayali Club cronies at Saravana Bhavan were to this pillar of the old school of publishing what Twitter or Instagram networking were to new kids on the digital publishing block.

Appams and Alleppey fish curry did for his book promos what retweets and hashtags did for e-publishing portals.

Luncheons powered by ghee pongal or ghee paper roast masala dosai made his Mallu brethren more malleable to seeing the myriad virtues of his new books. The next round of rava dosai and rasam or idlis and idiyappam catapulted the malleability of Mallu constitutions to the next level, of loosening their purse-strings or credit cards to actually pre-order Lasith ji's latest signature self-help titles:

- *Apple CEO Who Switched To Selling Appams*
- *Malabar Parottas That Made A Millionaire*
- *The Head Honcho Who Gave It All Up to Sell Idlis*

It would be but befitting, dear reader, to draw your attention to the side-effects of Lasith ji's marketing strategies—the idlis arriving at the luncheon table could be seen puffed up to double their size upon overhearing that their tribe had not only been shattering the ceilings of idli-makers but also the glass ceiling of Amazon-powered bestseller-hood.

So superbly were Lasith ji's marketing skills unlocked and so magically were his brethren's listening skills sharpened by these savouries from the South that if it were a Masala Magnum Opus being gingerly dished out to the crème de la crème of the Capital's Mallu community as a side dish between 12 and 2 on the third Sunday afternoon at Saravana Bhavan, it had every chance of not only being lapped up but also being ordered for a refill.

What the Malayali Club outings at the Mecca of gastronomic indulgence achieved for his book promotions among the culturally and literary inclined of his brethren, was accomplished among the more spiritually inclined sections of his targeted readership by his weekend trips to that high seat of Mallu piety and pow-wowing—Guruvayoor Temple.

Thus, it was at this Mecca of the Mallus that the gentry with more pious propensities, upholstered in crisp Kerala Kasavu sarees or starched Set Mundus and wreathed in the after-effects of pujai incense-bathed spirituality, became unsuspecting recipients of subtle promotionals for Lasith ji's sundry self-help titles.

Another stage for wooing the readership among the more spiritually awakened gentry had to do more with his Anglo-Indian better half, Alice Almeida. The Sunday post-Mass tete-a-tetes at his wife's church.

These post-aarti tete-a-tetes with Mallu brethren at the Guruvayoor Temple or the post-Mass hobnobbing with the spiritually minded Christian sections of the Capital's Mallu community, thus, served as an unofficial stage where Lasith ji subtly but surely managed to promote or even sell his books. The Sunday morning pontifications about the political climate of the country or of God's Own Country or the small talk about the floods or fallouts of climate change were gently veered towards more literary confabulations. Soon, the unsuspecting denizens, whose thoughts were prone to revolving more around God, or, at best, if stretched to literary allusions of godliness, to *The God Of Small Things*, would suddenly find delicately being thrust into their vision, or even into their hands, copies of Lasith ji's latest spiritually elevating self-help titles.

This banter and bonhomie born of believing in the same God somehow obligated his fellow Mallus into buying his books in the earnest belief that there was a divine hand in Lasith ji's supplying to the spiritually confused populations such life-altering titles as:

- *The Mallu Millionaire Who Became a Monk*
- *The Monk Who Sold His Set Mundu Empire*
- *Who Moved My Varghese*

Given this exalted standing of his in publishing circles, it, therefore, meant a lot to Lollita when, as they sealed the deal, his gifted gab, gilt encased in gold chains and the glitter of Govinda pendants, gurgled, "We always like to give a chance to new writers…new voices. So, Lamba ji landed you at the right door!" As he delivered the last part of his utterance, Lasith ji's astute, agile eyes swept over the flamboyant picture that Lamba ji presented. As if the latter was one of those feathered friends that wing it to the Kerala beaches from other continents.

"Oh yes," Lollita seconded that wholeheartedly.

"So, the good news is that we would like your writing to be the new voice," Lasith ji preened in his seat. "But there is some not so good news, too…," he added, fingering the egg-sized Krishna pendant with the bejewelled excess that was his hand. Making 'Krishna', fondled by fingers studded with king-size topaz, emeralds, and moonstones, peep like The God of Big Things.

"Ohh…bad news?" Lollita exclaimed.

Lasith ji looked less Bappi Lahiri and more Manmohan Desai as he reeled off formula.

"Es, es, the bad bit is you'll have to kill some characters and spice up the plot like Masala Dosai!" Lasith ji merrily mouthed the formula, again fidgeting with the Krishna pendant lording it on the landscape that was his pug-skinned neckline. As if to constantly reassure himself that he was in the good books of the galaxy of gods and goddesses.

"Masala…?" Lollita sounded befuddled.

This time, it was Lamba ji butting in to bestow enlightenment. "What a bikini is to the Bollywood blockbuster, exotica or erotica is to a Bestseller!"

"Hmmm...," Lollita weighed the challenge. "Well, erotica may not be as tough as *revisiting Mythology*!"

Lasith ji looked a little nonplussed, but sallied off on his own trip, "Ah, revisiting? Reminds me, I have to revisit my hometown in Kochi, for a meeting to plan the next edition of our Kerala Litfest."

"Litfest? Kerala?" Lamba ji's ears pricked.

"Oh yes, I'm part of the organising committee," Lasith ji puffed up with pride like the plumage of a Pygmy Goose or Pipit, the native avians pottering on Kerala beaches. Trust Lamba ji to have seen in it another kind of gold. A golden opportunity.

"Sir, do invite one or two of our authors," Lamba ji pounced on what clearly looked like a business opportunity for future literary networking. "Kochi litfest will be a great stage to give them visibility."

"Aaah, 'es, 'es...we will try to do something," Lasith ji. "You send me the names of some of your authors you'd like to be invited."

Lamba ji's parting shot the next minute was what made Lollita's Trishul nosepin and Lasith ji's eyebrows shoot northwards, as if scooting off on an expedition for scaling a Mount Mukteshwar.

"Yes, done, done, my author list will be with you by evening, sir," Lamba ji had been saying. Then, guffawing as exuberantly as a Haryanavi bus conductor taking off on a trip of colloquialisms, as they scrambled up to leave, he spouted his swag, "My *balls* are in your court now, sir!"

12

The Curious Case of Raas Meets Rumi

Somewhere in the side-stage of 'City Beautiful'

Cupid has a strange way of landing one back to square one. Sometimes literally, sometimes figuratively.

As Cupid was scripting his narrative beyond conversations and cappuccinos, beyond iced mochas and ice-breakers, Lollita and Ruhaan found themselves setting out for a Sufi spectacle soon after. Again.

They drove down those same boulevards in bloom.

Ruhaan was a picture of rakish informality in his Fab India black kurta sported over his pet pair of denims. To resonate her mood for the evening, Lollita had fished out her silver tissue Kasavu with its exotic tapestry of Radha-Krishna Raas Leela.

The promenades of giant Gulmohars now taking on the hues of a blushing sunset to radiate a more pulsating palette.

Passion red. Passion red of capillaries throbbing with platelets of desire.

Bridal red of an Altaa-smeared beloved bedecked for her lover.

Lipstick red of a pouted pretty inviting a lusty kiss.

Lollita couldn't help but bask in this Mother Nature's regalia of radiant redness as they drove by.

Ruhaan delicately placed his hand on hers.

The blood red of the Gulmohars now refracted in the choppy churning in her veins. A churning like the Yelaganga yearning to flow up to the Grishneshwar.

Ah, but as Cupid's plot propels forward, dear discerning reader, it may be pertinent to remind here how the raconteur of romance spends countless restless moments pondering how to prod the plot along. How many nights the raconteur spends sleepless, poring over (what else?) scenes from *Sleepless in Seattle* or from a *Roman Holiday* or *Breakfast at Tiffany's*, for just that inspiring iconic line or turn of events or phrase that could play the muse for his or her own plot. Lines such as these....

Holly Golightly (Audrey Hepburn) to Paul Varjak (George Peppard) in Breakfast At Tiffany's: "I'm like Cat here, a no-name slob. We belong to nobody, and nobody belongs to us. We don't even belong to each other."

How many rewinds and forwards the raconteur of romance races through in the hope of searching that perfect setting and screenplay, as in *Sabrina*...visiting and revisiting that iconic Hepburn-esque or Humphrey-esque moment of *"...gentille petite amie"...*

Linus Larrabee (Humphrey Bogart): How do you say in French, 'My sister has a yellow pencil'?

Sabrina Fairchild (Audrey Hepburn): "Ma sœur a un crayon jaune."

Linus: "How do you say, 'My brother has a lovely girl'?"

Sabrina: "Mon frère a une gentille petite amie."

Linus: "And how do you say, 'I wish I were my brother'?"

Or that iconic *"la vie en rose"* moment...

Sabrina: "Maybe you should go to Paris, Linus. It helped me. Have you ever been there?"

Linus [thinks]: "Oh yes. Once. For thirty-five minutes."

Sabrina: "Thirty-five 'minutes'?"

Linus: "Changing planes. I was on my way to Iraq on an oil deal."

Sabrina: "Oh, but Paris isn't for changing planes, it's for changing your outlook! For throwing open the windows and letting in...letting in la vie en rose."

At the end of each such cinematic revisiting, how the raconteur gushes and gasps, "Wish I could create magic like this in my script!"

There's more revisiting, till the raconteur reaches this and flails the forearms in Eureka-ean ecstasy: "This is it… this is my muse!"

As follows…

George Down (Rupert Everett) to Julianne Potter (Julia Roberts) in My Best Friend's Wedding:

"…What the hell. Life goes on. Maybe there won't be marriage… maybe there won't be sex…but, by God, there'll be dancing."

And, so, dear discerning reader, here we are, the romance raconteur in one suitably stirred for inspiration by all those cinematic revisitings, hoping to sidestep clichés whilst one propels the protagonists to that exotic and exciting stage of Sufi poetry amid serene settings.

The same stage where they had first met. Back to square one. Literally.

"The Saturday Sufi Bazaar seems so much bigger today!" gushed Lollita.

She cast a keen eye around at the studded Sukhna-side bazaar that seemed so much more packed tonight. Both in terms of the larger number of stalls selling organic produce or ethnic trivia, and in terms of the swarm of Sufi lovers converging at this kitschy spectacle in the heart of the lake forest.

"The Dervishes are the big draw. Guess it's got to do with the superb splash they got in the papers last time."

"Is it the same performers as previously?" Lollita asked as Ruhaan threaded her through the throngs, his camera in one hand and her hand in the other.

"Nah…they have a much more renowned artiste tonight… That's why I invited you… She is not to be missed!" Ruhaan's grip on her hand got firmer as the jostling got more frenzied.

Most of the charpoys and stools were occupied by the time they burst in upon the scene of action. There was some place on the durries sprawled across the semi-pucca forest floor, while some spectators parked themselves on the wooden fencing hemming in the courtyard.

Lollita and Ruhaan, too, gravitated towards the fencing, as sitting on floors for long stretches of time when one is on the plus side of forty isn't the sort of rigour the bordering-on-the-brittle bones much relish being subjected to.

As dusk descended, lanterns flickered open their eyelids. Like glow worms blinking upon the bosom of the surreal skyscape. Like gota-patti and sequins studding the velvety veil of the night.

The warp and weft of the woods strained their ears. Awakening again to the strains of mid-eastern music. The Kudum, Kanun, Ney, and Rabab stirred to strum to readiness.

A sweet voice pierced the night's shroud of expectant stillness.

Seeing that the spectators were getting a tad restless, the cultural ambassador behind the show sauntered to centrestage, her lehariya dupatta sported over an ethnic Jaipuri mirror-work kurti and flowing white palazzo, brightening the darkness like gay streamers.

"Till the artistes are ready, we have for you recitations of Rumi by local poets..."

Cheers of excitement rent the air as she made this announcement. "If you could all just settle down..."

A young poet-student from the local university came close on her heels and perched himself on the tall stool centrestage. An antithesis of aged, bespectacled, scholarly-looking and jhola-toting *'kavis'*, he looked kitschy in his Lucknavi kurta worn over jeans.

The magnetism of his voice started releasing Rumi into the air thick with bated breaths and breathlessness of the breeze. A throng of throats rose to rent the air for this rendezvous with Rumi. As if to propel the recital, strains from the Ney or Oud being tuned backstage strayed onto the breaths of the awaking night.

"Only Breath...," the young bard began.

Loud cheering tore through the cloak of the night, as a chorus of collective cords rose in chanting.

"Not Christian or Jew or Muslim,

Not Hindu, Buddhist, Sufi, or Zen...

I am not from the East or the West..."

The young poet started swaying, sinking into the spirit of the Sufi night,

"...I do not exist, am not an entity in this world or in the next,

Did not descend from Adam and Eve..."

Lollita, too, swayed from side to side on her perch on the fencing as the chorus crept up to a crescendo and her nude matte-lined lips spouted the lines she knew so well, had read and re-read countless times. Ruhaan had been perambulating all over the forest square, his camera crazily clicking away at candid frames of the Sufism-soaked spectacle for his coffee-table book.

Having done one round of photography, he joined her at the fencing as the chorus scaled the heartbeats of the pulsating night.

Both these Rumi lovers at the back erupted into echoing it. The spring breeze bestirred the Raas Leela in the layers of her pallu. In the latent layers of her pores.

"My place is placeless,

A trace of the traceless..."

Lollita and Ruhaan resonated the soulful silkiness of the poet's recital in their blithe voices. She slowly felt Ruhaan's hand on hers, its brawny bushiness brushing the depths of the soul of her skin's softness.

The energies were electrifying. The high-voltage energy emanating from the stage resonated in their own blood and curdled with the current coursing through their veins to erupt like a magical mellifluousness hovering on their lips as Rumi united the two, for better or for verse.

"Neither body or soul...

I belong to the beloved..."

By now Lollita's head deemed it fit to hover in a state of belongingness somewhere upon Ruhaan's boyish yet strong shoulders, spelling a restful repose that comes from two souls in sync.

Ah, the temptation is great, dear discerning reader, for the raconteur to now succumb to clichés and treat you to all that mumbo-jumbo "Time stood still..." blah blah. But to spare you that assault of cliché-ism, here's deftly side-skipping the solidification of the soft emotions that were now suffusing the stirred souls of the two protagonists (best to leave the hormones to do their talking, isn't it?), and here's steering you to the next scene.

The strumming of the instruments moved from backstage to centrestage as the main artistes took position on the semi-circular stage carved out for them, with embroidered Phulkaari baaghs (huge shawls or sheets) making the curtained backdrop.

Slowly, the stray strumming first lulled into a silence, before it took off again for a rhythmic resonance as the performance by the Persians unfolded.

Tonight again, a black form swathed in a black robe silently strolled to centrestage and after the customary salutations, started step by step its whirling.

Gentle at first. Then, as the strains of the Mewlana's magic got strewn around into the air, like pollens from some exotic petals scattering into the soul of the darkness-veiled evening, the whirling became high voltage.

This exquisite dervish spelt sheer magic. Nothing like what Lollita had beheld before. From the porcelain-like Persian facial features to the depth of devoutness that poured from her every single pore, she spelt sheer poetry in motion. Rumi's poetry in motion.

The magic of the moment was too much to resist. Spectators started standing up from their charpoys to sway along with her.

This collective urge stretched its hands to nudge Lollita near the back fencing. Her spontaneous instinct was to reach out for Ruhaan's hand and surge slightly forward, pulling him along.

Before she knew, she was swirling like much of the crowd, the way those fashion commercials show models levitating over *sarson* or tulip fields in fashion's finery and slow-motion floating-ness.

The pallu raised its arms as if to make an offering at a Mahakaleshwar or Meru.

The Raas Leela wrapped its arms around every twine and thread of her churning capillaries.

But that's where the catch is. Those models in those fanciful footage of fashion brands are not forty plus dames with bad backs that have begun creaking like rusting bathroom doors with non-lubricated nuts and bolts swaying in the dead of night by unsuspecting winds.

Barely had Lollita indulged her middle-aged anatomy to these circular perambulations for a couple of minutes that she felt her head swimming and her back's brittle vertebrae letting out an orthopaedic orchestra of protest.

She frantically reached out for Ruhaan, who, seeing her flailing arms, lunged to steady her.

The pallu brushed upon the brawn of his being. Then, bowed its head in surrender as a faithful at Vaidyanath or Vrindavan.

"Oh Ruhaan...my head," Lollita gasped, her swimming head and torso relieved to have found a speed-breaker in Ruhaan's strong arms as they steadied her.

Blame it on the darkness or the madness of the moment, or both.

The fact is, dear discerning reader, this is the moment raconteurs of romance die to reach in order to serenade their script to the next level.

As much as the adrenaline pumping in her veins, Rumi's verse throbbed through Lollita. The molten kohl-inkiness of her eyes gaped up at Ruhaan and his hands slowly slid up to the sweaty softness of her mouth.

The pallu squirmed in the sandwiched thermostat of their bodies.

Lollita almost lost her balance.

Raas Leela meets Mid-Life's hormonal imbalance.

Every breath, every pore of Lollita's pre-menopausal self stood stirred by the peaking hormonal orchestra as much as the Dervish-ness of desire.

Her Trishul nosepin bestirred into a breathlessness. Then, erupted into an erotic exhalation. Unleashing of its Urongana.

The pallu with its resplendent tapestry of Radha-Krishna half slipped off her supple shoulders. Like a lavish lace curtain half drawn.

As her warp and weft throbbed to that onstage recitation of her favourite verse of Rumi, *IT* happened:

"If anyone wonders how Jesus raised the dead,

Don't try to explain the miracle.

Kiss me on the lips.

Like this. Like this."

LOCKDOWN 1.0

"If light is in your heart,

you will find your way home."

—RUMI

13

The Curious Case of Life's Lemons and Laukis

Somewhere in the suburbs of Gurugram

On the patio outside Lollita's window, Bholi Punjabban's brood of kittens was frolicking, chasing the pigeons scouting for scarce grains under the gargantuan Gulmohar. But Bholi Punjabban didn't seem her sprightly self, content instead to warily watch over her flock, content to contemplatively gaze out at the landscape.

She was tickled by an inexplicable uneasiness. Engulfed by an eerie edginess.

The antennas of her black-brown Calico ears were curiously cocked. The moist perkiness of her snooty nostrils sniffed at something. The chartreuse green paleness of her pupils peered out, as if seeing something yonder.

Hither, inside the apartment, the modernist Home Centre 'Butterfly' coffee table in the living room was hosting its own narrative.

Its foldable flaps had been pried open for a larger spread. A butterfly spreading its wings.

It stood perched on its lean legs as an embodiment of the modernist minimalism defining condo living. Where space constraints governed furniture, that could be folded into a corner when not needed, as could be an unwanted family member.

A coffee table that on other weekend nights mostly played host to takeaways from Zomato or Swiggy. The food on wheels fashioned on their Butterfly Table mostly by Domino's Pizzas to KFC Zingers, Dunkin Donuts to Belgian Waffles.

A table that tonight staged a painstakingly rustled up dinner, a lip-smacking labour of love, awaiting next to microwave-safe, cobalt-blue crockery. Gaily embossed ceramic plates from the terracotta potters of Haryana that Lollita had once picked from Dilli Haat.

A third plate had elbowed its way on to the customary table for two.

Ever since Lollita had introduced Ruhaan to her son, Sidak, they had hit it off pretty well. Credit it to their shared love for gaming and sports, especially watching Wimbledon and IPL. The staple guy stuff.

Soon after, the trio had started going out for coffee or dinner together. Later, that led to Ruhaan dropping by at their rented apartment in the suburbia every now and then. Whenever Lollita shuttled to the Capital to be with her son, who was balancing a corporate internship with an online MBA program.

Things had been speeding to the next level and Ruhaan had sort of given feelers of how serious he was about her. It was just a matter of time that one of them would move in with the other.

Given Lollita's situation, it was most likely for him to do so.

But neither of them was in a hurry to rush things, so they were taking their own sweet time.

For the weekend, Ruhaan had come over from Chandigarh to spend time with Lollita and her son.

All three were enjoying a cosy dinner at home and watching *F.R.I.E.N.D.S.* on TV.

"Ummm, never knew simple dal and ghiya ke koftas could taste so yummy-licious," Ruhaan gushed as Lollita dished out a second helping of the stuffed bottle gourd curry.

"Wait till you fall in love with the lauki, the way our neighbour has!" Lollita teased him.

"Lauki? Love?" Ruhaan crinkled his dreamy eyes in wonderment, not yet getting the full import of her banter.

During the break in the serial, Sidak just casually reached out for the remote and surfed the channels.

The eyeballs of all three were arrested by the life-altering narrative unfolding on the 'Breaking News'. For, emblazoned on the tickers of all news channels were these tidings:

"PM announces Lockdown from midnight."

Ruhaan's first reflex action was to glance at his watch. It was almost eleven. There was no way he could reach the bus stop to catch the next Volvo back before the stroke of midnight, even if he were to race as frenziedly as a Formula 1 racer.

Lollita and Sidak exchanged glances, both could read what was going on in Ruhaan's mind. Sidak gave a faint nod to his mom and on the cue, Lollita just reached out and squeezed Ruhaan's hand reassuringly across the couch.

The air was rife with an uninvited 'visitor' knocking on their doors.

"Chill...you are most welcome to stay," Lollita said invitingly to him.

"As long as you can fit in..." Lollita looked at Ruhaan teasingly. "...into Sid's pyjamas, that is!"

That was that. It took an alien 'Trespasser' to rush their life to the next level.

Ruhaan suddenly stooped.

He dropped on his knees and with a look of mock seriousness, held on to Lollita's hand with the ardour of a Prince Charming in the throes of theatrics, "At the risk of uttering a future Cliché-ism of the times to come..."

That was that.

When life's doors were bolted.

When life came home.

As the fumbling and fragile silkiness of Ruhaan's voice lipped the inimitable and impromptu proposal:

"Darling, will you be my Quarantine? Till Bored to Death Do Us Part!"

14

The Curious Case of the Lin in Lockdown Ritualism

Lollita grimaced as she placed her cup by the now fettered windowsill. Lollita's life had migrated to the Lockdown window, lock, stock, and barrel.

The parade of paraphernalia from the Present—her ThinkPad pregnant with her Work In Progress—the *Wannabe Bestseller*; her bedside books; her charging cords, her reading spectacles. Even the props of her long-forgotten tea ritualism. Migrated along with slices from her Past—her Maa's daaj chest from Dabbi Bazaar, a rosewood trousseau box inlaid with peacock and barley straw motifs crafted from camel bone, now housing priceless laces and pure zari *gota-kinaaris* that she hoped to hem on to some sarees, and such excavated treasures. Buried pieces of the Past that it took a Pandemic to bring back to life.

Lollita contemplatively surveyed this new migrant population upon the metamorphosed landscape that was now her fettered French window ledge. Her lens to the locked world outside. Her eyes fell fondly on the newcomer on this landscape. The Canon DSLR camera. The lens through which the outside world came in visiting Ruhaan.

The Lockdown windowsill also had another migrant. A migrating population that sensed the future. Not one to lag behind, Bholi Punjabban and her brood had moved from their pet place by the kitchen door to the windowsill, her sixth sense telling the queen cat that this was where the action would be.

Lollita's petite face squiggled as she took a sip from the cup. She just wasn't used to such a high level. Of sugar in her morning cuppa, that is.

"Honey, hope the sugar's not less?" Ruhaan's singsong voice had sailed forth from the kitchen.

Lollita almost sputtered on her first sip, even as she managed to spout a faint "Noooo". She didn't have the heart to tell him that when it came to levels of sweet, she liked it just right. Neither syrupy strong sweetness, nor the dullness of sugarless or Sugarfree.

Lockdown had afforded her that leisure time that had seen a revisiting—return to the ritualism of tea drinking.

Lollita sprawled out languorously at the Lockdown window as an embodiment of this return to the tea ritualism.

Come quarantine, she had delved deep into the long forgotten heirloom chest of drawers making up the mantlepiece and dug out her mother's antique bone china tea set. A fragile fragment of a priceless legacy. The porcelain facade of a long-lost life of leisure buried into oblivion in the hustle bustle of life in the fast lane.

Surprise of surprises, when her dainty fingers had today rummaged into this other treasure trove of heirlooms to retrieve a slice of the lost past, what should they have stumbled upon!

Tea cosies.

Tea cosies, tumbling out of the trousseau chest like pressed petals pouring out of the pages of a dog-eared classic read long ago.

Tea cosies sprinkled with satin stitched posies, dainty daises to pretty pansies, crafted by the nimble hands of her Maasi Maa and Naani Maa (affectionately called 'Bade Beeji' and 'Beeji').

Tea cosies fashioned by the fragile fingers of a generation familiar with only the pangs of one 'P'. Partition, not Pandemic.

Tea cosies, embodiments of embellished exquisiteness from a generation whose vocabulary was defined by hand-artistry 'unlocked', not by an intruder hand called 'Lockdown'.

Lollita tugged out a tea cosy crafted by Beeji and Maa for her trousseau. An embroidered canvas of a Spring boulevard in bloom. Similar to the scenery stitched by Maa on silk handkerchiefs for their eldest cousin, Sureeli Di's, 'daaj' summers ago.

Tapestries threaded with cross stitch, satin stitch or lazy daisy stitch. Faded stitches frozen on the cheeks of Time like dew drops from the dawn bygone.

Tea cosies, redundant relics relegated to requiems, like much else of the Millennium that had become stowaways in the annals of archiving. Buried like the Box Breadwallah, the Bunta Soda or *Binaca Geetmala*. Gone like Beeji and Bade Beeji's 'Cheeni Wali Choori' or *Chitrahaar* nights of Doordarshan days.

Lollita's long, Lockdown-unkempt hands then move on to finger the ivory tea-set.

Gilt-edged ode to a gone-by era. Gossamer gift-wrapped memories from girlhood's trunk.

The fragile face of a girlhood fed on a diet of Chinese author Lin Yutang's famous literary odes to the ritual of tea drinking in *The Importance of Living*. Fed on the flavours of Oriental tea treatises from the Poster Boys of the leisurely life—Lin Yutang to Lu Yu to Kakuzo Okakura. The advocates whose writings had elevated tea taking to a fine art. 'Teaism'.

As Lollita sipped her saccharine suffused first cup of the brew, she soaked in the spirit of the Yutang-esque 'art of doing nothing'.

Yutang had likened the 'first pot of tea' to a girl of thirteen; the second to a damsel of sweet sixteen; and the third pot to an older 'woman'. Not as desirable as the sweet sixteen-like second pot of tea!

Lockdown's leisurely tea ritualism caused Lollita to lapse into idle contemplation—was mid-life or middlescence to a woman what that 'third pot of tea' was to Yutang's tea treatise?

Was a woman's sensuousness and attractiveness in the Forties akin to these relic teapots—out of fashion now?

Lollita could be called an unsung yet ardent practitioner of Yutang's tea philosophy, wherein the perfect cuppa was meant to be a 'clear, pale, golden yellow' and 'never dark red like English tea' (or never brownish, burnt red like the *kadak* chai that most Indians loved).

Lollita took another sip of the *kadak* masala tea that Ruhaan had rustled up, missing the customary taste and texture when she prepared it—that Yutang-esque subtle goldenness. She realised another thing was missing.

"Love, can you please hand me the cookie jar?" she called out to Ruhaan, as she let her tea get mellowed to a lukewarmness that was easy on the tongue, not stinging like a piping hot cuppa.

Chai drinkers can be a curious tribe when it comes to quirks about how they consume their morning cuppa. There's a legion of chai lovers who love to dip the crunchiness of cookies or clones into their brew before the first sip.

Lollita was of the breed—the Britannia or Parle G generation—who had grown up on this bed tea ritualism of dipping glucose or Marie biscuits or crunchier clones, called the ubiquitous 'rusk', into the liquidy molten-ness of their chai.

Lollita tucked into the contents of the cookie jar to pick the crispest of rusks and dipped it into her cuppa.

Now, the tea-with-rusk ritualism is a fine art that calls upon the connoisseur to exhibit an acute sense of timing. The perfect timing to pull the rusk or Parle G clones out of the liquidy molten-ness to save them from death by drowning.

Lollita retrieved the rusk with a flourish. Like those brawny *Baywatch* babes bobbing up on the beachy goldenness just for a fraction of a nano second before bobbing back again. Nymph like.

The smell of freshly unpacked rusks was invitation enough for Bholi Punjabban to come caprioling for her game of cookie 'fetch'.

As Lollita poured the second pot, she fingered the fragility of this heirloom bone china set.

Like much of life's other stowed-away treasures, it would not have seen the light of day, had it not been for Lockdown's Big Long Return to Leisure.

"Here, honey...your fave aloo bhujia," Ruhaan handed her another jar as he too settled in on the chaise lounge by the window-side.

Lollita settled the tea cosy with dainty daisies, embroidered by Beeji, firmly on top of the teapot.

#LockdownChallenge1 showed signs of popping up with Ruhaan about to broach a matter plaguing him, "Darling, would you be having a coffee-maker?" Just then, distraction flashed before his eyes. His concerns were overshadowed by the showstopper of the tea ceremony.

"What's that?" Ruhaan asked intrigued as his eyes fell on the tea cosy. His generation that had perhaps never set sights on this relic of tea ritualism.

"Tea cosy, darling," Lollita looked amused.

"Wow, didn't know vintage tea cosies can be so exquisite!" Ruhaan said.

15

The Curious Case of 4G

Thud! Plonk! Lollita looked up from her new-found position on the patio outside her Lockdown window—rolling on the floor not with laughter but with litter (ROF-L).

Ah, dear discerning reader, lest you think the writer has mislead you into thinking that 'Lollita' is the real name of the protagonist, this is the opportune moment to defog the mists of misunderstanding that may be settling upon the reader-ly brow.

'Lollita' was an acquired moniker, the real name was as far removed from it as Wales is from Witherspoon. As is wont to be the case in many Punjabi households, her real name was as far removed from the official name as 'Pinki', 'Babli' or 'Ginni' are wont to be from a Parveen, Baljinder or Guneetinder.

Her real name was Laasyanga Mansingh. When her mother had noticed her middle offspring announcing her arrival on the planet in a dance mudra, she had been inspired to name the child 'Laasyanga', after the graceful dance form 'Laasya' synonymous with Goddess Parvati. Laasya being a dance symbolic of happiness and healing and denoting the feminine energy, as opposed to the brute masculine energy of Lord Shiva's Tandav.

In the hope that she had given birth to a future danseuse, Lollita's mother had even enrolled her for classical dancing in girlhood. Lollita had over the years, however, shown a propensity towards using her limbs less for Laasya, more for lolling. This decided tendency towards toppling or lolling is what, since girlhood, had earned her the moniker 'Lollita'.

Lockdown had only served to solidify her propensity towards lolling. Whilst trying to balance the roles of Bai meets Budding Writer, she had hoped to live up to her name by essaying these duties with dance steps that would spell a revival of her girlhood's lessons in Laasya. Alas, this return to classical dance in Quarantine saw her mostly toppling. When she was not toppling, she could be seen lolling.

Lolling across Lockdown's living room, laptop in one hand and broomstick in the other, as positional symbolism for her balancing act between Quarantine's Work In Progress (#WIP) and Work Of Home (#WOH). Behavioural propensities that she'd proudly posted on her Instagram videos of Lockdown Life.

This had earned her, from Insta fam and friends, the moniker 'Lollita'.

Thus was born 'Lollita'—a creature of Quarantine—to whom the moniker had stuck as badly as the pigeon poop stains that were solidly stuck upon the balcony floor she was now striving to scrub.

Minus maids—Lalitaa ji & Co—Lollita had started scrubbing and mopping the house since early morning and was now lending her final hurried strokes to the balcony. She was almost done with proving her strength on the floor of the house—mop stick in hand—and was hoping to switch from her #WorkOfHome to #WorkFromHome time. But Bholi Punjabban and tom cat Socrates Singh's litter of kittens had other ideas. Their playtime had just begun. They started plucking at the threads of the mopping stick and just as she was trying to free it from their cute clawed clutches, she managed to kick the bucketful of *pochaa* water. And there she lay, like a mighty WWF participant tripped and toppled by a mosquito-sized opponent trying to figure out what the heck hit her and where.

As she was sprawled in this state of ROF, she became conscious of certain pairs of eyes from neighbouring balconies bestowing undivided attention on her state of half undress—if you consider her tee flown off half way up the torso and the palazzo too doing a northward darting up her un-exercised plumpish legs.

The looks that she was at the receiving end of none other than the Lockdown special—Gaze of Gupta ji and Ganguly ji (4G).

It may be pertinent to mention here that the balconies had been turned into India Quarantining's new mall lounges or living rooms—be it as a stage for the Great Return to the Evening Tea Ritual or the Reinvention of the Couch Potato Into Netflix-a-holic. It were these facades of middle-class cramped condo living that were now mirroring most the Life in Lockdown. It was here that the action lay.

If Alfred Hitchcock's *Rear Window* had the fortune to be remade in India Quarantining, it would perhaps have run into nomenclature feuds. Punjus would have pressed for it to be titled 'Rear *Vehra*' (courtyard). Bongs would have taken out street processions, egged on by 'Didi', for it to be named 'Rear *Chhaad*'. Mallus would have seen 'Red' had it been named anything other than 'Rear *Poomukham*'. And TamBrahms would have made much sound and fury staking titular claim on the 'ground' that it was the 'Rear *Thinnal*' of their Besant Nagar that had cradled the maternal roots of the then future vice-presidency of the United States, Kamala Harris.

If the remake had had the sheer good luck to still survive these India Quarantining's 'Dis-unity in Diversity' speedbreakers, its star cast would surely boast a desi twist, too.

Starring next door's *golu-molu* Gupta ji or Ganguly ji, in place of a Stewart. Crippled not by legs that are plastered a la Stewart, but by legs that are luxuriantly haired and caged by Lockdown, conducting their sleuthing about neighbourhood doings or misdoings from the ramparts of their Rear Verandah. Never mind that the comparison of Gupta ji or Ganguly ji to Hollywood hunk James Stewart is as odious as likening Karelas to Kiwis.

For those partial to spirits, not the spiritedness spilling from diabetic Gupta ji and Ganguly ji (G&Gs), as they keep count of cups of sugar-loaded tea consumed on neighbouring balconies or a count of 'cup' sizes of female laundry fluttering next-door—but the spirits that spark riots outside liquor vends when Lockdown lifts, this comparing of G&Gs to Stewart at Lockdown's *Rear Window* may sound like seeing cousinly resemblance between *desi thharra* and Sauvignon Blanc.

Gupta ji could mostly be seen doing one of the two things his system was programmed for over the years. Firstly, his job of a *sarkari* officer in suburbia had trained his nostrils for a pastime that only Indian officialdom has the knack for—snoring.

So it was that at most times spent lolling on his Lockdown verandah, Gupta ji could be seen, rather heard, snoring.

It started as a repressed rumbling trickling out of his hairy nostrils, as a Yamaha mobike kickstarting in first gear. As it escalated to the higher octaves, Gupta ji's densely cropped head could be sighted bobbing up and down. By the time his snoring sputtered to work itself into a Raag Bhaiyy-ravi (Fearful raga), it had all the likeness, in terms of noise pollution shattering the suburbia, to a Yamaha in fourth gear. A Yamaha minus a silencer.

When he was not snoring, he was mostly sleuthing.

In what resembled a roaming ritual, when Gupta ji settled down for his morning or evening cuppa on his cramped verandah and whilst Mrs Gupta's eyes were engrossed roaming restlessly over her WhatsApp messages, Gupta ji's eyeballs got ample opportunity to do a neighbourly roving. To air his inner Wannabe Sherlock.

His inner Holmes had been honed to some measure by his stint in *sarkari* service. A sleuthing propensity that came from peering up and down the corridors of power with an inner magnifying glass. To keep an eye on the Who's Who who gallivant in and out of the Burra Saab's room. To detect clues of the goings-on of fellow officers whose carpal muscles work less over the files on the table and are wont to work more proactively under the table. To train extra-sensory antennas to detect disturbances, caused by Cupid's capers in the staid *sarkari* stratosphere, when a junior lady officer, angling for out-of-turn promotion, fogs the corridors around the cabin housing the Big Boss with copious fumes from her faux Chanel or Calvin Klein.

Thus it was in sleuthing mode that his gaze first gallivanted over all neighbouring balconies, in what resembled a random roaming.

This entailed darting his eagle eyes hither thither on Lockdown's terraces-turned-living rooms to detect clues for suspicious goings-on—was the neighbouring Srivastav ji's son trying to woo Subramaniam ji's daughter by darting out with his yoga mat into the balcony in his brawny best every time she sauntered out into her terrace next door, cooing into the smartphone? Was the newcomer to the neighbourhood Pandey ji a Modi bhakt, AAP bhakt or simply a Hanuman bhakt? Had the IIM professor-turned-management author Agarwal ji had a hair transplant or was that wobbly crowning glory a wig he had started sporting of late over his balding pate? Was Khullar ji having an affair with or harbouring rather un-sisterly feelings towards his Gujju neighbour's wife Kokila Ben?

Aha, but the moment the gaze of Gupta ji spotted on any verandah a member of the fairer sex, it displayed blinking behaviour that caused his cornea to catapult from roaming into roving.

It propelled his pupils to dilate and dance in action that could best be described as goggling and gaping as wide-eyed as a Bharatnatyam artiste depicting 'Raas Leela' mudras. The catch here was that his Glad Eye carried out its operations quite unabashedly in the presence of his better half. But the roving was camouflaged by and couched in a vocabulary of double entendre that caused his pretty and much younger (in)significant half to presume that he was appreciating the flora and fauna of the neighbourhood, when what he was doing had less to do with fauna and more to do with fawn.

It is another story that the gallivanting of his Glad Eye was sometimes accomplished not just despite the better half by his side but also despite the gurgling and gaping imp of a grandson on his lap. For, a footnote in his profile was that Gupta ji was a granddad to not one but a battalion of budding Gupta Sub-Juniors.

When a grandson—Gupta Sub-Junior—was perched on his lap, the 2G operations (Glad Eye of Gupta ji) got further camouflaged in a vocabulary of double entendre. Gupta Sub Junior could oftentimes be seen brandishing his toy binoculars to conduct his favourite Lockdown pastime, bird watching. The quintessential retired Punjabi Dadaji and his Potaaji could thus be seen conducting their own respective forms of 'bird' watching.

The double entendre conversations, which were totally lost on Gupta ji's better half, ran on these lines:

"Mor...Mor," gushed Gupta Sub-Junior on sighting a beautiful bird on Lollita's patio, where this well-endowed Punjabban lay sprawled in a state of half uncover in a pool of *pochaa* water.

"Yeh Dil Maange More," Gupta ji discordantly did the jingle while his Glad Eye did the neighbourly mingle.

Ganguly ji's gaze, on the other hand, displayed a discreet demeanour of roaming the neighbourhood. Unlike Gupta ji, Ganguly ji, a retired defence officer, possessed a higher devotion quotient to his better half. This could be gauged from the fact he would not commence his cuppa till his Monali ji took her seat on their lush verandah populated with potted micro greens and through the day, the twosome could be seen clicking cosy selfies of couple time. He being of the tribe of Tweeple whose social media posts were incomplete without mooning over Monali ji. Be it Instagramming about her incredible Ilish Patturi or tweeting about her baking successes, err excesses.

When Ganguly ji was not chilling on his patio with his first love, both treating quarantine as a blessing in disguise to catch up on cosy couple time, he could be seen, from Lollita's lockdown window, pampering and primping his second love—his showstopper of a Lamborghini.

His besotted-ness with his 'lady in red' made Gupta ji tease him oftentimes: "Dada, *aap Fauji log ki do baatein toh khoob hain—Gharwali ko chipka ke rakhte hain. Gaadi ko chamkaa ke rakhte hain!*"

Interestingly, his beauty on wheels was not the only thing that glistened on the Ganguly porch. Two other things rivalled it, to outshine it.

A moon that shone in the sun.

Ganguly ji's bald pate that glowed in the suburban sunshine like a skinned silvery Hilsa.

The other, a crowning glory.

The sparkling set of 32 studding the toothsome smile of Ganguly ji. Lo and behold, all that glittered was not his original enamel, but erected architectural wonders landscaping his entire jawline. Crowns that bespoke of polish.

It's another story that their polish owed itself to another Bong. Orthodontist Dr Sujoy Banerjee, aka 'Banjo'. Sujoy, the Bong, who did not give to Ganguly ji much joy. For, the former managed to polish off most of Ganguly ji's monthly pension in return for a smile studded by porcelain with plenty of polish.

Given these two loves of Ganguly ji's life, digressions of his Gaze were few and far between. When distraction did present itself, particularly in the form of a Punjabi damsel well endowed with charm as much as chutzpah, Ganguly ji's Gaze was wont to go gallantly agog with admiration. A Gaze decidedly discreet and decent even in its distractions, in deference to his devotedness to the better half. The Gaze of a gallant knight ever ready to spring to the service of a damsel in distress. Or a Quarantine's damsel in ingress and egress.

That said about the behavioural propensities of the G&Gs, it may be pointed out that at this very moment the Gaze of the G&Gs was pointedly fixated upon not the fluttering laundry but the flailing lady on the balcony across from theirs. The lady in question was trying to disentangle from the kittens doing a hop, skip, and jump on her exposed belly while she lay prostate in the puddle of *pochaa* water.

As Lollita managed to scramble back on her feet and returned a frosty look to these gazers, the Gaze of the G&Gs pronto changed its direction from travelling over the contours of Lollita. Gupta ji and Ganguly ji now pretended instead to interlock eyes with each other as part of a profound debate about other kind of curves.

The contours of the Covid 19 curve.

16

The Curious Case of Laukis Versus Lamborghinis

Lollita heaved a sigh of relief as Lockdown's #WorkOfHome neared its end and she was free to switch over to her other role #WorkFromHome, which meant returning to her manuscript.

She gazed at the Gulmohar standing as a solitary summer sentinel outside her Lockdown window. The tree's crimson couture an exception to this harsh Summer's bare-bodied barrenness that resonated the narrative of Death and Doom being scripted in every pore and pistil of Mother Earth, whose Coronascape's corpses were shedding faster than dead leaves.

Before settling down with her laptop, Lollita waddled to the porch again, to put out the laundry to dry.

She noticed that instead of all that usual neighbourly gazing and gossiping, Gupta ji had now settled down for a chat session, albeit with his plants this time.

For the only time Gupta ji's jarring vocal cords, resembling at the best of times an outdated and obstinate transistor that won't slam shut, lulled into a state of sublime sentimentality was when he telepathically communicated with the budding *bhindis* or bottle gourds in his patch of green.

As Gupta ji's uncultivated vocal cords hummed paeans to his horticultural *haseenas,* his pupils simultaneously slipped into sleuthing mode and scanned neighbouring Khullar ji's balcony with interest. Khullar ji was pacing up and down his balcony ostensibly guffawing gregariously into the smartphone, but beaming as brightly as a neon hoarding the moment he sighted Kokilaben shimmying outside to sun her laundry in the next door balcony.

The detective in Gupta ji now spotted suspicious movement—Khullar ji's calf muscles switching from an up-and-down walkathon to legging a sort of circular ring-a-ring-a roses in that corner of his balcony that bore the best proximity to Kokilaben's laundry stand.

The suspected undercurrents of ardour emanating from these neighbouring terraces stirred Gupta ji's own ardour, hitherto suppressed into the sleepiness of his subterranean desires. It was this bestirring of underlying passion that he could be seen channelising into his cultivated beauties, whom he could now be seen crooning to with a renewed vengeance.

All his suppressed fantasies had a field day the moment he stepped into his kitchen garden, as he serenaded the budding beauties as if they were the Katrinas and Kareenas of his kingdom. He would finger the contours of the pumpkins and bottle gourds as if they were the voluptuous Vidya Balans and Rekhas in his repertoire. He would glow at the glistening skin of the brinjals as if it was the lustrous epidermis of a bronzed Bipasha or Malaika.

"*Bhalo...bhalo,*" Ganguly ji would chirrup from across the wall upon finding Gupta ji stroking the slim contours of a *bhindi* or bottle gourd fondly.

"Beauty, isn't she?" Gupta ji would gush. "Wait till 'she' breaks a record," articulating his fixation.

The time that Gupta ji spent directing the hose pipe to irrigate his kitchen garden, that was also the time Ganguly ji could be seen directing a section of the water supply of this suburbia to a beauty bath. Of his 'second love', the Red Lamborghini.

Lest it be thought to be an idle pursuit to kill the time hanging heavy on his hands in Quarantine, more light needs to be cast on the small dream driving this fixation of Ganguly ji.

For the past many seasons, since his retirement, Ganguly ji had devoted himself to the serious pursuit of his passion—fashioning himself into a car rallyist to reckon with.

This passion saw him participating in some sundry car rallies, but his coveted destination was the Himalayan Car Rally, that culminated in the quaint colonial hill town of Kasauli.

He owed his initiation into this rarefied social stratosphere of Himalayan car rallyists to his cronies Gen Chintan Kapur and Col Shresht Joshi, with whom he had once found himself steering down the sylvian climes of the Lower Himalayas in what was an unforgettable Boys' Day Out.

Seasons of rolling down the hill-scapes had seen him evolve into the top-10 vintage car rallyists and last season he had even progressed to make it as the third runners-up.

Making it as the winner of the vintage car rally was the passion propelling Ganguly ji.

Being the first to make it to the finish line in his four-wheeled 'Lady in Red'—that was the small town India's big dream driving this retired denizen.

The Himalayan Vintage Car Rally Awards Night... Ganguly ji's sights were thus set on a different red carpet.

Pottering about their patios, Gupta ji and Ganguly ji presented a picture in contrast.

The contrast in the vegetation extended not only on the Gupta and Ganguly patios, but also their pates. It was a contrast as striking as the cliched chalk and cheese. Or better still, the Gupta and Ganguly scalps boasted vegetation as contrasting as the Tropical forests of the Brahmaputra and the sand-dunes of Bikaner.

The dense crop atop the cranium of Gupta ji was of such a proliferating nature that its offshoots could be seen sprouting even from his earlobes. Like that wild Curtain Plant creeper that crawls out of every nook and cranny.

In contrast, Ganguly ji's was a case of follicle deficit. His scalp was getting as bereft of vegetation as a sand-dune of the Thar desert-scape. And, though no amounts of herbal oils scrubbed into the surface yielded fresh vegetation, it did cause his balding pate to glow and glisten like a pomfret profusely marinated in mustard oil.

As for the thriving vegetation in Gupta ji's kitchen garden, it would be but befitting to mention that he was not in the grip of an idle itch to be a green thumb. Rather, his passion took on aspirational hues. The way aspiring authors dream of making it big on bestseller lists, Gupta ji had his own little big dream. What the Booker is to budding authors, a coveted Book of Records was to this sexagenarian with the Glad Eye and the Green Thumb.

Gupta ji thus personified Small Town India's Little Big Dream—it was his stated ambition in life to one day make it to the *Limca Book of Records* as a proud owner of the country's longest lauki.

A small dream that could be his only big ticket. Out of mediocrity. Out of middle-class anonymity.

At this point of time, as Lollita lolled out to air her laundry, Gupta ji across was airing his lungs. His humming to the greens in his kitchen garden an ardent articulation of this very middle-class, Mungeri Lal-esque dream:

"Mere anganey mein tumhara kya kaam hai...Jiski lauki lambi..."

17

The Curious Case of the Catch in #CoupleGoals

Lollita sighed softly like a pressure cooker out of steam, as she put her ThinkPad, parked on the chaise lounge, out of the way. The Trident on her nose-stud did not bestir, sticking to its *sthayi* status.

It was one of those mornings when Lollita didn't feel propelled to bustle about like an over-industrious Metro or Shatabdi train tearing from station to station, racing against the clock to trundle towards trysts with time-tables. Rather, she was content being parked in idle restfulness, much in the manner of an idling engine detached from its cavalcade of coaches.

Bholi Punjabban resonated the mood of the morning by idling on her pet spot by the window. Her demeanour echoed much the manner of her mistress. There being days when even the most sprightly and springy of cats likes to cool her heels, idling like a mini rail coach taking a cue from the mother engine.

On days when Lollita was not labouring over her Work in Progress, her carpal tendons tended to be torn between twiddling on touchscreens for her twin passions—Netflixing and online saree shopaholic-ism.

These two passions defined Lollita's mantra to dish out Life's proverbial lemons into not just lemonade but martini. What in the spirit of the New Normal vocabulary boasted a new name.

Quarantini.

What this meant was that OTT was figuratively her New Quarantini. The newest addiction that she was getting drunk on.

What this translated into was that she was using Lockdown as a blessing in disguise to consolidate her status as a sworn member of the new species called Obsessive OTT Surfer. Or, New Normal's Netflixing Couch Potato.

Shaken, not stirred.

When applied to Lollita, this signature swag a la James Bond denoted a Pandemic-shaken Lollita's literal absence of stirring from the position of Netflix Couch Potato position for hours together, sometimes being glued to that position 24×7.

Thus, it was that the Netflix-a-holic in Lollita spent the morning watching *Masaba Masaba* and *Manikarnika* in bits and parts.

Done with that, her carpal tendons then twiddled towards Instagramming.

"Rooh, look…aren't these Insta posts picture perfect?"

Lollita scrolled her smartphone Smartie's screen to show Ruhaan the Instagram picture postcards of celebrity couples in Lockdown mode.

There was one hashtag that was threading together all these portraits and popping out of all these posts. It was this one hashtag that kept niggling at the back of Lollita's mind, casting her into candid contemplation of her own relationship status.

#LockdownCoupleGoals.

There was Katrina experimenting with Punjabi *ishtyle* halwa to impress younger partner Vicky Kaushal and to dish out cultural confluence.

There was Anushka Sharma giving Virat Kohli a haircut.

There was Ranveer Singh cooking up lip-smacking treats for Deepika Padukone.

There were Priyanka Chopra and beau almost half her age, Nick Jonas, twinning in Lockdown wardrobes.

There was Bipasha Basu and her younger husband Karan Singh Grover bonding in quarantine over Harry Potter movies.

There was former Miss Universe Sushmita Sen cementing chemistry with her younger boyfriend over biology—yoga. Garbhasana, of all the poses.

The subtext of all these Cupid narratives: #CoupleGoals.

"How hot this Bollywood couple looks doing their workout together," she was peering enviously at a picture of Sushmita and her hunk of a boyfriend levitating in the air as lightly as if both were barely twenty somethings, belying the fact that theirs was an autumn-spring romance wherein Sush was on the wrong side of forty.

"They don't even look as if they have so much age gap," she muttered more to herself than aloud.

Age is just a number, goes the cliché, but she felt between her and Ruhaan it looked like a tell-all number.

She felt suffused by shades of doubt: nothing in her narrative of coupledom seemed to match the tinsel town scripts, except perhaps the similar sounding beau monikers.

"These celeb couples seem to be cosying at everything," Lollita marvelled. "Are we low on #couplegoals quotient (CQ)? Forget twinning, we're not even together at tread-milling!" she wondered as she watched Ruhaan plodding at his push-ups while she lolled lazily in bed.

Bholi Punjabban and tomcat Socrates Singh were engaged in a workout of their own. Canoodling upon the Lockdown windowsill.

"Even they are better at couple goals!" Lollita rued, enviously.

It would be but befitting to mention here, dear discerning reader, that in this age of digital natives, couple chemistry came riding newer nuances. Hashtags were now the new anthems driving couple chemistry galore the way *Cosmopolitan* Quick-fix Quizzes were to yore (you do remember, don't you, dear reader, those quickie quizzes in girlie glossies—*Femina, Elle, Cosmo* & Co—that were wont to dish out balderdash like those Top Five or Top 10 tell-all signs:

- 5 steps to land a hunk as handsome as Tom Cruise;
- 7 'handy' hints to ignite or reignite the sparks on a Cruise;
- 10 signs to tell if your guy was instead 'cruising' towards another woman.

Well, Generation Instagrammers seemed to have sort of distilled all that *Cosmo* kind of relationship wisdom into a new vocabulary of hashtag-ism—the couple chemistry hashtags.

As Lollita browsed the hashtag more, a couple of contemporary blogs popped up, reminiscent of the diet of *Cosmo* quick-fixes their girlhood was fed upon for navigating the relationship roadmap:

- 5 signs to tell if that office guy by the cooler has the 'hots' for you or is hanging about only because it is damn hot;
- 3 signs to check if the hunk in CCD was staring because he was smitten or because he wanted to know the funky hair colour you used;
- 7 signs to know if the guy in the Metro is stalking you for your tooth-some smile or for the Bluetooth on your ears.

The only change was that these quickie quizzes now came clothed as digital clones.

The blog that had popped up before Lollita's eyes looked like one such *Cosmo* clone—MissMonalini.Com.

It was full of footage on the Lockdown life of celebrities and in the middle of hashtagism there was this title, "Seven steps to check compatibility with Couple Goals", that caught Lollita's eye. It was a quickie quiz of a few parameters by which to measure a couple's compatibility. If 6–7 of the boxes got ticked, the quiz said, it meant you were a made-for-each-other couple.

Lollita was doing a mental checklist of the quiz questions when Ruhaan came canoodling up to her.

"Ummm...what's it, love?" Ruhaan suddenly was peeping into her smartphone, ambling up to her with his sweaty torso.

Lollita looked up at him with a twinge of envy. There he was, all brawn and bustle, not missing even one day of #WorkoutFromHome. And, here she was, just lolling in bed or at the laptop most days of Lockdown, not able to heave herself to so much as do some yoga. Sheer lassitude and lack of super-charged attitude was driving her fatten-the-curve narrative.

As they both pored over Sush and beau's Instagram pictures in couple workout mode, Lollita suddenly made a resolve. A resolve that tickled her Trishul nose-stud into 'Chaali' mudra.

"Time to amp up on #CoupleGoals!"

18

The Curious Case of Vatna Under My Veil

Lollita's skin pricked from the peculiar pack pasted on it as she plodded away at her *Wannabe Bestseller* on her laptop, embedded upon the plushness of the chaise lounge by her Lockdown window. Her face felt as taut as an over-starched Kota Doria saree. A few drops from the golden paste blotched up the clinical whiteness of her mask resting carelessly on the recliner's arm. Un-erasable stains? Or, indelible patches of sunshine on the starkness of the mask? The new Reverse Veil.

This homemade facepack was none other than a beautification regime rooted in the folk wisdom of Punjab.

This return to the roots, this reviving of the *Daadi-Naani ke nuske*, was a blessing in disguise of Lockdown life, born out of sheer necessity.

It was the little grooming luxury to be afforded in a season when all salons and beauty parlours were packed up.

The #stayhome protocol had rekindled in Lollita girlhood memories of an ethnic ritual fashioning the folk traditions of Punjab, popular in folk parlance as the 'Vatna ceremony'. The folk tradition that entailed a bride-to-be or groom-to-be being barred from leaving home prior to the D-Day to protect them from any evil eye lurking beyond the threshold, and being beautified during this enforced stay-home with a homemade herbal paste. An auspicious concoction culled from haldi, sandalwood powder, and mustard oil or curd.

Vatna.

The folksy resonance of that ritual of girlhood now returned as a prism through which Lollita refracted the ritualism of the New Normal.

#LifesLemonsIntoLemonade. Vatna ritualism.

Vatna. The paste that had paved the rites of passage from girlhood to womanhood for Lollita and her sisters, Meeraya and Radhyaa.

Summers ago, this same paste had suffused the air with its heady scents of sandalwood powder and turmeric being wedded to the pungent odour of mustard oil. Sisters, sundry assortment of aunts, and childhood chums had all congregated for pre-wedding rituals.

Sureeli Di, Jasmehar Di, Arshu Di to Gulnaar Di. Jasneer Bua, Babitaa Mami to Triptaa, Dolly, Jolly, and Minni-Binni Maasis. Childhood chum Manikarnikaa with Muskaan from Garhshankar and more had poured in to enliven the revelry and rituals, along with Radhyaa and Meeraya Di.

At their sprawling ancestral bungalow on the Panchkuian Road of Lutyen's Delhi. EKKAANTH. Silent solitude.

Spelling anything but silence or solitude that long-ago day as giggling girlhood got ready to smear the Vatna paste on to the painfully bony girlishness of the bride to be.

Lollita.

On the threshold of an arranged marriage. A romantic, starry-eyed Wannabe Writer being tied to a pragmatic, hard-boiled Bombastic Banker.

The mild scent of the sandalwood powder being muted by the pungency of the mustard oil.

Vatna being whipped into readiness.

Its signature scents jostling with the sharpness of the fragrance of freshly plucked mango leaves with which it was to be applied.

Beeji and Bade Beeji pounded the paste faster to stir it into a smoothness. Specks of sandalwood or turmeric offered rebellious resistance to the impending blending. The practiced hands of the matriarchs schooling the stubborn lumps of sandalwood into conforming. Patting the sandalwood into losing its individuality, its signature scent, for attaining a blended oneness with the mustard oil.

Lollita's skinniness had stood smeared with the goldenness of this #StayHome ritual of a lifetime ago. A golden goodness replete with the cooling power of curcumin in the haldi that had played the balm to calm her pre-marital jitters at an arranged alliance, at a blending of a cheese-chalk contrast.

In the midst of all the giggling and gurgling of wedding festivities that ensued, the siblings tried to smuggle out Lollita for a secret rendezvous with the groom to be. The groom desperate to steal a pre-nuptial kiss.

Repressed machismo longing for a foretaste of the free conjugal outing that Indian marriage-hood is.

The moment the girls were trying to steal out of the house, the eagle eyes of Guddi Maasi Maa, and Chaandini Maasi Maa, had frozen them in the act.

"Vatna lagan de baad...Vyaah toh pehle, dulhan gharon bahar nahin jaandi," Guddi Maasi Maa's sweetly stern voice had played the speedbreaker, as she had imparted folk wisdom to the girls. ("Post the Vatna ceremony and prior to the wedding, the bride-to-be is barred from leaving her home.")

"Buri nazar lag jaandi hai," Chaandini Maasi Maa had endorsed the wisdom inherent in the Vatna folk rituals. ("The bride is subjected to stay-at-home to save her from the evil eye.")

Bitter truths mouthed by a matriarch, whose own marriage had run into rough weather on the nuptial night itself, when her groom had callously informed her that he loved another woman and had entered this marriage only to please his patriarch.

"Eh kedi Hoor Pari hai," was the snide remark spouted by Jasleen Maami. ("She's hardly a princess to attract an evil eye.")

Beeji pounded the paste more forcefully. As if to hasten the blending. Maa didn't say a word. Maa was too mild, too gentle to say anything. She patted the mango leaves into readiness. The pungent sap from a mango tree stem dropped its trickling tartiness on her skin. Maa bristled silently.

The lionesses sprang to their sibling's defence.

"Hoor Pari toh kum nahin hai saddi behan," Meeraya Di and Radhyaa chorused as cheerleaders.

"So soft skinned...*Shukr hai saddi behan thick skinned nahin*!" Gulnaar Di spoke up in saucy defence as she started to smear Vatna all over Lollita's leanness.

"Hai, nazar naa lagey iss Hoor Pari nu," Sureeli Di chimed in, to champion the cause of little sis Lollita, in her syrup-sweet voice.

The trickle of acrid sap wasn't done yet.

"Sukki jehi nu kii nazar lagni," Candy Maami trilled tartly in her thin voice, casting a proud matronly gaze at the voluptuousness oozing out of her bounteous beti Babli's choli. ("What evil eye will her size zero skinniness invite!")

Maami's snooty gaze had pierced the pointed tininess beneath the padded bra of the then twenty-something Lollita. Maami had made her point.

Lollita smarted under the prick. From the barbs of Biradri. From the Vatna pricking her skin as it parched to a dryness.

The parchedness was still the same, the pricks were gone.

The pungency of mustard oil was gone, too. From the Vatna, as from Lollita's life.

A whiff of mint after-shave and the faint fragrance of Parachute coconut oil from his ponytailed locks teased her nostrils as Ruhaan's face brushed past her Vatna-plastered visage to pick his photography paraphernalia.

Lollita dropped dollops of curd into her Vatna paste to make it more moist. Curd, her substitute for mustard oil.

Plastering her un-threaded Quarantine face now with this same Vatna paste, was perhaps Lollita's symbolic schooling of herself to see the social distancing protocols as Mother Earth's own version of the 'Vatna' folk wisdom. To protect her human populace from the evil lurking at the doorstep—the Coronavirus Pandemic.

"Looks like Mother Earth wants us to use Lockdown to beautify our souls, the way the 'Vatna' folk custom beautifies the face!" Lollita said sunnily to Ruhaan, who was labouring over the lens that had captured slices of Sufism for the coffeetable book he was working on.

As Lollita patted another layer of the herbal moist-ness to soothe the parched plaster pricking her face, she exclaimed philosophically.

"Quarantine is the New Vatna Ritualism!"

"Honey, how about twinning with Vatna!" Ruhaan tossed up his own twist, as he smeared some of the Vatna paste on his face, too.

The scent of sandalwood serenaded his skin.

Its understated, subtle fragrance erased the pungent hangover of yesteryear mustard oil from the labyrinths of Lollita's memory. Forever.

His face now plastered in the pallor of the same Vatna paste, Ruhaan then preened with her for an Instagram selfie.

The parched paste on her face, the parched soil of her soul, pricked with surprise, then crackled into a smile. And, Lollita ticked the first box of the MissMonalini couple quiz in her mind.

#LockdownCoupleGoal1. It Takes Two to Twin.

19

The Curious Case of Dum Maaro Dum

"Rooh, let's spice up our CQ!"

This was a resolve that left Ruhaan looking a little nonplussed as Lollita egged him on.

"CQ? What in the world is that?" Ruhaan looked at sea, as if it was all Greek to him.

"Haha...#CoupleGoals quotient," Lollita enlightened him. "But, you leave out the vocabulary, let's get the action rolling."

"Action? Right now? Right here?" Ruhaan goggled gleefully, only to warm up to things.

"Honey, I'm talking of spicing up things in the kitchen," Lollita teased. Just as Ruhaan was beginning to get ideas and drip all drool, she tossed the speed-breaker, "Let's do fusion food today—a mix of my Punjabi and your Mallu cuisine?"

Ruhaan tweaked her nosetip fondly, "Don't you wanna take it easy today, like a pampered princess? A total break from writing...and from #WorkOfHome...and just order me about?" he teased her.

"Nooo, today is our CG day," she cooed as Ruhaan looked a tad nonplussed. "Let's do North-South fusion food," she said, excitedly.

Interestingly, Malabar menu had been making steady inroads into not just Lollita's kitchen but also into the *rasois* of India Quarantining. With house helps and maids migrating to their villages, a staple of the Punjabi platter—the parantha—had gone for a toss. With no Lajjos or Lalitas to roll out the day to day Big Fat Punjabi Parantha *"makhan maar ke"*, an enterprising substitute being rolled out by enterprising entrepreneurs had made it to Lockdown's kitchens as much as to Lollita's—frozen Malabar Parotta.

"Why not us experiment with Malabar recipes using our staple north ingredients?" Lollita was bubbling with ideas as she browsed YouTube for fusion recipes.

Thus, it turned into a moment of Dum Aloo meets Malabar Biryani. They spent the afternoon dishing out their own experiments with fusion cuisine. Tossing out Appams with wheat flour instead of rice flour. Rustling up Reshmi Kebabs in Coconut Curry, gurgling with glee at epicurean eureka moments when they got it right.

The fusion food that took the cake was the two of them doing Dum Aloo and Malabar Biryani done in *dum* style.

Culled from Mughlai cuisine and popularised in particular by Nawab Asaf-Ud-Daulah, the wazir of Awadh, in the 1700s. Ironically, it's a culinary tradition that was cultivated to cult status in the time of deprivation—a famine. Later, the craft of 'Dum Pukht' was catapulted to iconic standing in Hyderabadi and Kashmiri cuisines. A culinary tradition that entails cooking ingredients, be it meats or veggies or rice, in huge handis (clay or metal pots) sealed with dough. The folk wisdom driving this tradition is to let the ingredients cook in their juices, oftentimes overnight.

Lollita fished out the pots she had picked from Dilli Haat, placed them on low flame and tossed in the spices.

Ruhaan spiced up the mood with Rumi. His brawny embrace encircled her from behind.

Lollita stirred in the whole spices into the first pot. The spices sputtered to a new life. Ruhaan wrapped her gently from behind, sturdy as a pillar, as his hand stretched to toss in the spices into the second pot.

The flame flickered. The low flame leapt. As if with longing. A longing to leap higher.

His warmth brushed her skin as Ruhaan stirred the spices. The "Radha" in her stirred.

The flame simmered in softly. The "Parvati" in her stirred into awakening, like a seeker at Nageshwara.

Lollita's nimble fingers worked on the onions, to be peeled and sauteed to a glistening goldenness. Ruhaan's fingers worked on peeling the layers of her being, the layers of embedded apprehensions of age.

Layers upon layers. Peeling off.

Inhibitions, of mid-life baring before a younger lover, shedding away. Inhibitions, of middlescence brushing its flab upon youth's well-toned abs, peeling away.

Hormones, that had seemed on the point of petering off, now peaking. Hormones that had lay latent, now dancing to bare their new inner skin.

Lollita tossed in the baby potatoes, then poured in the coconut milk to mingle with the baby potatoes. The micro souls flowed to merge into the sea.

Lollita felt a current snake up the back of her neck, as she tossed in the *potli* of whole spices swathed in muslin softness.

Ruhaan's lips naughtily nibbled the milkiness at the nape of her neck, as his hands shepherded the marinated chicken chunks into the second pot.

The plasma of her pores pulsated as though staging a Laasya like Parvati's. Her capillaries churned like a Krishna river longing to flow up to the Mallikarjuna jyotirling.

The Trishul nose-stud preened to her pulsating breath. Then, took a deep breath to let loose its 'Ladhi' mudra.

The bronzed bushy brawn of his hands slided to stack the layers into the skin of the Biryani. Slided back to un-stack the layers of her skin.

Atop the sputtered bay leaves and other condiments, he strewed in a layer of the Jeerakasala rice peculiar to Thalassery Malabar Biryani. In went a layer of the curd-marinated chicken chunks. More layers of rice, succulent chicken, and seasoning.

Sheets upon sheets, as he tossed in soaked saffron strands, sautéed onions, and spices to blend into the juiciness of the marinated meat.

Layers upon layers, piled on.

As Ruhaan's fingers returned to shepherd her atoms to an awakening, Lollita felt her own being's sheets sliding off.

Peeling off, layer by layer.

Her middle-class inhibitions peeling off. Her hangovers from failed relationships peeling off. Her middle-aged hormonal speedbreakers shedding off. Her strands of midlife blues shedding off in the saffron goldenness of the soaking.

Her old skin peeling off to unfurl the new skin of the inner core. As had the epidermis of the sauteed onions shed itself to reach the goldenness.

The awakened pores of her new skin glistened as her hands moved to roll out ropes of wheat flour dough. Her nimble fingers frolicked with the ropes to ready them for clamping the lids of the pots.

She felt Ruhaan's fingers rising up the ample-ness of her waist, and up the sculpted suppleness snuggling in the heart of her spaghetti.

Her heartbeat stretched its altaa-adorned hands to stage the 'Dhasaka' *bhaav*.

Ruhaan's fingers rose to send flames leaping up her pores.

His fingers unfurled their feather touch to serenade the suppleness of the lipper-bereft nudity of her lips.

Lollita's fingers reached out to tug the ropes of dough round the pots in an inextricable embrace. With a deep breath and sweeping embrace, she sealed it.

Her latent hormones leapt up into a Latabandha. The embrace around her tightened and Ruhaan sealed it.

Sealed it with flames of molten desire poured on her lips.

'Dum', the breathing in. 'Pukht', the simmering on slow flame.

20

The Curious Case of Reshmi Meets Rumi

Into this reshmi kebab meets Rumi moment walked the proverbial 'haddi'.

"Anything cooking?" Sid suddenly popped into the kitchen as the two disentangled just in time.

Cooking, it was.

Sid lingered to lend his touch here and there, with a *MasterChef Junior* sort of swag, before disappearing into his room for his #WFH Webinar.

Much sweating it out over pots and pans later (a workout Lollita certainly hadn't minded), they sank into the living room recliners to relish their labour of love.

"Umm...this tastes so different!" Ruhaan gushed, chomping on the Reshmi Kebabs in Coconut Curry. "I think this fusion brings out the best of both sets of spices...," the fusion food was stirring the poet inside him to new levels of eloquence.

"Wow...the baby potatoes actually taste super with a touch of south spices," Lollita was dipping into the bowl of Dum Aloo in Coconut Curry.

"This is sheer poetry for the palate...," the poet in Ruhaan was reasserting itself again and again, looking for suitable articulation.

"Ummm...this is what PGW would call the 'sunlit' moment," the humourist in Lollita was looking for parallels in the Pasha of Prose of the sunshine sort.

The "Dum" culinary tradition stirred in Lollita a folksy resonance.

As she dipped into the fusion food, Lollita couldn't help philosophise aloud thus, "Mother Earth looks to have locked us all into a proverbial clay pot and is letting us cook in our creative juices to bring out the best flavours in us! What say, Rooh?"

"Divine...divine...," Ruhaan raved, propelled towards the pinnacle of poetic expression as he tucked into the Dum Malabar Biryani and Reshmi Kebab Curry. "Guess what would Rumi call this?"

"What?" Lollita was only half listening.

"You are not a drop in the ocean, but the entire ocean in a drop!" Ruhaan said, unlocking his inner Rumi.

Lollita was busier ticking a mental box from the MissMonalini couple compatibility quiz:

#LockdownCoupleGoal2. The couple that cooks together stays together.

21

The Curious Case of Patturi Versus Pattod

If Vatna was the beautification regime that Lollita was having to bank upon and that was her lens for filtering folk wisdom, the other lens that was her Lockdown glasspane, was showcasing another beautification narrative.

"Rooh, how I wish Gupta ji grew cucumbers instead of those boring laukis! At least, I could have begged, borrowed or stolen some for a face pack," Lollita naughtily remarked to Ruhaan as she looked across, patting more curd on to the Vatna plastered on her face one morning.

It was a morning that showed signs of not only her outer beautification, but also 'inner' grooming.

It was a day devoted less to Netflixoholicism and more to her twin passion—e-shopaholicism. Lollita's fingers tapped away animatedly on Myntra.

She was browsing some Mangalgiri sarees and mayur motif blouses to team with them when some alluring inner wear pictures popped up.

Her fingers strayed. And stayed.

It was as if strangers stared back at her.

Lacy lingerie. Corsets to camisoles. Oozing oomph.

It was ages since she'd shopped for sexy lingerie.

Her fingers strayed to a piece of loud lace.

A Victoria's Secret "Bombshell" babydoll in lipsticky red.

Was this too flashy for the Forties?

Her hand next e-lingered over a Bwitch bralette full of fuchsia frilliness.

Terribly Twenty-ish?

A corset boasting Bucket Berry bling popped up.

Tempting but too Thirty-ish?

Would Ruhaan fancy her in this bit of bling? What's the stuff that would turn on a younger beau? Which lacy lingerie would be an eye-catcher that would keep his eyes riveted enough, away from the Lockdown 'tyres' that had housed themselves on her waistline or the midlife flab bursting out of the seams of her skin, like extra cheese dripping from a Domino's Pizza?

Her fingers clicked on a colour that never went out of fashion. A colour that one could never go wrong with.

Black.

Black camisole with plenty peek-a-boo lace. Naughty at Forty.

Just as her fingers were hovering over 'Add to Cart', a head popped over her shoulder.

"Mom, did you receive my Amazon…?"

One look at his middle-aged mom's shopping cart and Sid's sentence froze in the air.

Beyond the Lockdown window, too, beautification was happening on the Gupta and Ganguly patios.

The window revealed only laukis, more laukis and greater greens sprouting and being scrubbed and sorted in Gupta ji's kitchen garden as he could be seen buried in the wilderness like a grizzly bear pottering about the Prairies.

Grooming was on Ganguly ji's mind, too. But, of a different kind.

It was Ganguly ji's Day Out to wax eloquent. His 'Lady Love' was getting a full-fledged facial. Car waxing.

Car wax was to Ganguly ji's four wheels what spraying and manuring was to Gupta ji's flower beds.

Each scrubbing of the skin of the red Lamborghini lubricated Ganguly ji's cherished dream. To one day be the first to make it across the finish line with his lady in red as the winner of the Classic Car Rally.

The glint and glassy look in his eyes as he saw his beauty glisten bit by bit imbued to him an uncanny resemblance to the day-dreaminess of that fabled character in *Mungeri Lal ke Haseen Sapne*.

So lost was he in his Mungeri Lal-esque day dreaming about the car rally that when a spurt of liquid wetted not only the rear of the Lamborghini but also his own posterior, he imagined it to be Durga Maa's divine blessings in the shape of an unscheduled condensation of Cumulonimbus to cool the scorching summer.

It was only when he realised the shower had skirted the rest of humanity and only showered benediction upon him that he looked up in disbelief over his shoulder. Only to find that spoiling the car wax of his beauty was not sheets of rain, but torrential spurts from the neighbour's hose that were a pain.

Gupta ji was busy bathing his greens, and some of his irrigation inadvertently had strayed on to Ganguly ji's porch and person.

"Dada, careful…!" Ganguly ji called out aloud, while under his breath he muttered a long list of curses in Bengali which he knew Gupta ji couldn't decode.

"Sorry, sorry, Dada…," Gupta ji muttered.

"Your laukis' beauty bath is not good for my waxed beauty…" Ganguly ji rambled.

"Awww, isn't this one a beauty," Gupta ji by now was holding up a plucked piece of his fresh crop of laukis.

But, Ganguly ji's mood had been soured by the splashes on his freshly waxed Lamborghini and he wasn't taking too kindly to this neighbourly overstepping.

"Arrey Dada, so much of the society's scarce water resources wouldn't be used up if only you would treat your taste buds to the pleasures of Rui Machher Jhol or Bhetki Patturi instead of munching on these mundane greens! These...these...leafy greens!" Ganguly ji spouted, sardonically. His bespectacled eyeballs scoffingly surveyed the humongous heart-shaped herds sprouting all over to eclipse lesser greens in Gupta ji's kitchen garden.

Arbi pattas. Cultivated copiously by the Gupta household to make that staple savoury, 'Pattod'.

Ganguly ji's culinary preachification touched Gupta ji to the quick. Such that the ruffled raw nerve quivered in the innards of the strictly vegan Gupta constitution like a Leftist smarting under a Right-winger's parliamentary pontification to the former to give up Red.

"Dada, but at least we have our laukis in Lockdown, we're not starving...with no fish supplies coming in," the vociferous vegan in Gupta ji shot back.

As happens in much of social discourse of cross-cultural India, an innocuous banter between neighbours, this micro narrative of a Lauki Lover versus Non-Lauki Lover, a Pattod versus Patturi subtext, amplified into an animated macro debate.

As the 2G's squabbled, the cultural clash travelled through the air to sound a ring of resonance in the sigh of the newly converted vegan, Lollita. Stroking her cracking skin pack, she sighed soulfully, "If only Lockdown life could be as cool as cucumber."

22

The Curious Case of Life Out of Tune and Tuna

Bholi Punjabban was smitten. Lazing in Lollita's lap by the Lockdown window as her mistress keyed away at her Work In Progress, the cat gazed out unblinkingly with a new-found longing.

The Ballerina of a Bird became a frequent visitor on their patio and Bholi Punjabban's fascination for the creature grew day by day, so regal was its costume and so stately its gait as it strutted on the catwalks that were the Gulmohar's barren boughs braving the scorching season. Watching awestruck this creature of the wild, who had strayed into their urban-scape in the Lockdown, had Bholi Punjabban so smitten that she thought if there were to be a fashion show of the avian populace, this Ballerina of a Bird would surely be its show stopper.

Smitten though she was, but Bholi Punjabban still pined for the pigeons that used to congregate for their customary peck at the grains under the Gulmohar. And, she was beginning to miss the familiar smells of fish being cooked daily in the Ganguly household, as those aromas now seemed few and far between, becoming as much a rarity as the smells and supplies of Tuna that her mistress hitherto had ample stocks of, but which was now almost absent from Lockdown's kitchen shelves.

In Lockdown, looking at Bholi Punjabban sniff at the substitutes—Kurkure cheesy Puffcorn and Monster Paws—as acceptingly as she had hitherto hankered after fish titbits, Lollita wondered, how often it is that our pets are the ones proffering lessons in living, especially in unprecedented times such as the Pandemic.

Now, with Lockdown bolting life's doors and supplies of Bholi Punjabban's packaged fish food, in particular tinned Tuna, trundling to an unceremonious halt, her snooty nostrils were smelling new opportunities.

After the initial sulking and sullenness, Bholi Punjabban and her battalion of kitties, had taken things in their stride and shifted gastronomic affiliation to lesser food.

#LifesLemonsIntoLemonade: When Life tosses Lemons, treat Twisteez as the new Tuna.

For, by the end of Lockdown's Month One, Lollita had realised that quarantine life was not only going to be out of tune, but also out of Tuna.

#LockdownChallenge2 had presented itself.

When stocking up her refrigerator with frozen foods—chicken nuggets and luscious seekh kebab supplies for sonny dearest, and mostly potato smileys and hara-bhara kebabs for herself—little had Lollita anticipated the arrival of a compulsive fish-eater among them.

The only fish she'd stocked up was for her Bholi Punjabban and the kitties—tins and tins of marinated Tuna.

Lockdown soon became a stage for a battle as dramatic as a *Baahubali*, one that no pet mom wishes to be subjected to—to be torn between a loved cat and the new love of her life.

For, with all deliveries unceremoniously coming to a standstill in Quarantine, no fish supplies were forthcoming.

Which made Ruhaan like a fish out of water.

Slowly but surely, she saw the stocked supplies of Tuna depleting. Not because her cats were having a Tuna party, but because, life for somebody else was suddenly on a roll. Tuna roll.

That became the staple sandwich for Ruhaan's subsistence.

This presented a new challenge for Lollita—to find her cats a new substitute that would seem somewhat as delectable as Tuna.

One morning, she was doing up a Subway sort of sandwich of greens for herself, when the idea struck her the moment she was stuffing her own sandwich with the packed stuff.

Why not try the Tofu instead of Tuna!

So, she tossed some peppered Tofu at Bholi Punjabban. She at first came and sniffed and scrutinised it with some misgiving, for her smell and sights were set on the Tuna tin Ruhaan had left half finished.

Then, like a reluctant adventurist, she partook of some Tofu and didn't quite mind its cheesy goodness.

That was it.

For the cats, Tofu thus became the new Tuna.

#LifesLemonsIntoLemonade: When Life tosses Lemons, treat Tofu as the new Tuna.

But the Battle was waiting to happen.

It was not only the ongoing battle of the Vegan versus Non-Vegan that had been unfolding on the kitchen shelves and refrigerator stockpiles.

There was another Battle in the offing: Tuna Lover 1 versus Tuna Lover 2.

And, it did, the day Ruhaan uncorked one of the last few tins of Tuna.

Not that he had not been magnanimous in sharing the spoils with the felines every time he had dug into the stockpile of tinned Tuna meant for them. It's just that Bholi Punjabban and her kittens didn't much relish a 'hooman' digging into their supplies or having to share their goodies with a new 'hooman'.

So, that day as he uncorked the much coveted goody, Bholi Punjabban leapt up as if to snatch the tin of Tuna from his agile hands. Ruhaan was bit taken by surprise at the swiftness of her action.

He hurriedly scooped out the tinful needed for his roll and with the last few chunks left over, he decided to share with her. He was all to share the spoils but not without subjecting Bholi Punjabban to an arduous workout in the form of a game of 'fetch'.

He tossed some fleshy chunks of Tuna out into the patio, hoping Bholi Punjabban would be in time to lap them up.

Alas, Bholi Punjabban missed the bait meant for this game of 'fetch'. After all, like her mistress, she too hadn't been bestirring herself much for #WorkoutFromHome, hence her calf muscles weren't as sprightly in reaching the bait in time.

On missing them in the air, Bholi Punjabban presumed Ruhaan had tricked her by not throwing them at all. And, in a mood of revenge, she uttered a loud war cry and charged back at Ruhaan to grab the tin in his hands.

The Tuna chunks, meanwhile, meandered further yonder, like a Seeti Bomb hissing through the stratosphere aimlessly, only to be arrested by what looked like quite a cushy landing spot.

It was only when Ruhaan was greeted by an inexplicable bout of cacophony that the import of the misadventure revealed itself.

That very moment an uproar erupted from the verandah across. Dripping vexation and volubility like the grunts of a pig that finds himself stepping into a puddle packed with pests. Gupta ji across was exercising his lungs in the only workout he portrayed a partiality towards—ejecting expletives that any Punjabi would be fully familiar with but those which might have left a half-Punjabi a tad nonplussed.

As they did Ruhaan.

The thing was that the chunks being directed at Bholi Puñjabban had flown off to go do some neighbourly visiting in gross violation of social distancing protocol and the landing spot the forces of gravity had finally propelled them towards was none other than the person of Gupta ji as he was bending near his gate to lend his green thumb to some of his prized petunias and pansies. And so, to be precise, the Tuna had landed on the strictly vegetarian Gupta ji's oversized posterior.

Bemused at this misdirected battle of the Tuna lovers, Lollita burst into a bout of laughter, as she mentally ticked another box of the MissMonalini couple quiz.

#LockdownCoupleGoal3. "Love Me, Love my Pets..."

She added to it her own rider for Ruhaan. "...but not my pets' meat."

23

The Curious Case of Strings Attached

"Rooh...Sid...where the heck are the earphones? Desperately need them for my family dhoom on Zoom!" Lollita called out dramatically to both the guys.

Ah, but there was slim chance of her being heard, for the cochlear compartments of the recipients of her frantic pleas were at that moment encased in earphones themselves. The younger, millennial pair of ears was receiving blaring music of the Ed Sheeran kind "I'm in love with your body", while the older, mid-thirtyish pair of ears was tuned in to Sufi love with Nusrat Fateh Ali Khan's "Mere Rashke Qamar".

"Gosh, just when I have back-to-back Zoom meetings coming up, I can't find the earphones," Lollita ended up muttering more to herself as she exercised herself in out-of-syllabus yogic asanas that might've captivated the attention of Baba Ramdev for their innovation—from stretching one arm under the bed while stretching the legs on the floor in the opposite direction to crouching on all fours like a squirrel nosing around for nuts—only ending up to dislodge dumped wrappers of chocolates or chips residing under the couch or the bed instead of the earphones.

Having barely recovered from near yoga like stretching, Lollita straightened up only to find her prized pair of earphones dangling, from where else but Bholi Punjabban's mouth. Needless to say, they resembled a corpse of cords that breathed their last on account of chomping, being mistaken for some blackish version of the Chicken Chowmein that Bholi Punjabban simply loved.

"Oh no…you naughty girl," Lollita chided even as she retrieved the mangled corpse from the cat. Ruhaan walked into the room just then and Lollita virtually grabbed at his earphones.

"Darling, lend me your ears…and also your earphones," she implored. She even tried the tack of hashtagism. "Remember, honey, it's part of #couplegoals, the new-age 'Forty Rules of Love' of Rumi?" she reminded him.

Eager to facilitate her Big Fat Indian Biradri Dhoom on Zoom, he supportively supplied her his brand new Sony Bluetooth earphones.

"Such a sweetheart you are!" Lollita said, gratefully.

Having acquired the earphones, she hurriedly set up her laptop for the Zoom meeting with her commissioning editor. For the next 20–30 minutes they were brainstorming about the changes the editor wanted in the script—which character was to be murdered (out of the script), who and who had to be made to meet, and which character had to have more meat.

The thing about Zoom, Google Hangouts & Co—where the Virtual was the New Real—was that it robbed half the joy of a face-to-face conversation. Especially when that conversation gave rise to tectonic shifts in the fellow conversationist's facial reflexes. And, so it was, throughout the Zoom meeting, how Lollita missed the live crackling of Paroma's crisp Kasavu or Taant sarees that had always been as much a part of the conversations Paroma and she had had. Alas, this crackle of couture had suffered an unceremonious burial, thanks to the Lockdown.

For, the biggest cosmetic changes that the pandemic had ushered in was not in downsizing vanities, but also downsizing of vanity boxes. Zero cosmetics was the New Normal.

And so, the Zoom meeting with Paroma ended on a write note but not a rather right note, replete with the requiem to the Sarees' Day Out.

The next Zoom meeting of the day was more a family reunion, all cousins were coming together globally for the extended family's Grand Patriarch's 90th birthday, Zoom being the New Banquet Hall of the New Normal.

The family had all decided to host the Zoom party as a surprise, with Kaavya playing the emcee. The culinary code for the evening: everybody was to cook something special, to be showcased and savoured virtually. Except for the birthday boy, there was a dress code—black and red.

Lollita hurriedly showered and rummaged out her black and red border Venkatgiri saree. She hadn't really baked any stuff in ages, so she rustled up a quick Caramel Custard, garnished with Oreos. She parked her laptop on the patio for a nice chat session of connecting to the global Biradri.

At the stipulated time of 4 pm, one by one, all the grids started coming alive, as all the cousins who'd been sent invites for the Zoom meet came online. The time had been so chosen that kith and kin from all continents, Australia to America, could join in.

"Hi...hello everybody...can you all hear me?" Kaavya was getting the conversation rolling.

"Hello...yes, yes...Kaavu...but I don't see your mom?" it was Sureeli Didi smiling up in between her Bridge session.

"She'll be online any minute, Mausi...."

"Hi darlings, so lovely to see you all beauties... Can you see me?" that was Inderpreet Singh, aka Indy, from Maharani Bagh. Not to be missed, peering out of the tiny Zoom grid next to the nattily dressed Indy, in a black shirt and red striped tie, was another handsomely dressed face—his chit of a chihuahua, Chulbul, in a Candy Cane Tie!

A tapestry of turbans and countless cousins came alive on Zoom grids. Ashok ji, Ashwameet, Akram, Jassi, Sarbyy, and Bharat Bhais to Ajit, Pushii, Mandy, and Sattu uncles to Tanishaa, Reuben, and Nayaraa bhabhis to Sonyaa, Bindyaa,

Taara, Naanki, Nehaa, and many more. Relatively speaking, the Dhoom on Zoom narrative spelt more the merrier.

Amritsar Shahi to Patiala Shahi to Barnala wali Pagg to Morni Pagg. The grid was a gallery of the grandeur that was the Sikh headgear.

Into this tapestry of turbans arrived the showstopper.

The lehariya pagg.

The Grand Patriarch popped up on Zoom.

Dapper and debonair Kawi Mama, aka Kawalmeet Singh, the former bureaucrat and now a Bridge champion. The Patriarch, who presided over their extended Big Boisterous Punjabi Biradri as also their WhatsApp and Zoom family chat groups called 'Ekkaanth'.

Much cacophonous crooning of birthday greetings later, Kawi Mama zeroed in on Lollita.

The lehariya pagg lorded it. "Where in the world have you been, darling?" he enquired.

"Where can one be in Lockdown…except travelling… indoors…from one room to the other?" Lollita laughed.

"Sweetie, why are you missing in action on our WA cousins' group?" another cousin, Gulnaar Di, sweetly chimed in from Jalandhar. She dripped not only sweetness but also solitaires. Where else to showcase the solitaires she just bought before Lockdown than at this family dhoom on Zoom!

"Was wondering where you've run away," teased her sister Radhyaa.

"Or, whether you're stranded on some exotic runway!" bantered her niece, Kaavya.

The Barnala pagg bobbed from Belfast. "Don't you know, darling, if you're not constantly writing on WhatsApp, you risk being written off!" joked Sarbyy.

"Who in the world does the vanishing trick from WhatsApp?" demanded Sureeli Di.

The Patiala pagg butted in. "How can you survive without WhatsApp...that, too, in Lockdown?" Indy boisterously bantered, as his chihuahua bow-bowed as though in agreement. Though the cousin and his chihuahua hogged up most of the Zoom grid, Lollita could see smiling sunnily in the background her stylista of a sister-in-law, Reuben.

Now, this was a question that Lollita had much practice in fielding from Biradri, BFFS & Co who took much relish in propelling her on a certain trip, even in these times of zero travel—the guilt trip.

"Haha...Well, I'm surviving without WA the way Shakespeare survived the plague or Walt Disney the Spanish Flu!" Lollita shot back her standard reply, copy to all.

All this caterwauling and chirruping went on among the cousins connecting across cybersphere in the time of social distancing.

Small talk may not be your cup of tea, dear discerning reader, so not to bore you with any more of the jollifications being staged on the virtual stage, let's take you behind the scenes to the real action.

Looking at the grids, Lollita let out a sigh, as she saw that every kith and kin was with a partner and she was the only one going solo.

Now that soulful sigh was perhaps heard by Providence, who might have been passing by or even eavesdropping. You know how curious Dame Fate can be!

So, just as the family reunion on Zoom was in full swing, Ruhaan had finished bathing and came out in a semi-clad state, tiptoeing tentatively to park his laundry on the clothes stand somewhere in Lollita's background. The photography pro that he was, so as not to photobomb into the Zoom grid, he was manoeuvring to materialise his migration by crouching cautiously on all fours, much like monkeys at a Hanuman Mandir crawling to creep off with your Chanel clutch without being spotted. Alas, Ruhaan's perambulating pate and bare back somehow strayed onto the screen to stage a guest appearance.

The paggs popped forward. The grids goggled. At first, a studied silence as all soaked in the sight.

Thereafter, unlocked a barrage of grilling, like back-to-back volleys hurled by primetime's Rajdeep, Rajat & Co.

The Amritsari pagg peered from Panchkuian Road. "Who is that behind you?" Sweety Mama quizzed.

"Whoa… Who's that nude dude?" Indy teased.

The lehariya pagg loomed again. "Goodness, is that your son? Handsome hunk!" Kawi Mama sounded stunned.

The nok wali pagg squirmed. "Look at *aaj kal ka bachchas*… Why isn't he saying a hello to us all?" Pushii Mama chided.

"Er…Nah…Er…," Lollita's mind was racing fast on how to save the situation. She was hoping to pass off Ruhaan as Sidak since his face hadn't really photobombed.

Till then, that is.

Bingo, that very moment the pets of the household—Bholi Punjabban & Co, who were sprawling on the verandah in half siesta mode, were distracted by a dangling object. The pyjama string dangling from Ruhaan's lower wear as he was ducking down. The string sort of struck a chord with the cats.

Bholi Punjabban made a dash for the curious object as her kittens clapped about Ruhaan's heels dying to tear their teeth into it too. Leave alone photobombing, now there was noise bombing behind Lollita, too.

For, the felines began to 'belt' out their own cat chorus driven by the sentiments stirred for the string, "Till Death Do Us Apart…"

Attracted by the felines foraying into Lollita's grid, Indy ji's canine Chulbul too joined the chorus with a bow-bow, which if translated was meant to convey his ardent appreciation at the felines string dance, "wow wow".

In all this melee, Ruhaan couldn't quite accomplish his migration from the backdrop and found himself doing a towel dance with the felines, on the lines of Ranbir Kapoor's dalliance with bath linen in *Saawariya*. And, instead of migrating out of the scene, he photobombed, up, close, and personal.

If the look on Lollita or Ruhaan's face were to be described as 'sheepish', it would be an understatement.

Whilst confused emotions mapped their faces, all that Lollita was able to utter aloud was, "I…Er…Nah that's Sid's friend…."

The silence in the other grids was suddenly so pregnant, that had Donald Trump come and told the assembled congregation "I am Barack Obama", they would have found it easier to believe.

Later that night, Lollita mentally ticked another score on the MissMonalini couple quiz. #LockdownCoupleGoal4, but not without learning its comic life lesson.

Lockdown live-ins may come with strings attached.

24

The Curious Case of Being My Cup of Tea

Lollita's chai drinking household's encounter with a coffee-holic, had its roots in a morning few weeks into the automatic live-in called Quarantine.

As Ruhaan had strolled out of the study room-turned-guest room that morning towards Lollita's room, she had still been lolling in bed and called out, "Hey, honey, help yourself to any tea or coffee..."

But, the moment she uttered it, she knew they had a situation on their hands.

#LockdownChallenge1, Part B, had now re-asserted itself fully the first thing that morning. The chai drinker versus the coffee addict.

Though her kitchen was pretty well stocked with stuff the mother-son needed—since her deliveries from Big Basket had just arrived a day or two before Lockdown, coffee, that too filter coffee, was nowhere on the wishlist ordered nor were there coffee-making contraptions on her kitchen shelf.

He softly knocked at her bedroom door and she invited him in, feeling a tad sheepish at him seeing her in her unkempt situation.

But, what the heck, sooner or later he was going to see her like this and even beyond this.

"Honey, I'm so sorry but there's no provision for filter coffee...what to do?"

Ruhaan grimaced. For, if it is 'cutting chai' or kadak chai that refuels a Northie the first thing at daybreak, it's filter 'kaapi' that does it for a southerner.

Never mind, if Ruhaan had trotted the globe from Venice to Venezuela, you could take him out of his coffee plantation boyhood but you couldn't take the coffee out of him.

He was as passionate about his coffee as he was about Rumi's poetry. If Rumi was the food for his soul, coffee was the food for his senses.

Lollita's coffee deficient kitchen shelves saw him brooding about like a fish out of water. Or, to put it poetically, he moped about much in the manner of a Devdas pining for his Paro.

"Awww, honey, can't do without my 'poison'… We need to figure out fast how to stock up. What does Punjabi jugaad have to say?" he prodded her, pecking her on the lips.

"Punjabi jugaad is grappling with grogginess just yet," she had mumbled back, rubbing her eyes sleepily.

"But hey, lemme get you your cuppa while we figure this one out," he hovered over her bed, before making it towards the door, to rustle up her 'bed tea', as the Punjus love calling their morning brew ritual.

When he returned with a laden tray, she couldn't help but beam from ear to ear. It felt so good to be pampered like this, after ages.

"So sweet of you!" she said fondly as she offered him some coffee-flavoured cookies instead as consolation for the absence of coffee, not letting him know how high was the sugar level in her chai.

An overdose of saccharine levels once in a while wasn't going to kill (Given the fact that most of her ancestors were fabled foodies who'd met their end more from the side-effects of too much greasy butter chicken and malai tikka than from diabetes. It's another story that one or two of them had met a not-so-sweet end from choking on the chicken legs they were chomping, right on the table).

As long as life looked to be taking things to the next level.

What had been bothering Lollita was not the high sugar level in the bed tea Ruhaan made for her. The thing niggling away uppermost at the back of her mind was—when were things going to move to the next level.

Hoping to egg on the languorous pace of Lockdown life to the next level, Lollita thought of killing two birds with a stone.

Firstly, cheer up the coffee addict brooding without his customary cup of cheer. Secondly, speed up and spice up things between them.

Ruhaan had been looking for a chance but didn't want her to feel rushed into it. Besides, Lockdown meant they were never alone in the apartment. Three is a crowd, as they say.

"Rooh darling, why don't we watch some breezy RomCom in my room tonight?" Lollita suggested seductively over dinner, when Sidak strolled off from the dinner table for few minutes to take a call.

Thus, Quarantine's rendezvous was all set up.

Lollita laid out her assortment of scented spa style tealights and aromatic candles in various nooks and crannies of her tastefully styled room. Fished out from the depths of her closet was lacy lingerie, which had virtually been given an unceremonious burial during lockdown in favour of New Normal's National Lower Attire—pyjamas and palazzos.

As the night got younger, Ruhaan looked for an opportune moment to slip into Lollita's room.

Thus far, the opportune moment was not presenting itself since Sidak could be sighted strolling up and down the living room, ears pasted to his smartphone, chattering away, with nary a sign of the call nearing its end.

Every time Ruhaan smelt an opportunity, thinking Sid had slipped back into his room, there he gambolled back, still prattling into the damn device.

If you've been a keen observer of sports, you will agree that Ruhaan's antics resembled those of an Olympic sprinter poised at the start line, all set to do the leap jump sprint the moment the whistle goes off. Alas, the get-set-go whistle shows no sign of going off.

For the umpteenth time, Ruhaan braced up for his Usain Bolt like act of bolting into Lollita's bedroom. Just then, he heard Sid popping out of his room, also for the umpteenth time, to perform across the length and breadth of the lounge his aimless walkathon meets talkathon.

Ruhaan propelled every rippling muscle of his gym-sculpted torso to perform the marathon of a lifetime. Whooosh, he went sprinting towards Lollita's door before Sid had fully ejected from his own room, only to land not so much at the door as upon a squiggly bundle. The said squiggly something, not taking kindly to nocturnal trespass, meant to make mince of the intruding limbs that landed upon it, but in a passing moment of mercy, let go of the said stamping foot with a mere bite.

"Ouch ouch ouch!" As a chorus of such hushed exclamations of agony escaped Ruhaan's lips, he swooped down to scoop up the squiggly something he had stepped on and whose slumber he had sinfully cut short, which he had been meted out a meaty style of crime and punishment.

Life could be said to have been in kick mode to prod things to the next level when Sid had sallied into the living room in his walkathon-talkathon mode, for the sight that had presented itself to him was this.

Ruhaan had been limping into Lollita's room with not only a foot that was lame, but also an excuse, that to her sonny dearest within earshot, had sounded even more lame.

"Honey, here, Bholi Punjabban was desperately looking for you!"

Deeper into that night, as life literally kicked things to the next level, Lollita was busier mentally ticking another box to notch the next score on her MissMonalini compatibility quiz, #LockdownCoupleGoal5, even as Ruhaan whispered Rumi into her ears,

"When someone quotes the old poetic image
about clouds gradually uncovering the moon,
slowly loosen knot by knot
the strings of your robe
Like this."

25

The Curious Case of It Takes Two to Thaali

Lollita stifled a lazy yawn as she gazed out of her Lockdown window, sighing like a pressure cooker out of steam.

She was in zero writing mode that afternoon. She anyway wouldn't have been able to do much writing at her usual post-tea hour that day.

For, the Prime Minster had given a call for cheering the Corona Warriors that Sunday evening.

Now, you may wonder, what that had to do with a writer's life or with their writing. Well, the thing is that when Prime Ministers get it into their head to bring the nation to a standstill for a couple of minutes for an act of symbolism, it is but natural that writers too would be dropping their pens or ThinkPads for action that presents more pressing concerns than Writer's Block.

Just as well Lollita and Ruhaan had done the dishes together that afternoon and scrubbed away piles that had been accumulating over the weekend, for they would now be required to dish out some of the pots and pans they'd scrubbed squeaky clean and stowed away to drip dry.

There are three things that Punjabis are famous for being loud with—Gaali, Taali, and Thaali. (Not necessarily in that order, though.)

Today, Lockdown was thus going to be a stage that would be a litmus test at least for the last two trademark propensities—Taali and Thaali.

For, dear discerning reader, if you hadn't heard of this new form of theatre, who can blame you. It hadn't existed till that evening.

This was going to be an evening of Taali meets Thali Theatrics.

At sharp five that evening, all those utensils that citizens may have been discarded into disuse or dumped, but which may have possessed a high acoustics quotient or musical vocal cords, those were to be rummaged out for a theatrical outing on the promenades and patios of India Quarantining.

For the citizens of the country had been given a clarion call for coming out on their patios to bell out or bang out any utensils with a metallic propensity towards music in support of the Corona Warriors—the caregivers or workers battling the pandemic from the forefront putting their own health at hazard. To complement the performance with pots and pans, the citizens had been called upon to put their carpal tendons to use to stage cameo performances in the form of that subsidiary form of theatre—clapping.

The staging of a new form of theatre. Taali meets Thaali.

And so, when the clock was about thirty minutes short of the hour of five, Lollita and Ruhaan were seen scrambling through the kitchen shelves for the appropriate instruments of steel that might be inclined to musical renditions.

Ruhaan pulled out some steel plates and pots (*katoris*) to be drummed with steel spoons for the desired results.

"Nah, they're tad too tiny, sweetheart," Lollita called out, bending on her knees to rummage through the cardboard box in which she had just stowed away kitchen paraphernalia no longer in active use.

Her hands groped at something substantial that seemed like a *peetal paraat* (a larger, rimmed version of the plate, used usually for kneading dough). She tugged at it to dislodge it from among the piles it was embedded in.

Ah, but what she also dislodged was a family of cockroaches that had sort of established residence in the cardboard box and had particularly parked themselves on this *paraat* owing to its resemblance to a sprawling suburban roundabout.

She let out a screech that was almost so penetrating and piercing that Gupta ji and Ganguly ji, already positioned with paraphernalia on their patios, perceived it to be a call of calamity. The result was that their eyes and ears, hitherto attuned to each other in an across-the-wall conversation, now detached themselves from each other and attached themselves to the goings-on on in the Lollita household.

What the 4G (Gaze of the Gupta ji and Ganguly ji) beheld through the open windows of the living room smacked surely of suspicious conduct.

Lollita was ducking up and down all over the living room while Ruhaan was darting behind her with something in his hand that looked as suspicious as a weapon of attack.

And, the 4G also beheld another suspicious object in Lollita's hand which she wouldn't let go even as her lungs were letting loose a volley of shrieks and screams, while Ruhaan was trying to snatch it from her.

This 'weapon' was none other than the Hit anti-cockroach spray which Ruhaan was trying to squish upon the utensil but somehow was managing to spray more on Lollita than on the object of intent. This made her scream as much at the insects as at the showers of the repellent.

"It's sitting right there on the neck of your top," Ruhaan was trying to play the role of GPS for the whereabouts of the cockroach, but Lollita was squirming and squiggling so much from terror that she wouldn't even crane her neck towards the side where the abhorrent creature was perched.

When Ruhaan saw that the repellent nor his GPS-style navigational commentary were producing results of dislodging the creature, he lunged forward to tug at the spaghetti top Lollita was wearing.

Now, you can jolly well imagine, what this vision must have appeared like to the 4G. Perceiving this to be an act of forcible disrobing of the damsel in distress, the 4G goggled and gaped.

"Was this an act of domestic violence? Should it be reported to the police?" These were some of the thoughts crossing the sleuthing minds of Gupta ji and Ganguly ji, since they had been reading reports in the papers and seeing shows on Tamasha TV dwelling on the rise in domestic violence during Lockdown.

Gupta ji's Karamchand-the-detective type nosiness and Ganguly ji's Feluda-the-famous-Bengali-spy sort of sleuthing were probing these possibilities mentally when they heard a shattering sound. A sound that spelt the death-knell of their alternate career as future Feludas or Sherlock Holmes.

As Ruhaan's tugging at her top dislodged the petrified cockroach and it started inching from her neck towards her face, Lollita, in sheer terror, just dropped the *paraat* that she had been clutching at as a sort of shield. It landed with a loud thud in this utensil version of Metallica, as Lollita went plonking after the *paraat* on the floor in a reflex action. Ruhaan, who had his fingers entwined in the strings of her spaghetti, too, was pulled by this chain of actions, and they both collapsed on the floor in this clang of cacophony and unplanned canoodling.

As Ruhaan landed atop Lollita in a theatrical leap and the two resembled an inseparable heap, they became conscious of not just 4G but all neighbouring gazes peering at them with a mix of suspicion and curiosity.

As their peering pupils pondered, in the bosoms of Gupta ji and Ganguly ji were bestirred buried roles—knights with steel ammunition, "Is this a damsel in distress?"

By the time Lollita and Ruhaan appeared on their terrace in answer to the clarion call, obviously, with the controversial orchestra in tow—*paraat* and the paraphernalia, the 4G was already in position to behold the unveiling of the new theatre.

Gupta ji was lording it on his verandah with his eclipsed significant half, three married sons in tow with their better halves, and Gupta Sub Juniors, with a centre-table holding the contents for their collective performance. This formed the picture called the Gupta gharana of music-to-be.

Ganguly ji and his better half were parked on their cane garden chairs, along with his aged mother, all attired in traditional Bengali wear, spurred by the sartorial knowledge that this was the only outing they were going to have in a long, long time till Lockdown.

Bringing up the backdrop was their canine called Bruno, a daschund who couldn't quite comprehend what all the commotion was in this time of Quarantine's zero action. From time to time, he would let loose yelps as if beseeching enlightenment about this curious evening. This constituted the Ganguly gharana.

As Lollita and Ruhaan took position on their terrace armed with their ammunition, Gupta ji could be heard bending over his wall engaging Ganguly ji in political pontifications.

"Modi *hai toh mumkin hai…*," he prattled.

"Mamata Didi *ko match na kor sokey*," Ganguly ji countered. "*Bhalo bhalo*, how Didi has controlled Corona… Kolkata has one of the lowest casualties."

"What a brainwave of Modi ji to unite the country in support of those Corona warriors…," Gupta ji's staunch support did the talking.

"We're doing it more as solidarity for the warriors than as solidarity for any sarkar," Ganguly ji clarified his stance, lest his musical rendition be misconstrued and be music to the ears of Modi bhakts.

Their political ramblings were cut short as at the stroke of five, there rose in the air a collective chorus of a zillion Thalis and Taalis, and the two scurried to preside over the performances of their respective gharanas in this theatrics.

The Gupta Gharana announced its presence with metallica powered by 3G. Three generations.

In between his clanging and clapping, Gupta ji's gaze was travelling back and forth from balcony to balcony, like that of a budding maestro who from the corner of his eye scans the contents of a concert hall to ascertain the attitudes of the audience. Thus, it was that Gupta ji's gaze was keeping count of balconies that paraded full participation—which he translated to spell as the inmates' inclination towards the ruling party; whilst the empty balconies, to his sleuthing mind, spelt either apolitical approach or an affinity to rival parties.

The Ganguly Gharana, on its part, was treating this limited outing as if it were an 'express' and dress rehearsal for Durga Pujo. Its amateur musicians were clanging their collection of metallica with the same gusto which Bongs are wont to bring to their Dhunuchi ritual.

Gupta Gharana's *paraat, thaali, chimta,* and *chamach* versus Ganguly Gharana's *thala, chamoch, hata,* and *bati.*

Lollita was lending to this musical rendition all the energy that she had missed expending on her writing the whole day. Thus, the *paraat* found itself being catapulted to the exalted position of star performer in an instrumental band, its sentiments smacking similarity to that of a sitar that has gathered dust and rust for months but is suddenly strung back into eloquence. Such that the sounds it emits resemble less a practised mellifluousness and more a staccato squeaking.

Ruhaan, on his part, was more content just clapping in tandem with her sonny dearest.

He was anyway not much in the mood for clapping either, as his push-ups in the morning had left him with little stamina for extra-curricular exercising. After a bit, even his clapping panted and puffed to a lull and he just stood there a silent spectator.

The Taali and Thaali theatrics ended as abruptly as it had erupted.

Later that night, as she uploaded selfies on Instagram of the Taali and Thaali Theatrics, she hesitated over the hashtag #couplegoals.

Mentally, she had to un-tick the next box of the MissMonalini compatibility quiz: #LockdownCoupleGoal6... It Takes Two to Tango (In this case, It Takes Two to Thaali).

"Heck!" she exclaimed, making Ruhaan look up nonplussed. "Damn these relationship quizzes! Damn this #couplegoals hashtagism!" she muttered more to herself, as she saw her love life's rating drop on the MissMonalini.Com compatibility quotient quiz with that one un-ticked box.

But, the moment she saw the love of her life's drop-dead drooling eyes, she couldn't help gushing aloud, "Damn, who cares if we're a flop on #CoupleGoals or CQ!"

Planting a peck on his puckered brow, she spelt out the sentiment that was the bedrock for cementing compatibility, "Sweetheart, you're the best thing that happened to me... Never mind, if you're a half partner in chime!"

UNLOCK 1.0

"...The heaviest rain comes

out of the darkest clouds."

—RUMI

26

The Curious Case of the Missing Migrant

Somewhere in the suburbs of Gurugram

Peering petulantly out of the window, Bholi Punjabban felt a surge of an alien emotion suffusing her bosom, like a stranger creeping in from the back window of her being. Unheard. Unseen. Unknown.

A yearning that had gingerly tiptoed in to make home in her heart when life had been busy locking their homes.

The stirring of a hitherto unfelt longing, like when a tiptoeing stranger stumbles into a still piano to send springing to life unheard of staccato notes. A symphony of sublime pining.

It was many days since she had sighted the Ballerina of a Bird.

A pang pierced her innards as she heard the orchestra of thunder rumbling in the distance.

Bholi Punjabban was about to turn away the emptiness of her Peridot pale gaze when she spotted some stirring in the bough-laden bosom of the Gulmohar.

As Mother Nature rolled out its rock band of lightning and thunder, there, the grand Gulmohar's scaly arms from a searing summer staged their own extravaganza.

Rain's rock concert.

Bholi Punjabban gaped spellbound at the show stopper strutting about in the tree's greenroom.

Swarovskis started dripping from the eyelashes of a bereaved Mother Earth. To stud the rusty runways of the Gulmohar.

Lo behold! The Ballerina of a Bird preened, pirouetted, and unveiled the full glory of its plumed couture. Mother Nature's theatre at its best.

Hither, Lockdown's fleeting migrating population from the wooded wilderness into the cityscapes, Pandemic's mascot for the reverse migration—the Peacock—unlocked its spell.

The winged migrant unfurling to Mother Earth's Mian Ki Malhar.

Giddha on the Gulmohar.

Gulmohar. The Peacock Flower.

Mother Nature's Dance of Life amid Monster Pandemic's Dance of Death. Hand in Hand.

Thither, for Lollita, Unlock spelt another kind of unveiling.

Some days later, to propel this Unveiling to the next stage, Lollita landed again at Shahpur Jat.

In an Unlock landscape, it resembled a cat crawling out of a stretched hibernation. Peacock Lane rubbed its eyes to douse the drowsiness. Reminiscent of a hitherto crackling-with-energy cricket stadium, that had been lulled into languor when rain played spoilsport, spring back to the suspended game.

The business of making books in Unlock bespoke New Normal's ground reality. Virtual was the New Real. Be it the virtual conferencing and connecting to authors over mail or brainstorming boom with commissioning editors and art editors on Zoom. None of the briskness and business of Before Corona.

It is into this somnambulance that Lollita sallied forth, having been beckoned to see the first proofs of the book. Her heart was as aflutter as that of a wannabe starlet legging it to the preview of her debut flick. Starry eyed yet skittish.

As Paroma thrust the first proofs under her nose, Lollita fingered the script so gingerly as if she would touch it, it might do a vanishing trick.

"Here, the first proofs of your book," Paroma proclaimed in a matter of fact, dull tone, since this was not the first time some first proofs were passing through her hands and it was an everyday task for her.

"Wow," gasped Lollita, the contours of the countenance contorting with much the same sentiments as that of a player poised for a milestone moment. "Can't believe this...finally it's taking shape!"

"So, you can take two weeks or so to go through the proofs and after the corrections, if any, we send it to print," Paroma shut the folder as resolutely as she shut the discussion.

The next couple of days saw Lollita ploughing through the proofs. She had barely turned in the final proofs, when soon after she got a frantic call.

'Smartie' vibrated animatedly and Lollita saw Paroma's number flashing on the phone screen.

"Hey, I'm afraid there isn't very good news," said the voice at the other end.

Lollita's heartbeat almost came to a pause mode.

"What happened?" Lollita asked with bated breath, like a player poised on a pitch waiting for the umpire to make the crucial announcement of whether or not he is run out.

"Err...some unforeseen eleventh hour hiccups," Paroma said nonchalantly, sounding as blaise as if she was used to encountering speed-breakers in the book making. "The printing your book and a couple of our other titles will have to be put on hold for the next three months or more as our regular printer has not yet returned from the village. Due to downsizing after Lockdown, another printer we checked with has been compelled to relocate his workshop to a cheaper location," Paroma dropped the bombshell in a voice that was too calm and cool for Lollita's hip-hopping heart.

"Three months? Oh no!" Lollita almost screamed, if screaming is doable when your mouth cavity is stuffed with steamed momos and your lungs let out a sound so loud that it threatens to disgorge the contents of the oral cavity. "What do we do now, it turns our launch plans all topsy-turvy?" Lollita voiced her concerns.

"Well, with the Lockdown taking a toll on the printer, what we can do is an e-launch... And soft release the book for the time being...*only on Amazon*."

Paroma signed off with the air of a senior surgeon who has many 'babies' to attend to and can't be bothered too much with the birth pangs of one book.

Birth pangs on an unimaginably long and dark night. A night that will not be blanked from the bookmarked pages of memory for as long as memory breathes.

27

The Curious Case of New Kids on the Blog

Somewhere in the NCR

It is one thing to lust for Litfests, but quite another to have Litfests lusting after you.

Post Lockdown and post a digital launch on Amazon, Lollita's lusting for Litfest outings looked more like a case of longing for the moon. For, the wait for Litfests to resume their season kept getting longer and longer. Litfests were still playing it safe than sorry as every other day saw spikes and surges in Covid19 casualties.

Where the previous season had seen some Litfests seeing their death-knell sounded, riding on the recession and shrinking of sponsorships, Pandemic season saw death itself staring at Litfests.

What it all translated into was—Lull in Litfests.

What it spelt for Budding Authors and Wannabe Bestselling Author was that hopes of getting breaks at Litfests looked as far as Timbuktu was from Tuscany.

"Aww...yours is such a rollicking write... But, maybe its timing just isn't right," Meeraya Di was on the phone and both sisters were engrossed in discussing the after-life of a book that looked in need of promotional ventilators to survive, and the high hope of breaking into the Litfest circuit resembling more the Covid's flattened-the-curve narrative and the economy's Great Depression script.

"Di, but I didn't know all this was going to happen when I started writing the book," Lollita lamented. "No packed-house launches, no Litfests to look forward to, no rave reviews... How's a budding author to survive?"

The last bit caught Meeraya Di's attention in all this lament. "Rave reviews? But who's stopping you from getting those?"

In the post-Pandemic literary landscape that had scripted the epitaph of Old Normal's book biz, the rules of the game had changed. It had triggered a tilt. Bibliophilism's Big Fat Tectonic Tilt towards social media as the main stage, perhaps Pandemic's only surviving stage, for book marketing. On Lockdown's literary graveyards—bookstores—had burgeoned a breed.

The burgeoning breed of bright young things called Book Bloggers. The bridge between a Wannabe Bestseller and Bestseller Charts.

A Wannabe Bestseller's best bet—to peep out of as many book blogs and bookstagram frames as possible. Accessorised by Photoshopped book jackets to book shelfies, by cappuccinos to cheesecakes, petals to pearls.

"What do you mean, Di?" Lollita was all agog.

"Sweetie, which world are you living in? Rave reviews are all out there on offer!" Meeraya Di mouthed market intelligence with every word. An alumnus of IIM-A, she was the biz whiz of the family. If you wanted to know business trends, be it the stock market, or how GST was going to impact solitaires from De Beers.

"Really?"

"What else do you think this whole new book biz is all about?" the Big Sis was in her element now, it didn't take her much prodding to get started about new-age businesses and start-ups.

"But, how does one break into this book promo circuit?" Lollita was all agog.

The answer came in the form of IIM alumni networking.

"Wait...one of my IIM-A batchmates is heavily into the book collab biz...Let me connect you to her," Meeraya Di came to the rescue.

Lollita felt the heartbeat of hope rising from the ashes of its flattened-the-curve narrative in this literary script.

Meeraya Di was prompt in connecting her to a book blogger friend. By that very evening the two had connected, both on call and Instagram.

Unaa Ray.

"Hey, I heard a lot about your book from Meera. Hmmm... So, how do you want me to help?" Unaa didn't beat about the bush much and came straight to the point.

"Ah well, it's a new domain I don't know much about... So, you tell me how it works," Lollita was candid in confessing her ignorance. "You understand how it is, Litfest don't really look to be happening as of now, so I just want to use this lull to give some visibility to my book."

Lollita had been quick to pick up the new book lingo. That good ol' world of bagging book reviews on prestigious book pages of Sunday papers was passé. These were the times of instant action—Instagramming (no wonder, the world itself boasted the letters 'Insta').

And, the new catchphrases and hashtags driving this world of book blogging ran on these lines: #bookcollabs #bookpromos #bookvisibility #bestselling and all that.

"Worry not... We'll do the best we can for your book. I'll just DM you our packages...," Unaa chirruped.

"Packages?" Lollita's voice betrayed bafflement.

"Yes, my dear, depending on what the author wants, we have Short Review or Full Review...then, we have the bronze, silver, gold, and other packages, too!" Unaa offered enlightenment on the blogging dynamics.

"Ohhh...really?" Lollita was wonderstruck at how structured the system was.

It was a wait of a week before Lollita could witness a socially distanced unveiling of the face of this hot and happening new tribe. Till then she had to be content with goggling at a bloated-ness, not of her book sales figures, but her DM becoming bloated and bloated with book blogging content.

A couple of days later, Lollita trundled towards Dilli Haat with Lamba ji in tow, the latter adamant upon accompanying her so as to give his own special push to their marketing plan.

Lollita and Lamba ji were ferried forth by an Uber, the clinical coldness of its protocol-driven plastic curtain partitioning the Before Corona era from Unlock. Zipping along the avenues leading to Dilli Haat, greeting their eyes was a different carpet.

A carpet of uncrowned citrine chandeliers. Fall's fallen summer lanterns. The army of Amaltas breathing their last in the lap of a landscape that had been panting for breath.

Rolling into the ramparts of Dilli Haat, Lollita almost tripped on the undulating terrain, the desi carpets—durries. Unwrapping and unfolding for the Fall fest.

Lollita unfurled her black Maheshwari saree, with a poppy red temple border, rummaged out of her Pandemic-packed wardrobe. Her temple motif pallu caressed the cobbled cheeks of the pathways like the Godavari sweeping upon the shores of Trimbakeshwar.

On a landscape strewn with slayed skeletons from the armies of Amaltas, her Frida blouse was the lone portrait brimming with blooms. The embroidered Frida's floral hair-band bursting with red roses.

Rose red blush returning to the sallow cheeks of an unlocking Mother Earth. The culturescape blinked its eyelids to awaken from the Curse of the darkest night, from the Curse that the Guruji had ordained would consume the city.

The Restarting India narrative rolled out, trumpeting the return of footfalls.

As Lollita and Lamba ji's footfalls forayed further, this Unlock narrative revealed that beneath the surface though, the subtexts bespoke a new vocabulary.

The stall of state awardee, T. Mohan from Telangana, saw shoppers now bargaining for two Kalamkari stoles at the pre-Pandemic price of one.

Madhubani artists Kamini and Mamtha, camouflaged behind self-painted Madhubani masks, had, during Lockdown, switched from sarees to painting Madhubani pouches, clutch bags, men's ties, and masks. Stuff that was lighter on their pocket as much as on the depleted pockets of Dilli Haat's middle-class shoppers.

National Awardee Punjab's Phulkari artist Lajwanti's stall now had takers more for easy-on-the pocket salwar-suits and lighter-embroidery Phulkari dupattas. National awardees Nazir and Aleya, as also Shilp Guru Awardee Alima, from West Bengal, were finding fewer footfalls at their stall of exotic and exorbitant Kantha sarees and were trying to reinvent by showcasing stoles suited more to post-Pandemic pockets.

Pattachitra artistes Noordin Chitrakar and Kalpana from Purba Medinipur in West Bengal, were reinventing, too. With hardly any buyers for their Pattachitra canvases, they were dishing out souvenirs such as coasters painted with 'maachh' motifs and more.

The puppeteer from Rajasthan, Vicky Bhat, who had turned to farming during Lockdown, was back, but with refashioned livelihood. He was now peddling curios such as key rings or 'latkans' crafted from puppet faces, as his puppeteering had taken a beating, with hardly any big weddings happening in Lockdown or Semi-Unlock where he could stage puppet shows.

Downsizing stared them in the face from every twine and threadwork of the tapestry that made up Dilli Haat.

The most telling comment on the post-Pandemic micro narratives was perhaps being unlocked in the portico leading to the gateway.

Right at the doorstep of Dilli Haat.

The book vendor outside the entrance had returned. He was still peddling pirated editions of bestseller-hood. On the face of it, not much had changed in his livelihood narrative, but on looking deeper, the subtext had surely changed.

For, the book vendor had now switched to squeaking:

"Sau ki teen…Sau ki teen."

Lollita and Lamba ji trundled past him. Just as they navigated the narrow entrance, now replete with sanitiser and mask checks along with security checks, they bumped into Lollita's girlie gang.

"How wonderful to see you after ages!" chorused Tulikaa, Shiv Shaktii, and Avantii.

"Sweeties, so what have you been up to?" Lollita said, chattily.

"Window shopping only, what else!" Tulikaa said.

A little ahead, more familiar faces waved out to Lollita, while Lamba ji was busy booming to his bloke on the phone.

Upon spotting Lollita, her shopaholic friends, Madhurima Popli, Kirron Kapur, Purnimaa Pandya, and Neerjaa, waved out from the Odisha stall as they exited empty handed.

A few stalls away, Lollita met more of her handloom enthusiasts, Rathi Vaidyanathan, Mamatha Shaswat, Aarti, Mikuu, and Brindhaa.

There was one face though conspicuously missing on Corona's culture-scape. Missing forever. Missing like those festoons plucked by stormy winds on the Haat's caparisoned canopy.

Chiinaar Di's.

"Hey dears, what did you pick?" Lollita asked, all agog.

"Could pick just one simple Dongria," revealed Rathi, a passionate patron of these weaves from the Kondh tribe of Odisha.

"No sarees, darling. Only some Kutch cholis going dirt cheap," smilingly said Mamatha, who pre-Lockdown was often seen splurging on Rajasthani sarees, from Kota Dorias to Bandhinis.

They soon left, laden with only masked smiles, not their customary loaded saree shopping bags.

Pandemic's downsized consumer micro narrative telling its tale again.

Lollita and Lamba ji legged it into Dilli Haat's food court. It was there that the face of the new tribe did an Unlock. Seated in front of Lollita and Lamba ji was a bespectacled and bright-looking Bong specimen of this breed of game changers—the Book Influencer.

Unaa, the pure one.

A quintessential Bong beauty. Accoutred in a Gamcha ruffle saree strewn with *maachh* applique motifs. Long, lustrous tresses framing an intelligent face.

A spherical brightness beautifying the bridge between her thick brows—the big fat kumkum bindi.

A crimson sunrise smiling up from between a pair of shadowy sand-dunes.

"Hey, so finally we meet up...been hearing so much about your IIM days from Meera Di," Lollita gushed. Filtering her excited voice was a mask that had funky Frida bookmark insignias embossed on it.

"Lovely to meet Meera's li'l sis now," Unaa shot back from behind her white and red Gamcha border mask.

They made small talk over Thukpa and Momos, about Meeraya Di and Unaa's classroom capers, college crushes and all that. Then, as Unaa browsed through her book, Lollita stirred her Thukpa and steered the conversation to the challenge at hand.

"So, tell me about your packages."

"Well, it's all very structured. We offer the Short Review and Full Review Packages," Unaa elaborated, bending over her i-Pad to show the packages to Lollita, her bindi-bedecked brow plunging to browse.

A scarlet sunset dipping upon the domes of a raj baari or a Rajasthani fort.

As Lollita and Unaa pored over the packages on the i-Pad, Lamba ji shuffled in his seat restlessly and fished out his iPhone. Not wanting to miss the moment, he butted in with his boom.

"Selfie time," he egged them on, flashing his cheesiest smile for this marketing shot aimed for his Facebook and Instagram status update-ism.

Selfies done, Unaa picked up her plan pontification.

To Lollita, in nomenclature, it all sounded so much as if they were talking the Shortlist and Longlist of the Booker Prize. "So, Short Review is essentially a single review package. And, the Full Review?"

"That obviously has a broader reach and it covers reviews on Amazon, Goodreads, and a host of other book blogging platforms. Ah, but if it's fast action that you're looking for, then there's the Baap of Book Blogging," Unaa puffed up as if about to announce the winner at an awards night.

"Haha...I thought it was all about *ek ke saath ek free*... But this is a surprise...*Baap re Baap*," Lollita bantered.

"Wait till you hear about the Bulk Blogging package," Unaa teased and started to explain how bulk bookstagramming worked.

Lollita's large eyes danced from above the mask. Book blogging sounded like credit cards—gold, silver, and platinum. The more you swiped at it, the bigger and better your trolley of book reviews and bestselling ratings became.

Just as Unaa was holding forth, Lamba ji's glance fell on the table beyond Unaa and his face froze.

"Oh no!" was all that escaped Lamba ji's lips as he recognised the lady a few feet away on the table behind them.

"What happened?" Lollita and Unaa peered curiously at him.

"Nah, nothing, just don't look at the table beyond. Pretend to be talking..."

"Is something the matter?"

"Nah, nothing much, just that the lady seated beyond is a high-flying social butterfly turned author. She'd hired us to do her book... All went well, just that in the curtain-raiser post announcing her book cover, one of the novices in our social media team, by mistake, posted the cover of the book by her rival socialite."

"OMG," Lollita nearly choked over her coffee.

"We corrected the mistake, but she's been gunning for me ever since!" poor Lamba ji sounded like a hounded soul.

"It happens...it happens...such glitches happen with us all. Do you want us all to leave if you don't want to bump into her?" Unaa tried to proffer solace to Lamba ji.

By then, Lamba ji had already ducked his face behind Lollita's book.

What a blessing in disguise it could have been, a brilliant marketing gimmick for Lollita's book among the Dilli Haat onlookers.

Except that Lamba ji was holding Lollita's book upside down!

Reverse Marketing.

28

The Curious Case of a Silver Lining

Somewhere in the suburbs of Gurugram

Silver or gold?

Had it been their grandmother or mothers' age, this dilemma would naturally have been construed to cover contemplations about the yellow metal or white metal, be it for parking one's savings or be it buying for festivals like Akshay Tritiya or Dhanteras.

"Darling, what's the issue?" her childhood friend and soul sister Manikarnikaa Duggal, aka Manna, was trying to figure out what was on Lollita's mind.

"No, nothing really, Manna. Just that this is sounding so like the gold or silver dilemma that used to consume our moms when festival season came, remember?"

"Ah yes, how they would be hyperventilating about the soaring prices of gold and about how many *tolas* to buy on Dhanteras," Manikarnikaa reminisced.

Both their mothers—childhood neighbours—would weeks in advance start making rounds of their neighbourhood jeweller to shortlist the items they would finally go and pick up on the auspicious days of Akshay Tritiya or Dhanteras.

That was the age when gold and silver were terms that belonged mostly to metals. Ah, but these are times, when gold and silver found themselves denoting everything from credit cards to club memberships to even social media packages.

"This is sounding so much like the dilemma our mums would be faced with regards to the house helps—whether to buy Lajjo ji or Dhanno didi silver anklets or gift them a gold coin on Dhanteras," Lollita rambled on those lines.

"Yes, yes...but coming back to you, what's your confusion about, sweetie?"

"Manna, the thing is, Unaa, my Book Influencer, gave a choice of silver or gold package...so I'm just trying to figure out which one to go for," Lollita spelt it out.

"Haha...go by the Daadi and Naani *ke nuske* then," Manikarnikaa teased. "Remember when our Beejis got stuck about festival gifting, they used to stick to safe 'ol silver, gifting silver coins or silver baalis and payals (anklets)?"

"True that, Manna," affirmed Lollita. "So, silver it shall be, to start with."

Soon after, she signed up for Unaa's book blogging package—the silver *ek-ke-saath-ek-free* offer, which entailed that for every book review on Amazon, she would get a review on Goodreads, too.

The time now came when the first thing Lollita groggily groped for upon stumbling out of slumber every morning was not the customary newspaper with the morning cuppa or her smartphone for browsing through the notifications landed on it, but the Amazon book pages.

If she hadn't spent the night dreaming about her book sliding up and down ratings, like a pawn in the game of Snakes and Ladders, she was certainly waking up to Amazon notifications—to ascertain if any new reviews of her book had been posted and how many stars she had earned.

Things were proceeding pretty much on this course, till one day soon after she found one of her fellow authors, Jazz Sodhi, putting up a Facebook post about how his book had beaten competition to climb up the bestseller charts to being among the Top 10 in the satire genre.

"OMG!" was her first response, before her brow knitted itself into deep pondering.

"But, his book was published after mine... How come he's beaten me at it to make it to Top 10 while I'm not even in the Top 1,000?"

Her newly acquired wisdom about the book blogging biz, culled recently from the likes of Unaa and newer kids on the blog, made her brow un-knit itself. Instead, her brow now did a northward excursion as enlightenment dawned on her.

"Jazz in Top 10? Could it be...all that glitters is gold?"

29

The Curious Case of Game Changers on My Ginger Chai

Habits are hard to break, it is said. Lollita could be said to be a living example of another truism—compulsive habits can only be broken by even more compulsive habits.

The compelling habit Lollita had acquired lately—of scrambling to check the Amazon book ratings the first thing she woke up and as she sipped her morning cuppa of ginger tea—had assumed manic proportions. Such that the day she wasn't able to execute this new addiction, thanks to Ruhaan or Bholi Punjabban clamouring for cuddling or canoodling upon her awaking in the morning, she went about life with the same piqued and pained expression as a chain smoker who doesn't find his fags by his bedside upon awaking.

Lollita's carpal and cervical muscles had, of late, been subjected to a paradigm shift in their daily gymming regime.

Instead of exercising themselves to enable Lollita to ogle at OTT offerings, they were being put through more strenuous forms of workout. Workouts that entailed more stretching.

Stretching of the tendons, as much as stretching of time.

For, Lollita had now switched to less of Netflixing, more of Amazon gazing.

To conduct an in-depth study of her book's trajectory along bestseller charts. Her book being positioned to start with at the bottom.

Simultaneously, the pupils of her eyes could be seen over-exercising themselves, goggling and gaping at Amazon's self-help Kindle titles list for hours together in what resembled the meditative silences Buddhist monks were wont to lapse into in the pursuit of Nirvana.

The Kindle self-help titles that her pupils were now prone to pluck at read something on these lines:

- *How to Sell Solitaires to Sell Your Book;*
- *How to Get in the Good Books of Book Bloggers;*
- *How to Give Up Netflixing for Amazon Bestseller List Gazing.*

This bad habit of Amazon stalking had, of late, been overtaken by another early morning malady—of her eyelids twitching and brow knitting into a near frown until she had scoured the social media for curtain-raisers about any upcoming Litfests or online literary chats on Instagram or FB.

Not that there were invitations awaiting her—Litfests didn't even know of her existence, remember?—but she would surf through every Lit event, big or small, with microscopic scrutiny to look for the key persons—the Game Changers.

The Game Changers may have been too preoccupied redefining the rules of the game post Lockdown to have even bothered about budding authors but, interestingly, her publisher came to the rescue.

"Hey, since actual litfests are not yet happening due to stringent social distancing protocols, for promos we're connecting you to some book bloggers who stage online litfests," Paroma called up to say.

"Ya, the scene is bad still…I guess, litfests need to reinvent themselves for the New Normal," Lollita sighed aloud.

"So, we've suggested your name along with others for virtual book events that are coming up. You'll get a call soon," Paroma informed.

"Right ho!"

"By the way, hope you remember you must mention the publisher at least once or twice during the conversation and in the Bio you send them," Paroma's matter-of-fact voice reminded her.

Lollita was learning the rules of the game.

Rule One: You scratch my back, I scratch yours. Publishers wielded clout with Litfest organisers to get platforms for their authors; and the authors used that stage to promote their publisher.

Ah, so much like the sponsors of all mega sporting spectacles—from Wimbledon to World Cup. How the players showcased the sports paraphernalia—towels, kits, mineral water, aerated drinks etc., from the brands of their sponsors. Visibility was the key word here.

The whole week she waited with bated breath for her phone to ring and kept checking her mail.

By the start of next week, a voice dripping swag called.

30

The Curious Case of by Book or by Crook

Somewhere in the suburbs of Gurugram

"Are you good with Meet?"

The voice with swag chirped at the other end. It belonged to a young woman whose profile on LinkedIn and Instagram boasted many things—book club founder, Lit agent, bibliophile blah blah. But, the one thing that screamed the loudest from among those designer profile tags, like a mega billboard boasting a botoxed Kareena Kapoor Khan or brawny Shah Rukh Khan commercial emblazoned by neon lights, was the showstopper tag on her profile—Book Influencer.

As if book bloggers weren't enough, now Lollita was faced with another new species of digital natives and Instagrammers.

Ah, so this was the tag worn by the literary world's Game Changers that Lollita had been scouting for—Book Influencers.

This lady, who had introduced herself as Sudiptaa Bose, was the person her publisher had connected her to.

"Meet?" Lollita said a tad tentatively.

"Yes, that's a must," Sudiptaa sounded a bit suspicious, as if wondering whether Lollita was a digital native at all.

"Err...where do we have to meet?" Lollita sounded a bit uncertain.

"No, not that! Google Meet!" Sudiptaa's voice sounded a mix of amusement and impatience.

"Ah that," Lollita tried to sound intelligible, not wanting to betray that she wasn't too friendly to all those new platforms popping up all over Cyberia.

Sudiptaa then proceeded to apprise her of the date and timing of the virtual chat, waxing eloquent on all the Who's Who of the literary orbit they'd featured in the Web series they were hosting.

"Last weekend, we hosted Amodh Tripathi and Ashwamedh Sanghi along with some new authors, who're also climbing the bestseller charts," Sudiptaa announced with aplomb.

"Wow…so you're keeping the action going, virtually!" Lollita gushed.

"The week before that we had Anirudh Neelakantan and…" Sudiptaa was reeling off endlessly.

"Awesome…," Lollita kept butting in with her exclamations.

Her mind was grappling with interesting insights. "The literary scene sounds so much an A-listers club, literally," Lollita wondered. "Is the alphabet 'A' the lucky mascot to make it to the book bestseller charts? Ah, maybe there's more to it than meets the eye—Numerology!"

"Shall send you the web meeting link once everything is in place," Sudiptaa signed off breezily.

"Right ho!" replied Lollita, signing off.

Lest you be misled into believing that this whole world of web chats or literary chat shows was run purely by those sentiments of chumminess and coffee camaraderie suffusing the bosoms of the Game Changers, dear discerning reader, that's not even half the truth.

True, networking makes much of the literary action go round. But, where networking doesn't work, someone else steps in.

The web shows ran on more or less the same principles as the primetime shows and debates on tamasha TV—the more famous the face on your primetime panel, the greater the eyeballs enticed, the better the TRPs. So, you had all this rash of online literary events popping up post Lockdown in the time of the virus, driven by these dynamics.

Ah, but the Book Influencers, that's a breed you might just recognise were you to look more closely at your inbox. Rather, if you peered more perceptively at your Instagram DMs. There, among the so many inconsequential messages from food bloggers to content creators, if you are a budding author or an arrived author, you would spot the DM of consequence from this species called the Book Influencer. Penned with politeness as much as political correctness, the Book Influencer's DM informs and invites you to all those local literary action happening about town—at bookstores, Crosswords, malls, cafés, and all that.

But, there is a bottomline to it.

Fast forward to the next stage. Now the DMs you receive from that friendly Book Influencer, start inviting you to upcoming Litfests, keeping you updated about the literary calendar, as it were. You gush with gratitude that some kind soul is actually playing your guardian angel. You may even keep glancing over your shoulder in a delusionary demeanour whilst you conduct your Instagramming, just to ascertain if there indeed is a guardian angel smiling over your shoulder.

But, again, this delusion lasts till you get to the bottomline.

For, at the bottom of all such literary DMs is that crucial line: We would be happy to collaborate with you if you wish to participate in the upcoming Litfests or Web events. Please see our rate card for details.

So, to cut a long story short, the Book Influencer had politely inserted a DM into Lollita's Instagram account, informing about the price of literary appearances.

The top slot was for those budding authors who wanted to be on a web panel with A-listers.

Appearances with B-listers costed little less and so on, so forth.

Thus, Lollita had been given a choice of price packages in accordance with panellists.

Needless to say, Lollita couldn't afford appearances with the A-listers. And, so it was the economy pack—category 'C'—she opted for, a panel made up of all new writers barely breaking into authorhood.

Lollita could barely wait for Saturday to arrive. A wait filled, fruitfully, by Ruhaan.

The sweetheart that he was, Ruhaan again played the bridge between her generation of diffident digital natives and the constant overload of all things App.

A wait that saw Ruhaan rolling out a class. A crash course short and sweet, in navigating Google Meet.

31

The Curious Case of 'What's In a Name!

"We welcome you to this round of *Book Baatein*. I'm your host Sudiptaa Bose."

Lollita was squirming in her seat at home as the Google Meet screen went on air and nearly caught her twiddling with her earphones and giving gloss-stick grooming to her lips.

"We have with us a mixed bag today, a host of new authors from various genres—mythology, murder mysteries, and...," Sudiptaa paused here. Her crisp voice levitated like a Diwali cracker deciding whether or not to take off. Lollita almost thought she'd forgotten her and hurriedly waved into the grid as she saw the multiple screens blink on.

"And...we have humour, too," Sudiptaa chimed in.

Lollita heaved a sigh of relief, with the air of a steam engine articulating joy upon arriving at a platform.

After the customary ice-breakers, Sudiptaa got the conversation rolling.

Turning to the mythology writer first, she asked: "So, tell us about your journey, how did you turn to mythology?"

Mr Mythology Writer flashed a flossed smile as his South Indian face, framed by lustrous, black, coconut oil-fed curls, beamed. "Well, we grew up on a rich diet of *Amar Chitra Kathas*... That fuelled my fascination for those ancient princes and princesses..." He kept rattling off. "For many years, this idea of demystifying and de-villainising the Kauravas was filling my head... So, I started researching about it...," his Kannada accent asserted itself here and there.

Mr Mythology Writer looked the serious studious type who would skip going to the cinema to instead go skipping to libraries. "Then I met this publisher at the JLF (Jaipur Lit Fest) and when I pitched my idea to them, they at once grabbed at it... And there, before I knew, I'd been commissioned to do this book!" his voice was peppered with the childish excitement of a college kid who had managed to crack the IIT-JEEs.

"Lucky them, who didn't have to go hunting for a publisher!" Lollita thought in her head while her hands adjusted the earphones to listen better.

By the time the audio came on more clearly, it was Ms Mystery Writer who was reeling off the how's and whys of her literary journey.

Ms Mystery Writer: "The whodunit was what fascinated me since school... We would bunk classes to go sneak into the library for more doses of Nancy Drews and Agatha Christie's...."

Hers was the decided demeanour of a Diva, who if she hadn't accidentally tripped into typing out thrillers might have been a fashion model. Better still, she might have turned a yoga diva hosting and boasting her own power yoga channel on YouTube, so well-toned she was, in voice and waist both. The waist especially belied not only her age, but also her roots. No tell-tale gastronomic signs there of her Punjabiyat.

Ms Mystery Writer's suave voice further unfolded her story: "Post marriage, I was just so caught up in the usual stuff...travelling with my husband on his postings, raising kids and all that...I never could pursue my passion. It's only now that the kids are settled in their jobs and their marriages, that I had all the time on my hands, in between playing with grandkids, to pen my crime thriller...."

Lollita goggled into the grid upon hearing that the petite diva with a pint size waist was a mother-in-law but also a grandmother. One would have thought grandmothers would be more into penning memoirs than mystery thrillers unless they were dowagers of the Victorian era like Dame Agatha *et al*. And, one would have thought grandmoms would be more bothered about boasting solitaires and selfies with grandkids or antique Phulkaris and polkis than bestseller tags.

"Talking of bestseller tags, come to think of it...," Lollita suddenly seemed to notice the tickr running below their Google Meet screen frames. The bestseller tags were displaying on the tickr but...

Butting into her thoughts just then was Sudiptaa, "Now, let's hear it from our humour writer... What started you into this genre?"

Lollita made a flurry of movements to be sure her earphones and mic were in place. This unsettled her swivel chair which sort of started making all sorts of squeaky sounds. She hastily tried to silence its cantankerous lever and in doing so, she almost went off the screen and then clambered right back in. Just in time.

Just in time to see that she was back on the centre of her frame, and to also see that all her blow-dried hair were anything but centred, as they'd now betrayed signs of having strayed left, right, and centre.

The glitches of virtual as the new Real Litscape notwithstanding, Lollita determined to hold fort with spunk and style.

Her Trishul nose-pin did a 'Suka' to spring up as if taking off on an expedition towards Omkareshwar, the flag-bearer poised to lead a motley procession.

The next few minutes saw her dwelling pretty confidently upon her forays into humour. She peppered it with her punchlines, "A humour writer is like a MasterChef, having to dish out life's sunny side up..."

"After years of treading the 'middle' path, that is writing 'middles', by the time the mid-life crisis hit me, I realised hardly anybody taking me seriously—my maids didn't take me seriously, my son took the girls in his class more seriously, my partner took Pammi Aunty or Oprah Winfrey more seriously. This made me realise that my only nirvana lay in taking one thing seriously—Humour!"

Lollita must've delivered the lines pretty well for there erupted giggles and guffaws from fellow panellists as she could see one or two of the heads in the grid view bobbing up and down with nods of affirmation.

The conversation kept rolling back and forth till it came to that core existential question for authorhood.

"Now coming to that crucial issue," Sudiptaa propelled the chat to its last leg. "Should authors be expected to market books or should their job end with writing?"

The expressions visible in the grid—coy smile for Ms Mythology, knitted brows from Ms Mystery Writer. And well, Lollita's face must've betrayed a mixed bag of emotions. For, at this very moment the tickr once again brought into focus the tags with each participant's name.

"Oh yes, why not!" Ms Mythology's response was emphatic. "My publisher helps much with the promos, but I do my bit, too. I have more than a million Instagram followers, so I do reach out to my followers through interesting story contests from time to time, which boosts my book sales and bestseller ratings," she was boasting, her voice sounding as pushy as her promotion strategies. This was the umpteenth time in the conversation that she had flaunted her climb up the bestseller charts.

The subtext hit Lollita hard. More than a million followers!

Ms Mystery Writer was nodding her assent. "Oh, I'm all for it. I used the Lockdown to proactively promote the Kindle version of my book...since people weren't going out to buy books, nor were bookstores open, the Kindle version had huge takers. And, at less than half the price!" she sounded like a marketing whiz. "And, may I add, my Kindle edition made it to the bestseller charts at a time when books weren't really selling! All thanks to my 50K followers!" she added with glee, her chiselled face puffing up with pride like a saboodana papad that fluffs up to double its size.

Lollita didn't miss this subtext either. 50K followers!

She was beginning to read between the lines. It was not only about selling a million copies, but also boasting a million followers. The name of the game—Millionism.

"And you?" Sudiptaa's poser pierced into Lollita's reverie. Her morale dipped at the thought of her low count of followers. Less than 5K!

Lollita hastily shrugged off the sheepishness at My Big Fat Follower Deficit. Aloud, she decided to assert herself articulately.

"Perfect prose is its own best promotion...Dames Austen or Agatha hardly had any marketing blitzkrieg to push their books, yet we are reading them down the generations," Lollita clearly voiced her take. "I may sound a bit old school, being a believer in the supremacy of Prose over Promos. Well, an Author is like a Maestro, the essential role is to produce the perfect musical notes," Lollita struck a balanced note, emphatically yet elegantly.

"No amount of gift-wrapping can sell crappy content... But, if marketing be the call of the times, bring it on... We writers must play the game," she summed it up with style, sounding very much 'with it'.

What better testimony to the marketing overdrive defining Wannabe Bestseller-hood than the tickers of virtual book shows!

Lollita couldn't help but gape and grimace as the radiant red ticker once again danced on the screen as Sudiptaa wrapped up the chat with the customary thank-you note.

The ticker boasted bestseller tags appended to the author names, but there was only one name without that tag of bestselling author—Lollita's.

32

The Curious Case of Rotten Tomatoes

When the previous night you've been on a web chat where among the author names blinking on the ticker yours is the only one minus the coveted crown of 'bestselling author', life upon waking up the next morning surely doesn't look like an egg sunny side up.

And, when the millennial on that show has hogged half the talk time by boasting about her swelling Instagram followers umpteen times, life looks even worse than a scrambled egg.

Life then looks like a scrambled egg cooked with rotten tomatoes.

Add to that a virus that has come and pulverised and plundered the literary landscape beyond recognition, that the terms 'bestseller' were being redefined virtually. No litfests were happening nor book launches. The only place where book titles were being launched was on Kindle through Amazon & Co, the bestseller listings now spoke of Kindle versions more than physical books.

Online literary events from the JLF stable and others were the new face of litfests and were aptly driven by New Normal's hashtag-ism—#BraveNewWorld.

It looked that the only things likely to be competing for bestseller lists in the humour genre—in the absence of book launches, litfests, and all that action—could be memes about the New Normal; cartoons (even the Amul toon type that at least had their daily dose); or stand-up comedians who were having a blast of an outing on Twitterverse, having reinvented themselves as sit-ups on Google Meet for better or worse.

"Hey honey, why so quiet quiet?" Ruhaan joined her for the morning cuppa on the terrace, fondling her hair affectionately. "Too tired from last night?" he winked at her.

"Uhhh...just trying to grapple with new realities, love," she tweaked his nosetip which she found irresistible even on the bleakest of days for its protruding perkiness. "What's with all these figures 10K, 100K followers that every second author boasts of these days! Are so many people reading books to be following an author all over Insta?"

"Haha, so that's what's bothering you, is it?" he smiled his boyish smile.

"Nah, it's not bothering...I quite admired the unabashed aplomb of Ms Millennial every time she pouted to toss the 10K at us, like a sixer from Rohit Sharma!"

"But it's simple...you can have 100K too..."

"Really?"

"Ah, but more of that later... First things first, you may not have 100K followers but would you like a one-in-a-million breakfast?" he teased.

"Sure, sweetheart, as long as it's not scrambled eggs!" she shot back.

33

The Curious Case of Scrambled Eggs

Somewhere in NCR

Lollita tucked into her breakfast tray with a vengeance, like a bride who's not been able to nibble amid her own nuptials.

Thank God, Lalitaa was back in her life and those Lockdown days of trudging out of bed to dish out breakfast were way behind her. The return of Bai meant that she could slumber till the sun was way past poking a friendly good morning at Ganguly ji's laundry and Lamborghini sunning themselves on the patio, or beaming at Gupta ji's brinjals and *bhindis*, plus the perky chillis that his better half had left out to bake.

The baked beans and cheese pancakes on her platter were just what Lollita needed to pep up her spirits to spring out of the depth of melancholy into which they had sunk post the book launch which she had hoped would be designer, but had been more on the lines of disaster.

The thing about book events, virtual or real, is that they can so much turn out like eggs.

You may scramble through life all sunny tempered with a song on the lips, thinking you're tossing up an egg sunny side up, but what ends up on the platter instead is its scrambled version. And, what's worst, you scarce can spot what all has gone into making it the scrambled self it has shaped out to be.

Was it too much pepper, too twisted a tossing or too little buttering?

This tiny thought can spoil an entire morning or entire weeks to come, niggling and nagging at the soul's innards in search of existential enlightenment.

"C'mon, you can't let a little launch spoil your mood, honey!" Ruhaan cuddled his brawny arms around her to comfort her.

Little?

How oftentimes is it that words intended to proffer the balms of solace and succour to the suffering party can trigger quite the contrary emotions on account of an ill-timed word or phrase. Quite like a Boroline or Burnol gone wrong. That sort of aggravates the burning sensation.

So it was with Lollita. The 'little' in Ruhaan's well-intentioned bantering cut her to the quick.

But as with eggs, so with life. You've got to move on.

"Hey, cheer up...there's life beyond a launch," Ruhaan treaded tad cautiously with his words this time. "Remember my college mate, Chrissy? She's been calling to ask if you'd like to do a Creative Writing talk for schoolkids at the British Council Library."

Ruhaan's words sounded as sweet as maple syrup pouring over pancakes. Lollita managed to summon a smile in between chomping on her cheesy delights. "Interesting!"

"Yayy...that sounds better. You've been noticed for your book by whatever few stories the local dailies ran!" His fingers ran through her tousled hair and the back of her neck as he planted a peck. His touch somehow always sent electric currents charging through her epidermis, like a bullet-speed Metro tearing from Khan Market to Karol Bagh.

And so the next couple of weeks saw Lollita limping forward on the road of authorhood, being invited by the British Council for talks, by local schools for writing workshops, and the works.

Though ever second person was turning an author nowadays, and if not an author themselves, they went by the name storyteller.

But, there were hardly any humour writers. And, that placed Lollita in a league of her own in the crowd of authors.

There was a certain jauntiness in her step as Lollita spilled out of the crammed Metro, like the contents of a bottle of Dom Perignon scattering themselves the moment it is uncorked or unsealed. She trundled out of the station, propelled by the sea of humanity that surged ahead in the business of living in the fast lane.

Legging it from the Metro station to Dilli Haat, once again she stumbled upon the pavement vendor selling pirated copies of the latest book titles.

The air with which she approached the vendor now was not that of an aspiring author but that of a just-published author. The dreams harboured by her eyes had now taken a more definite form—from hopes of having a book to boast of to a hope of joining the ranks of the best-selling authors whose books were rubbing shoulders at the street-side stall.

"Well, if filmmakers have well-laid out pre-release promotion strategies, why can't I do so as an author?"

It was thus with some vaguely conceived marketing strategies in mind that she approached the vendor tentatively.

"If I give you some copies of a book, will you sell them?" Lollita plunged head-on into promotion mode, without beating about the bush.

The urchin peered at her curiously, "Are you a distributor?"

"No, no. Not a distributor," Lollita preened her hair and accent a bit to dispel any impression of belonging to the breed of distributors. "Err, I'm an author...a newly published author. My book will be printed soon," she corrected, stumbling, rather lamely limping, as closer to the truth as possible.

Now, it was the urchin's turn to blink even more curiously at Lollita, as she denoted a species he had not so far encountered—a Wannabe Bestselling Author whose book had not yet been printed but was already trying to sell it.

Day in and day out, various species of saunterers stopped by at his pavement stall to peer at the titles on display.

There was the species called Committed Bookworm, who knew which authors it wanted and got down to the serious business of buying. Then there was the tribe of Casual Bibliophile who stopped at this bookstall only to scout a title that was on a Bestseller List and which would be fashionable to carry for a quick read on the Metro. Not to forget the occasional Arrived Author, whose books were moving well on Amazon bestseller charts but who stopped by to ascertain the ground reality of how the book was faring on the streetsides. Then, of course, there was that species that weren't buyers or book lovers at all. Their only *raison de etre* to trundle to a fleeting halt at a pavement bookseller was because they were killing time—waiting for a beau who was late for a date, or for a spouse who was late for a pickup. Rather than making calls fast and furious to the unpunctual partner, they tried to kill time by picking up a random book.

But, never had this street-side urchin had had the chance to have a brush with this interesting new species called Pre-Printed Author on Promo Tour.

His expression, as he eyed her closely and curiously, bore an uncanny resemblance to that of a gardener who, gazing at his cultivated kitchen garden beds of turnips and radishes, finds a new species of radish sprouting in one of the beds that is neither the conventional tall white or the bulbous red on the colour palette.

"How can I sell a book that is not even yet printed, madam?" his tone took on a touch of mock amusement.

"Yes, yes, I understand that," Lollita tried to make him see the pragmatic side of promos. "Look, I'm just trying to work out a deal in anticipation," she changed tack and decided to babble the language of Mammon, "If I bring you 10 copies or so to sell, what'll be your cut?"

"Madam, you get the book first. We'll work that out," he darted an impish grin, as he got busy peddling some book titles to some young chicks who wanted quick reads to carry on the Metro.

The urchin's chuckle of amusement drove home to Lollita, better than any words, that she was yet a few steps away from being a printed author, as she stepped briskly towards the entrance and into the Dilli Haat ramparts.

Ruhaan was waiting for her at the Nagaland stall as she glided on to the marble bench of the open-air food court on which a cotton *chatai* stood spread out to cushion the customers from its cold surface.

"Here comes our author in the making," Ruhaan said with his boyish grin, "Autograph please," as he flourished a paper napkin bang under her nose.

"Huh, hardly an author," Lollita laughed as she settled on the *chatai* to browse the menu, ordering a plate of steamed momos while Ruhaan settled for steamed rice and Green Thai Curry. "Even that chit of a chap selling books on the pavement outside didn't take me seriously!"

"Ah, but there's one person who's pretty serious about you," Ruhaan countered with an impish grin.

Lollita dismissed his words with a generous smile but carried on with her train of thoughts. "If even a pavement seller isn't too keen to stock or sell my books, and all he wants is to flaunt a Shobhaa De, Shashi Tharoor & Co, what good is my becoming an author?" A growing sense of trepidation nibbled at her mind while the enamel of her nibbled at the greens encased in the steamed white-flour pockets.

"Who knows, you may be bigger than the Chitras and Chetans one day and find your titles eclipsing all others at these street-side stalls! Ruhaan teased her.

"I don't know what else, but you're surely good for my ego," she quipped.

Niggling at the back of her mind was the streetside book peddler urchin's parting shot. A reminder that now the fate of her future as a writer hung in the balance. In the hands of that species made so elusive by Lockdown—the migrant printer.

UNLOCK 2.0

"Behind the veil,

angels sometimes weep."

—RUMI

34

The Curious Case of 'Honey, I Shrunk the Guest List'

Somewhere in NCR

The thing about new beaus, who may come riding relationships with no strings attached, is that if they have the knack to pull strings, then the beloved's book is bound to see the light of day. In time or even before time.

As any man head over heels with his girl will tell you, if the lady expects the fellow to play a magician and juggle up a printer out of his hat, he jolly well does it.

Ruhaan, thus getting into juggler act, employed his networking in the book biz to ensure that Lollita's book was printed much ahead of the time that the publisher's printer would have taken. To be in time for the tentative actual book launch.

The Virtual being the New Real for book launches, and the Pandemic-pummelled publishing industry hardly able to do physical launches for authors, it was the Chandigarh Lit Club that came to Lollita's rescue.

The book was finally slated for a real launch. An Autumn release.

The thing about impending book launches is that they bring out the good, bad, and ugly in authors, depending on whether one is a Wannabe Author or Arrived Author.

The Arrived Authors may go about life as usual, as if the D-Day of the launch is just another day, and butterfly in the bellies are what happen to others.

An Arrived Author may trundle about as cool as a Frappe on the Rocks, as chilled as Jelly with Cold Cream, or as unruffled as a Bollywood biggie used to his or her films making it to the 100-crore club at the box-office.

Ah, but a Wannabe Writer or Author About to Arrive is as edgy as a cabbage rolling on pins or as jumpy as kittens upon their first foray into a flock of pigeons.

Lollita resembled an author straddling the space somewhere in between. She wasn't a debutante, nor was she in the ranks of Arrived Authorhood.

Lollita resembled a half-skittish cat on a hot, tin roof.

The memories of a certain pink jacket having a red carpet launch haunted her. That the particular book jacket had subsequently made it to the Million Copies Club only served to reinforce in her mind the importance of being a celebrity jacket. Or having celebrities endorse the jacket.

Thus, the next big challenge was drawing up the guest lists for the book launch.

As you know, dear discerning reader, guest lists can be of various types, depending upon your standing in the hallowed stratosphere of published authors or outside it. The guest list also hinges not so much on how well you've penned the lines of your book, but more on how well your pockets are lined.

At the top of the pile are Arrived A-List Authors who never have to bother about guest lists, for the Who's Who are bound to be at their launch if the author is a political heavyweight or their guest lists are longer than the number of pages in their high-profile book and the show is no less than the launch of a Box Office blockbuster.

Then, there are Bestselling Authors who by virtue of topping the charts and commanding huge commissioning amounts don't much have to worry about footfalls, as their publishers make sure the event is nothing short of a 'breaking news'.

Somewhere towards the bottom of the pile for whom drawing up guest lists is as big a challenge as a mofussil T20 drawing in spectators into a stadium, a new tournament that no big names want to inaugurate.

"So, who do we have as our Chief Guest and guests of honour?" Lollita looked thoughtfully at Paroma.

"Do you have any Bollywood connections? Nothing works for a book like getting a celebrity to launch it."

Now, asking a writer who hasn't been beyond the Central Plateau if they have contacts in B-town is like asking your neighbourhood subziwallah if he has seen passion fruit or zucchini.

"Bollywood connect? I...err..." Lollita was racking her brain for even any indirect or farfetched connections she may have to B-town. "No, not that I can think of," she finally blurted with certainty.

"Well, then, you may not get a great turnout at the launch, because a celebrity is the key to drawing footfalls," Paroma declared with a wisdom that comes from having presided over the fortunes of many a book on a journey of being born, as her brow knitted in deep thought. "Hmm... then can you rope in some local VIPs?"

35

The Curious Case of the Boom on Zoom

Somewhere in the suburbs of Gurugram

If life had begun looking like a scrambled egg with the Guest List Challenge of hunting for elusive A-Listers if she wanted to make it to the B-List, another thought that had been nagging Lollita lately was making things look worse—like rotten egg in the face.

It was just a fleeting, friendly remark tossed at her that was to blame.

That innocuous comment on the Zoom family reunion, where curious cousins had thought the photo-bombing Ruhaan to be her son, had pricked Lollita to the raw. Deeper than all those horrible pricks her dentist was adept at delivering to her oral cavities.

Strange, isn't it, how such barbs, unintentional or intentional, make that crappy cliché-ism about 'age is just a number' look as outdated as the Zara top one could fit into last season or the redundant contact lenses that one sported summers ago when the power number was less and one has had to ditch now in favour of good ol' high-power spectacles, even as the lens through which one is viewed gets Ageism tinted.

It is all good for the Priyanka Chopras or Sushmita Sens to flaunt a younger arm candy or beau, but if a lesser mortal have to be leaning on the arm of a younger dandy without being thought his aunt or mom, one has to either be oozing as much oomph as those Size Zero beauty queens, or at least not be oozing so many calories that the arm candy's forelimb runs the risk of a flexor fracture every time one is leaning on it.

"Maybe I should take some inspiration from Sush, who Instagrams about all those mind-blowing workout she and her younger boyfriend seem to be doing all the time!" Lollita tried to motivate herself.

Though Lollita cared a hoot about fitting into stereotypes and believed in being comfortable in her skin, yet Gupta ji's cursory comment had unsettled her.

Perhaps the passing prattle had pinched so much as it had driven home the truisms—Pandemic season spelt recession all around, not only in the economy, in the jobs, pay packets, malls, multiplexes or migrants' livelihoods, but there was recession elsewhere too, in the unsung or invisible indices.

And, one of these recessions was hitting Lollita at that very moment—The Big Fat Forties' Fall of OQ. Oomph Quotient!

Though Lollita was of the species that's happy being in their skin, she now had a niggling suspicion that all those fancy clichés—such as 'Forties are the New Thirties', 'Forties are the New Black' blah blah—had been coined by out-of-job social commentators or post-retirement pontificators who had nothing better to do than toss up terms over a game of bridge or over a lavish luncheon.

"All those commentators who call 'Forties as the New Thirties' jolly well need to go take a walk!" Lollita pooh-poohed the tribe and herself ended up doing just that.

Take a walk.

For, that was the easiest form of exercise she knew to drive away Lockdown's piled up pounds and get her OQ back.

As Ruhaan and Sidak were too engrossed in their Netflix game and Ruhaan had done his push-ups for the day, Lollita legged it outdoors all by herself. Mask in place, she rolled into the common lane running between the Gupta and Ganguly households across her flat.

She could see Gupta ji's kitchen garden more clearly from the lane. It wore a fuller look now with all the neatly manicured beds green with seasonal vegetables sprouting.

From red tomatoes to brinjals and *bhindi* popping their head here and there, it truly flaunted to the fullest Gupta ji's Lockdown labour of love.

The bottle gourds, of course, occupied prime pride of place.

There they were, a couple of them stacked away against the tree in the middle of the kitchen garden, their skin gleaming like future beauty queens all preened and primped for a pageant.

"Ah, those long *laukis* look all set to get Gupta ji his Fifteen Minutes of Fame in the *Limca Book of Records*!" Lollita thought to herself eyeing the mushrooming crop of leggy, long *laukis*, as she perambulated vigorously up and down.

The condo's common bylanes were now the Pandemic's new parks. With people still fearful of foraying into public places like parks, the common lanes were where much of Unlocking India, aired not only their limbs but also their lungs.

Lollita was hoping to air her lungs in more ways than one. By killing two birds with a stone—catch up with cousins on Zoom and bestir bloating limbs into downsized Zumba.

Behold, at that very moment, the neighbouring Gupta ji & Co sprinted out on a similar mission, except they're not only killing two birds with a stone, but doing bit of 'bird' watching, too.

The conversation went trundling somewhat on these lines:

One of her cousins had cooked up some designer dieting stuff and was proffering it to them for e-tasting.

Lollita aired not only her legs but her lungs too on the Zoom call as she gushed, "OMG, you've actually rustled up beetroot idlis and tofu cheese chilli?"

Gupta ji, also Zooming into his phone, treated Lollita's prattling as a prompting (with key words), to steer his own Zoom chat.

"Oye oye, Sheikh Chilli!" Gupta ji guffawed gregariously at some babbling bloke in his Zoom grid.

"And what's that...masala greens with peanuts?" Lollita goggled into the grid.

"Peanuts...that's what my poor, pandemic income looks like!" Gupta ji lapsed into a lament about recession on his Zoom, not forgetting its fallout on the density of his cranial crop.

"I'm going nuts...how the book's drained me!"

"How downsizing has sent our lifestyles down the drain!" Gupta ji babbled his boom into Zoom.

"How I needed to stretch my feet!" Lollita chirruped into Zoom.

"Five feet...*chalegi chalegi,*" Gupta ji jibber-jabbered into his Zoom call.

Half his sights were trained on Khullar ji's balcony where the latter could be spotted launching off on his evening walkathon and telephonic talkathon, exactly at the time that Kokilaben stepped out to spray her potted greens.

From the corner of his eye, Gupta ji was hoping to catch, from Unlock-facilitated closer quarters now, amorous glances flying hither and thither between Khullar ji and Kokilaben.

Lollita was, meanwhile, now chatting up her corporate cousin on the Zoom grid. "Sweetie, that deal, did you manage to close it?"

"Close…come close…give me a better view," Gupta ji cooed, ostensibly into Zoom.

Lollita goggled at him with a glare as glacial as the Gangotri glacier.

"These creeps, my foot!" Lollita thundered, half into her Zoom grid.

"How many foot?" Gupta ji chattered, apparently into his phone.

Lollita was dying to vent her angst in her girlie gang about all that clicheism about Ageism.

"BTW babes, do you believe all that bunkum about 'Forties being the New Thirties'?"

What she heard Gupta ji boom on his Zoom next, was enough to make Lollita slip from the scene.

"Forty by thirty… *Chalegi chalegi,*" Gugta ji prattled, ostensibly prodding a property dealer for some real estate 'specs'.

Having exercised not only his calf muscles, but also his Glad Eye, Gupta ji perambulated to his patio to retire for the day into his apartment's innards for a sumptuous dinner.

As he turned to go indoors, his eyes fell on Mrs Gupta's phone that she had forgotten on their verandah table. He was about to pick it up absent-mindedly when it began to vibrate with WhatsApp notifications.

Gupta ji hurried so that he could carry the phone inside for his significant half, but the moment he stooped to pick it, he froze as his eyes fell on the message box that was lying open.

"What the heck is this!" this was the pesky question that popped back and forth in Gupta ji's mind much like a bumblebee gone berserk buzzing round and round.

For the next few minutes, Gupta ji's actions could best be described as one big frenzy of scrolling up and down the open WhatsApp message inbox. In all the maze of messages exchanged back and forth between his better half and the sender, there was one thing that pricked and piqued him more than the litany of texts.

Staring at him were a string of scarlet emoticons. Smitten heart emoticons.

As if this was not enough, the next second the phone sprang to life again in a state of animated vibration.

The caller's name was flashing and flickering on Mrs Gupta's phone screen, much in the manner of a 'breaking news' tickr blinking again and again on a television channel.

The unsuspected caller's name hit him like a slap as horrible as rotten egg on the face: '*Khullar ji*'!

36

The Curious Case of the Three Mask-i-teers

"Ohh, the A, B, C of it all!" Lollita voiced the new challenge, dipping into a packet of Aloo Bhujia for comfort.

"A...B...C?" Ruhaan teased her. "Love, but I thought there was only an 'R' in your life!"

"The sheer angst of having to hunt for A-Listers if one wants to make it to the B-List!" Lollita looked at her shortlist.

"Awww sweetheart, so have you turned on our charms to rope in any A-listers?" Ruhaan poked her.

"Rooh, that's the vicious cycle! A-Listers don't wanna endorse or play chief guest for non-A listers. And, because they play hoity-toity, non-A listers don't make it to B-lists... and the cycle goes on!" Lollita voiced the truism.

"Ah, the irony of it all!" Ruhaan summed it, half teasing, half concerned. "The sheer un-Rumi-ness of it all!" he shook his head, the curly mop trembled with melancholy.

"Be a lamp, or a lifeboat, or a ladder...!" Ruhaan's lips breathed to life with Rumi.

Post-Lockdown, looking for an A-List chief guest for the launch of a book wanting to make it to the coveted B-List seemed as tough as scouting for exotic fruits in a local Subzi Mandi at its half-shuttered hour.

A post-Corona world makes it a tad tougher as people are a bit wary of public events and want to play it safe. Even if they're not playing it safe, humour book launches may just not be their cup of tea. Or if it's their cup of tea, they may not be happy playing guest of honour over a mere cup of tea, launches over cheese 'n' wine being more up their sleeve.

"Still, three people could fit the bill," Lollita looked at her shortlist.

"Who?" Ruhaan asked a bit disinterestedly as he felt nobody with a 'star quotient' could really materialise without high-powered connections.

Candidate One.

"Should we try this cricketer?" Lollita reeled out from her list.

"Cricketer? What's he got to do with a humour book?" Ruhaan looked nonplussed at her.

"Plenty to do with humour, if you recall that he's on the hot seat as a guest of honour of that TV comedy show, *Comic Nights with Cookie Sharma*. Don't you remember all his witty one-liners?" she smiled at the memory of it.

"You mean that former batsman Manjot Singh Sidhu?" Ruhaan retorted.

"Yeah, he's from this region and he's already doing this comedy show, so he could bring quite a star value!" Lollita sounded excited at the idea. But, would it work out?

The first challenge was finding and connecting to his secretary.

"Sahab is travelling...I'll try to fix a meeting when he returns...," pat came the standard reply of the PA over WA. And, over the next few weeks, these messages kept travelling back and forth on WA, like the first few friendly volleys between a Roger Federer and Rafa Nadal.

As you know, dear discerning reader, 'touring' is one of the pet excuses that PAs—to bureaucrats, ministers or head honchos—love to rattle off to cover up for the non-availability of VIPs; the others topping the Shortlist of Five

Favourite Excuses being *"Sahab meeting mein hain"*, "Sahab is busy with the boss" and all that, when all that the 'sahab' may be busy with, in between poring or snoring over office files, is twiddling on his touchscreen to navigate Netflix or porn sites.

Every time Lollita would call or WhatsApp the PA, she would get to hear this standard reply navigating new territory, "Oh ji, Sahab had to rush to Shahpur Kandi from Sangrur"; "Sorry ji, there was an unscheduled meeting that took him to Makerkotla"...so on so forth. Till last heard, Manjot ji was unreachable and gallivanting somewhere in the innards of Punjab, hardly mattered if it was Hallomajra or Daddomajra.

Thus, this thread of conversation on WA for chasing Candidate One met the same fate that befalls a mobike minus silencer that shoots down the street as if it's set to scoot off to a roaring start, only to splutter and stutter to a sudden stop just round the first corner.

Candidate Two.

"Then there's this stand-up comedian I'd met at some event... Should we give him a shot?"

"He'd probably be busy doing his shows and raking in fat bucks. Why would he want to come to a book launch?" Ruhaan was being practical about it.

"Let's give it a try. At least, he has a humour connect," Lollita felt optimistic.

The next couple of days saw Lollita trying to connect to him on WhatsApp and through DM on Instagram, etc.

By the end of the week he reverted with a polite regret. "So sorry, I've got back-to-back shows lined up for those dates. Hope you understand, how we've to make up for all the business lost during Lockdown."

"Damn," Lollita muttered to herself, "How I envy these stand-ups. Back-to-back shows, wow! And here, for us print humourists, putting up even one show is a Herculean task."

Candidate Three.

"Who else do we have?" Ruhaan asked, looking up from his laptop.

"The widow," announced Lollita a tad dramatically, as if reeling off the credits of a film cast and arriving at the point where enters the cameo.

"Widow? What in the world does a widow have to do with the book launch?"

"That's the catch. She's not only the widow of a famous comedian, but herself a television artiste," Lollita summed up. "That's the best part...being a fading star, she may have no starry *nakhras*!"

"Who in the world is this widow?" Ruhaan was all agog.

37

The Curious Case of Hari Jhariyaan Meets Dyed Daariyan

Somewhere in 'City Beautiful'

"Centre...right...bit left..."

Lollita looked as jittery and jumpy as a debutante showstopper caprioling on a catwalk strewn with a million joora pins.

The pallu of her Madhubani silk saree, an exotic tapestry of a majestic peacock inked with vegetable dyes, fluttered in the nippy breeze. As a streamer serenading a sculpture of a Yakshi at Omkareshwar. As billowy as a flag atop a Bada Mandir buoyant and bobbing in the air, knowing not which way the wind will waft.

Lest the 'right-left' be misconstrued, Lollita's ramblings, from behind a partially dismantled Madhubani mask with the handpainted 'Surya—the Sun God' motif, had to do neither with Baba Ramdev-esque power yoga posturing nor with political power leanings. All that she was trying to achieve by caterwauling change of positions to the chit of a chap on waiter duty was to get the positioning of the welcome bouquet right. To perfectly position it centrestage, before the Guest of Honour descended.

The day had dawned. The day of her dream 'red carpet' book launch derailed by a long night. The maple syrup goldenness of the muted sun beamed resonance upon the million suns smiling up from the bouquet.

The golden dawn after a deep dark night.

Spider chrysanthemums.

Lollita's only solace was that whatever the stage lacked in terms of frills and festoonery was more than made good by the breath-taking backdrop.

The scenic Sukhna lakeside. Shimmering like the sequined gown of a Cannes diva shimmying down the French Riviera. The perfect picture postcard setting for her book launch.

Thankfully, the Chandigarh Lit Club had volunteered to host the launch of her hastily and digitally printed book, in the wake of her Pandemic-pummelled publisher being unable to do a physical lit event and offering her only a soft launch.

Literature meets Lakefront.

Sukhna lakeside, the famous winter home to myriad migratory birds, from Siberian Cranes to Red-Crested Pochards to Yellow-footed Green Pigeons.

A lakeside where perhaps the winged visitors were the only guests returning to a post-Pandemic landscape with their lives un-singed, their flocks un-depleted.

A lakeside that had cradled to teenage-hood one of north India's leading literary galas.

Literatty.

Le Corbusier landscape's literary stage that with its fast growing footfalls of Young India had been subtly scoffing at the sobriquet of this being a 'city of *chitti dariyaan te hariyan jhariyaan*' ('city of white beards and green bushes'), popularised about City Beautiful by legendary writer Khushwant Singh in its nascent days as an ode to its geriatric gentry and greenery.

A literary outpost that had emerged as a lens to City Beautiful's curious confluence. Where the 'chitti dariyaan'—appended to moustachioed generals with muttonchops bigger than bank balances of pensioned life, biggies of bureaucracy big on bungalows as much as bloated egos, retired relics of judiciary, or to landlord scions of erstwhile aristocracy, who were perhaps left with only one thing heavier than privy purses, their silver beards—had, over the years, come to rub shoulders with many a Millennials' streaked mane.

A Lit landscape that had evolved to be emblematic of not only *'hari jhariyaan'* but aspiring authorhood's many a Harry or Hari.

It was in this luxuriant lushness of the Lakeview Club that Lollita legged it around to get things rolling. The club's waterfront shimmered in the bronzed mellowness of autumn's sun. What warmed Lollita's heart was another sunshine.

A zillion sun's rays sparkling upon the club's picturesque promenades.

A sunshine made of Beverley Gold to Buttercup Yellow. Gold Rush Yellow to Golden Cheryl.

A sunshine paint-brushed with Spoons and Snowballs, Pompons and Potomacs.

Chrysanthemums bursting back to life.

Life and Death going hand in hand.

Fall, in the same breath, also resonated a requiem to the grand Gulmohars parading on the Sukhna avenues, robbing them of their scarlet couture. Like a Mother Earth strewn with the Pandemic's graveyards from a summer of doom and gloom, the Gulmohars' burnt red corolla corpses rolled out autumn's carpet of jaundiced umber. Red rubies dropping from a diva's glittering gown that had once gallivanted in all its glory down the runways.

Alas, all the loveliness of the lakefront's flora and fauna paled the moment Lollita's gaze fell on another carpet. The ragtag carpet being rolled out for her book launch.

In all this hustle bustle to lend finishing touches to the stage, Lollita almost herself tripped twice over the undulating folds of the carpet. This durrie doubling up as a carpet was indeed a far, far cry from her dream red carpet.

Forget red, it wasn't even anywhere near it, looking instead not just a mousy colour but also a surface that the mice had perhaps been feasting and having a field day upon during the long Lockdown.

"Steady, my love," Ruhaan's arms reached out to arrest another one of her near-trippings on this ragtag carpet.

"What would I do without you," Lollita gazed into the depths of his soft brown eyes, her only oasis of calm and composure in this life-defining moment.

"I'll catch you in a bit, let me just look into the refreshments," he unlocked himself from the fleeting embrace to rush off to rustle things to place.

Barely had Lollita and the stage attendant bullied the bouquet into leaning left, right, and centre to preen it into a perfect posture of centrality on the stage, spruced up and studded with hoardings, leather sofas, microphones, micro mineral water bottles and, most importantly, those must-haves on the podiums of a post-Pandemic world—masks and sanitisers—when the guests started trickling in.

Her roving gaze came to rest only on a few familiar faces as she hastened to the entrance to receive the chief guest.

The club's sprawling lawns were strewn with stalwarts, socialites, and sundry gentry attired in that style statement of socialising in the New Normal—the Mask as the new Half Burqa. The Reverse Ghunghat.

The faces behind the masks were familiar. What was unfamiliar were the newly etched shadows mapping many of the masked faces. Shadows of a charcoal dark night.

The faces behind the masks were the same. What was not the same was that some resembled eclipsed orbs from the Pandemic's penumbra. The eclipse on humanity and history that the Pandemic was.

Among the faces few and far between dotting the greens, Lollita spotted semi-masked Executive Editor Raghav Vinayak pow-wowing with veteran former Editor Animesh Philip, Col Pradyuman Singh (retd), Raghubir Deswal, former supercop, and family friend Ashish Mehra. The latter's causal jeans-and-T-shirt look was a tell-all comment on the side-effects of the Pandemic. Gone was Mehra's suited-booted-tuxedo-ed couture as this head honcho from white collared corporate-hood now stood as the most visible face of an eroded India Inc who had borne the brunt of the Pandemic's downsizing—pink slips.

Downsizing peeped out elsewhere, too, from behind the warp and weft of masked reality. This throbbing tapestry threading the masked face of the New Normal looked resurgent and vibrant on the visage, but its fragile underlying texture bespoke a delicate downsizing.

Documentary-maker friend Rehmat's solitaires were missing from earlobes holding the mask strap, sporting instead gold-plated silver studs ever since her husband lost his real estate consultancy practice during the Pandemic, while fashion journo Kavery Reddy's customary one-tola gold jhumkas for socialite evenings had been downsized to plain gold hoop-baalis, mirroring the Media's Mean Lean Tryst with Recession—pay cuts or pink slips.

At a rear corner was her literati gang sharing notes on latest poetry and prose pennings from behind designer masks as they partook of immunity boosting drinks and dishes newly introduced into the menu post the pandemic—Amla Tulsi Panaka to Roasted Pumpkin and Turmeric Soup to Stir Fry Chicken with Peppercorn.

Behind a Kutch mirror-work mask and sporting her signature red rose in the tresses, poetess-socialite Raagini Singh was the blow-dried visage of local Rajput royalty tottering on its high-heeled legs for survival, a royalty for whom literary pursuits had been more a matter of leisure and social hobnobbing than of writerly bread and butter. But that Raagini's customary extravagantly embroidered pashmina stole now stood replaced with a more functional and flimsy lehariya stole was perhaps a statement that the erstwhile royalty nestling in the Himalayan foothills, hitherto subsisting on frugal earnings from converting their havelis into heritage resorts, was now gasping for survival in a tourism-deficit Corona-scape.

Giving company to Raagini were fellow poetesses Nazaakat, Lillette, and corporate bard Mandira Caur, all holding fort in resplendent regalia and ornate tussar silk masks. Rubbing shoulders with them were the bespectacled Prof Nirmaljit, who bantered from behind a thin khadi mask with Lollita's English teachers, Pari ma'am, Gurmeet ma'am, Gurdeep ma'am, and Reetinder ma'am. They were joined by Prof Kalha, whose kindly eyes crinkled above her home-stitched mask culled from her old Kota Doria saree, and Kishwar Singh with wife Naini.

In the forefront of the luxuriantly lush lawns were her BFFs, smiling and waving to cheer her, picture perfect in their semi-swathed, gaily coloured masks—Rasikaa in her Ikkat mask teaming well with her black Ikkat kurti over jeans; lecturers and authors Rita Kamra, Manikarnikaa, and Krrish peered from behind masked plainness; while college-time chum Ibaadat beamed from behind her Frida Kahlo mask.

"There comes our Humour Queen," chorused Rasikaa and Rita, blowing flying kisses to Lollita.

Along with her spouse Agasthya, lawyer-cum-literati Ananyaa Kashyap gesticulated a thumbs up to Lollita from behind her Kalamkari vegetable-dyed mask.

Her gaze fell on some faces hard to look at. Hard to look at as they were orbs from the epicentre. Epicentre of tragedy's Tauktae. Epicentre of an emotional Latur. Epicentre of the Coronascape.

Art influencer friend Leena's signature nosepin was the only thing that glinted above her Jaipuri block-printed mask. Her eyes had lost much of their mischievous glint since she had lost her mother during the Pandemic.

Beyond Leena was a pair of hollow, kohl-bereft eyes, half shielded by a sober tussar mask, that bespoke of a lost look meandering the bridges of past, present, and future. Eyes that were scanning the canvas called Life for answers, struggling to make sense of its subtext and script.

The once-dancing doe eyes that were now mere sockets of searing hollowness. Suhaani Uberoi. Lollita's family friend and food blogger who had lost her young, newly married son to Covid.

A face that was the palest moon from the umbra of a night of eclipse.

Damn, this social distancing protocol that one couldn't even say it with '*jaadu ki japphis*'. New Normal's elbow rubs just couldn't get the emotional vocabulary right like '*japphis*'.

Lollita parted her lips in a half smile as Suhaani's vacant gaze met hers. A half smile that didn't say much, yet said it all.

A half smile stranded from reaching Lollita's eyes by a Ganga going into spate on her lashes.

As Lollita was plunging forward to mingle with her guests, her smartphone beeped a string of notifications. Lollita was quickly browsing the messages and she nearly tripped on the ragtag carpet.

This time, not because of the carpet's undulating folds. But what her notifications did unfold.

One of their eminent litterateur friends, Principal Lajwinder, aka Lally ji, had that very morning lost the battle to Covid. The veteran vlogger, who was the life and soul of the Tricity's literary landscape and had affectionately anointed her 'Humour Express', was never meant to make it.

"Ho Ho...Benediction, benediction to bump into our Humour Express, whose peppered writing syncs salty phrases and sweet-sour neologisms with personal peculiarities," Lally Ji had gushed from behind black goggles, sported with a tomato red shirt and black polka dot tie, upon sighting Lollita as he sallied through Press Club's frosted engraved door, weeks before Pandemic had sneaked in through their doors.

"Remember, the first interview you give for your new book should be bequeathed upon me," Lally ji had spouted effusive vocabulary that could have put Shashi Tharoor to shame. He had exuded a joie de vivre for his advanced years that could have put many a younger literati to shame. "Remember, I'm the most ardent admirer to have made the ambrosia of your acquaintance!"

His sartorial statement in the resplendent red shirt resonated on Lollita's mindscape, like a flickering prayer flag upon a faraway Himalayan monastery, now that the moment of her book's birth was here.

"Gone like the Gulmohar!"

The curtains of her cornea fogged with a Cherrapunji. Her pupils pricked with microcosms of a million monsoons.

A Birth. A Death. To be seated side by side at her book launch.

38

The Curious Case of Phulkari on the Pandemic-scape

Lollita dragged her footsteps towards the other guests through the condensation on her cornea.

Bantering close-by were the Badshahs of Bureaucracy.

Swarmed by a string of social butterflies were the Queen Bees. Joint Secretary Srishti Misra, the life and soul behind Literatty, made a pretty picture in her powder pink crepe and pearls, teamed with a sequinned mask, as she engaged in a tete-a-tete with Lepaakshi, better half of the Chief Secretary, who looked stunning in a Sambalpuri silk saree paired with an Ikkat mask from Odisha. Basking in the sunshine as much as the spotlight, they sipped their Ginger 'n' Gooseberry Martinis over partially dismantled masks. Vivaan Agarkar, technocrat-turned-TedX speaker, ambled towards them to chat up the new Chief Secretary and his significant half.

In between munching on chocolate brownies, the small sprinkling of socialites and sycophants were making full use of this rare post-Pandemic social outing to also pile up brownie points. By gushing about the upcoming fiction book of the state bureaucracy's First Lady.

"Such gushing over a book that's not yet out!" Lollita couldn't help marvelling as she overheard all the raving.

Eyeing the socialites and sycophants already at work in promoting the soon-to-be-published book of the Chief Secretary's better half, Lollita turned tad green with envy, greener than the city's proverbial '*hari jhariyaan*'.

How Lollita wished that if not a Bollywood ride to bestsellerhood, at least Lady Luck could have lent her a helping hand in belonging to the Haut Monde of Higher Bureaucracy. By matrimonial berth, if not by birth or worth.

Had Lady Luck bestowed upon her such Advantaged Authorhood, Lollita could've commanded half the babudom to dance attendance and be her foot soldiers making up footfalls. Parading, rather 'mask-querading', as possible literati. To make good the non-fiscal shortage—My Big Fat Footfall Deficit. Behind the masks, who would have known at the book launch if it was a battalion of under-secretaries or underlings!

"Gosh, it's almost time for the Guest of Honour...but, where in the world are the rest of my guests?" Lollita grimaced, gazing at the half empty lawns.

Lollita looked around for the missing faces—of family and friends, peers and paparazzi—who were desperately awaited to lend the lush lawns a fullness of footfall.

"This is one day, when to boost the footfalls I would've even welcomed gate crashers...with *aarti ki thaalis,*" sighed Lollita.

Just then, piercing the placid lakeside was the decibelism of a deafening crash.

Somebody had knocked into a waiter ferrying an armload of plates.

Somebody in peculiarly permed tresses, who was waving out frantically now.

"Lollita...Lollita...heya!"

Lollita scurried to get up close and personal with the gate crasher.

"Youuuuu...," she squeaked with delight when a familiar pair of pupils peered from behind a masked countenance and its mangled maze of over-painted curls.

The one to crash-land was none other than BinduBee.

"How could I not land for your launch!" the fellow author-friend trilled in her TamBrahm accent.

In all the gush of greetings that ensued, there was one thing that rankled rather rudely before Lollita's gaze.

"What's with your hair!" Lollita couldn't help gaping.

"Oh that," BinduBee bleated, patting her permed profusion. "I was sounding so sick of looking like Lockdown's Plain Jane, that my Chinese hairstylist decided to give a makeover to my mane!"

"Chinese meets Chennai!' Lollita sounded startled.

BinduBee didn't much beat about the bush, the bush bobbing atop her brainy cranium, and dished out her hair-raising tale.

"Blame it on Lee!"

Lollita's eyes tried training themselves to the new vision, as one used to 2-D silver screen adjusts to a 3-D multiplex movie.

Before she knew, BinduBee was putting not only her best haircut forward, but also her best foot forward.

There, on the placid lakefront unfurled all the Salsa that BinduBee had been learning in the Lockdown. And, before Lollita knew, she was matching her step for step, spin for spin.

Salsa meets Giddha.

The Salsa spins were cut short as somebody came stumbling into them. Who else but Lamba ji.

Lollita almost collided head on with Lamba ji, who had one ear perpetually pasted to his smartphone. Lollita's gaze almost smarted under the feast of colour that Lamba ji presented, a far cry from his staple sartorial statement of blue jeans and white kurta.

His trademark white chikankari kurta was there, but, of all the days, today it was teamed with yellow cigarette pants. Perhaps, Lamba ji had been revisiting old Govinda flicks on

Netflix to have been inspired for this sartorial sunniness. Lollita couldn't get over the uncanny feeling that he reminded her of a radish that had strayed into a pumpkin's closet. As if to reinforce this resemblance, the canary yellow frame of his Ray Bans completed the pumpkin look.

"Come, come, remember to take lots of selfies while receiving the chief guest...for our social media promos," Lamba ji egged on Lollita.

BinduBee all this while had not uttered a syllable. Instead, she had been gaping at Lamba ji as open-mouthed as a school kid sighting a new species on a school trip to a zoo.

Mercifully, Lollita found Ruhaan at her elbow again as she sallied past her paltry parade of guests.

"Here, you need this desperately, dear." He had fetched acai berry and basil smoothies, an immunity booster which she hastily lapped up as if it was a nerve smoother.

He offered the other to her Lit Agent Lamba ji. "Ah, just what was needed," Lamba ji partook a few sips of the refreshment and then looking at Lollita, gushed gregariously, "What a handsome...!"

Just as he was mid-sentence, his smartphone decided to bleat and Lamba ji was again juggling the act he was adept at, babbling half into the phone to his broker bloke, half into the live conversation.

"Sun TV... *Uthha lo...uthaa lo* (pick it, pick it)," Lamba ji tattled.

"TV *uthha lo*?" Lollita looked a tad flabbergasted, casting a glance around the club lobby for any small screens and wondering what an Idiot Box had to do with the book launch.

"Err...no no...Sun," Lamba ji's de-cropped pate oscillated left to right as he returned to the conversation with Lollita and saw the nonplussed look mapping the faces of Lollita and Ruhaan.

"Sun?" Lollita looked even more befuddled.

"Err...I meant...," Lamba ji switched conversations with his trademark aplomb, the way one switches television channels. "I meant...what a handsome son!"

Lollita and Ruhaan exchanged quiet glances, as Ruhaan smiled at her reassuringly. "Hardly the time to let Lamba ji unsettle me with these unwitting reminders about age!" Lollita sighed like a beleaguered pressure cooker that simmers in silence and can't let out the pressure piling up inside it.

Fortified by Ruhaan's soothing smile more than the smoothie, Lollita plunged towards the patio.

Into the Ashoka-hemmed parking arena, there rolled in the much-awaited vehicle.

The Guest of Honour for this post-Pandemic book launch trundled in in her downsized car. A second-hand Maruti Esteem. Ferried forth not by a full-time chauffeur, but by a cabbie parading as chauffeur, on hourly hire. She was chaperoned out by this un-liveried chap, lanky and lean. Lean, not so much from the compulsions of constitution as from the after-effects of having lost his cab company in the Lockdown.

Peculiarities of Pandemic's new social life narrative being driven home.

Lollita's first impression upon setting sight on the lady behind the 'Half Burqa' (mask) and faux Gucci glares, was overwhelming. The Chief Guest stepped out, a spectacle swathed in the ethnic and exotic extravagance of the palettes of Punjab's Phulkari.

Sitaara Devi. Faded TV star. Wannabe MP.

Screened behind a mask that was also all Phulkari, Sitaara ji looked almost as vibrant as a partly gift-wrapped Amrita Sher-gil painting. Albeit a portrait gone wrong, as if accidentally strewn with spilt paint.

Upholstered in an ornate ochre-and-gold Phulkari embroidered dupatta with a matching phulkari-hemline mask, Sitaara ji was a picture of lissom-ness meets loudness, the only thing subdued about her being the now reticent demeanour, a glaring contrast from her exuberance of yesteryear when she had straddled the peak of their comedy career with her late husband.

Phulkari, the traditional handicraft of Punjab, was naturally a style statement among the city's socialites and fashionistas. Social butterflies often swathed the heavier versions of Phulkari on suits, dupattas, and now palazzos, too. The heavier the Phulkari work, the higher their standing in stylista circles. Then there was a section of the intelligentsia—academicians, artistes, arty wannabes and all those—for whom Phulkari was the style stamp for professional platforms, be it convocations, receiving awards from Sahitya Akademis or the President, Phulkari was the un-anointed queen of couture, the sartorial style statement for status update-ism and selfie-ism.

Like most traditional crafts, Phulkari had its street versions, too, which saw Phulkari work pop up on faux labels, with the street stylistas wearing its cheaper, machine-made versions embossed all over low-end suits, faux chiffon dupattas, as trims on juttis or hand clutches; and what not.

"Lovely to have you with us," Lollita stretched out her arms as if to squeeze Sitaara ji's hand in welcome and proffer her the mini potted plant meant as a welcome gift—as an emblem of Lollita's go-green mantra—instead of the traditional bouquet.

But mid-air, Lollita's forelimbs froze as social distancing protocol arrested their advancement, and the right hand was left levitating, much in the manner of batsman Virat Kohli sprinting half way down the crease and suddenly somebody comes out of the blue and into his ears does coo—Statue.

Switching out of handshake mode, the tapering tips of her fingers took charge and holding the pot gingerly with minimal contact, deposited its go-green contents into the hands of Sitaara ji. The latter, too, displayed the diplomatic body language of the New Normal—outstretching not her bare hands but hands politely veiled under the Phulkari dupatta to receive the green gift, smacking of a scare that the plant might be a carrier of the vicious virus.

The green gift was Lollita's gesture as part of the growing green brigade to go eco-friendly for festivals and fetes. Lollita had done her tiny bit by going minimalistic on paper, by sending out only e-invites and downsizing on posters (Ah, it's another story that the minimal presence of posters was partially to be blamed on a post-Lockdown lull, with very few printers back in business).

"Awww, what an environment-friendly gesture," Sitaara ji gushed, stretching her arm behind her to pronto pass on the potted plant to her chauffeur.

Now the thing with chauffeurs or chaperones is that more often than not they're not in attendance at just that very moment when their undivided attention or presence is crucial, gazing goofily perhaps at a passing bee or a spider spinning a cobweb on some nook and cranny. The said chauffeur, too, seemed to belong to this species and at the very moment that the potted plant left the hands of the Chief Guest in the hope of being caught by her Man Friday behind her, his gaze was glassily intent on a huge housefly hovering inhospitably over his frizzy locks, reeking of scented badam hair oil, the smell of which had distracted the said insect winging its way to the snack counter yonder to do a detour over the chauffeur's curly cranium.

As the pot spun forward on its stratospheric sojourn, it had no takers. Just then, divining the death blow that looked destined for the go-green emblem, a pair of hands that had been hovering in the backdrop lunged forward for the catch, bearing a resemblance to poetry in motion, in the style of a Bhajji or Bumrah at their bowling best—Ruhaan playing the perfect Knight.

The Mask of Zara. To the rescue of the Dieffenbechia in Distress.

Therefrom, they all trooped towards centrestage and a few flashbulbs popped, belonging to the stray media photographers who's just sauntered in, in the nick of time.

As Lollita passed Ruhaan on the way to the stage, she again nearly tottered on her Bata wedges, more out of nervousness than from her heel getting tangled in the folds of the apology of a carpet laid out.

Every time her gaze fell on the apology of a carpet, a stab of angst smote through her bosom.

Whatever happened to the Red Carpet book launch I'd dreamt of!

Ruhaan steadied her just in time and as he whispered best wishes in her ears, he couldn't help adding, "Wish we could have roped in that stand-up comedian instead...at least more media photographers and channel wallahs would have turned up!"

This remark of Ruhaan couldn't have been more bang on, as Lollita clambered up on to the stage and noticed from the corner of her eye barely one or two paparazzi clicking away. Ruhaan's remark put the finger on that unsettling feeling she'd been nagged by the whole morning.

Whatever happened to the Bollywood-like book launch with a million paparazzi flashbulbs popping that I'd dreamt of!

On the stage, the protagonists sank into the leather sofas placed apart, as per social distancing protocol. Words started flowing—the customary welcome speeches, keynote address, introduction of the Guests of Honour and all that.

Sitaara ji, parked on the central couch, presented an Amrita Sher-gil portrait spoiled by spilled paint, oozing the air of an overdone painting.

Commissioning Editor Paroma, who had flown in at the eleventh hour for a token guest appearance, perched on Sitaara ji's far right, cracked like a crisp saboodana poppadum in her starched Bengali Jamdani saree accessorised with a big fat Bong bindi. She exuded the exotic look of a Jamini Roy painting.

In between this overdone Amrita Sher-gil painting-meets-Jamini Roy exotica sat Lamba ji. He looked as much misplaced and a misfit as a pop art, street-side sketch in a Renaissance museum of murals.

Lamba ji's Ray Bans time and again threatened to do a downslide from the glistening gibbousness of his scalp towards his nasal regions, such that half his time was spent arresting its fall from grace and in twitching his tendons on the cellphone in an itching for all the calls to his broker bloke that he wasn't able to make.

The event rolled off with a two-minute silence in memory of the Pandemic's departed.

Soon, the whirr of voices from the customary speeches started swimming in Lollita's mind like a blur. As if it was mango chutney being pureed in a blender with the ingredients, one by one, losing their individual flavours to become part of a collective churning, a whipped whirring.

"So happy to be among litterateurs and writers today. In my college days, I too used to write for our magazine and would have become a writer if...," Sitaara ji was prattling pompously, more about her own journey.

Listening to the literary rhetoric-ism, only one thought niggled and nagged at the back of Lollita's mind.

Whatever happened to that star-studded spectacle with starry speeches fashioning me into a literary sensation that I'd dreamt of!

Sitaara ji's voice pierced into her reverie as, much venting of verbosity later typical of launches, they all clambered around for the unveiling of The Jacket.

"Can you help with this, the ribbon's stuck?" Sitaara ji said, as all guests onstage got down to unwrapping the gift-wraps and red ribbons packaging the book that had had little time to become designer, so busy it had been being born digitally.

The Guest of Honour was tugging at the ribbons as the flashbulbs were popping non-stop, capturing even this awkward moment, but the stubborn gift-wrap wouldn't come off. Acutely aware of the zooming lenses, Lollita first gingerly tried to twist and turn the ribbon into cooperating. But, when it appeared adamant at playing spoilsport, she just snapped at it so hard, that not only the shimmery cover fell off, but also The Jacket.

As Lollita bent down to pick The Jacket, she knocked off that same bouquet she had spent half the evening trying to position perfectly on centrestage.

Splish! Splosh! Water from the toppled designer bouquet from Ferns N Petals played true spoilsport not only on Lollita's exotic Madhubani saree, but also on the book jacket.

All this, on camera and on Facebook Live!

The worst had come true, not only did the launch look a damp squib, but even her new-born 'baby' looked damp—The Yellow Jacket.

Only one thought hammered harder and harder at her brain, as she surveyed the sight that spelt more disaster than things designer—the saree that went dripping, at The Yellow Jacket's unzipping.

What to talk of her shattering the glass ceiling of bestsellerhood, Lollita's dream lay shattered into smithereens like the fragile crystal flower vase.

As they all took their seats and the vote of thanks started rolling on the stage, Lollita looked back to scan the audience on the lawns from the corner of her eye.

Forget a chorus of wine glasses clinking in celebration, like at the unveiling of the celebrity Pink Jacket in the YouTube clip she'd revisited again and again, what Lollita's gaze encountered on glancing back over her shoulder was near-empty seats.

Even the few masked faces that had made it for the event, were discreetly legging it out in departure mode. Poof, there trickled out even her little chances of book buyers.

"Where in the world are those throngs of autograph seekers I had dreamt of!"

Upon one of the vacant seats, Lollita saw sitting that same potted plant she'd proffered as a welcome gift to the Guest of Honour—its shiny leaves that had been all perky and primped in the morning when Lollita got it, now looked all droopy and wilted.

Dieffenbechia in Double Distress.

The sight made Lollita sigh so loud, like a pressure cooker fizzling to its last whistle, that even Sitaara ji looked up from the Yellow Jacket of the unveiled book she was politely browsing through.

"Red carpet book launch, my foot!"

Only one consolatory thought crept up to comfort Lollita.

"Guess, My Big Fat Footfall Deficit can all be blamed on that gatecrasher of a Game Changer—Social Distancing!"

39

The Curious Case of Shades of Grey Under My Gulmohar

Somewhere in the suburbs of Gurugram

Bholi Punjabban sat by the window enveloped in an audibly amplified stillness.

Unusual. Unbecoming of her.

The amplified silence of an auditorium deserted after staging a Mian Ki Malhar by a maestro. Hers were the empty eyes of the theatre that now stares at the desolateness of emptied seats.

The Ballerina of a Bird no longer pranced in the unfrilled arms of the Gulmohar. Beneath its shorn canopy bereft of jewels, there rolled out another carpet.

A carpet threaded with beads of a biscotti brownness.

A canvas spilled as if with specks of sandy matte acrylic.

The carpet of golden grains that heralded the return of the pigeons under the gargantuan Gulmohar.

Bholi saw the pigeons flocking back, yet the lime paleness of her pupils did not see them. Her eyes searched not now for this sea of slate greyness, but for the fieriness of that plumed palette of bluish-greenness.

She licked her litter harder. As if to still the restlessness of her riveted retinas. As if to divert the aching-ness in the arterial bylanes of her heartstrings.

She showered most of her attention on her ginger kitten, who had looked listless for the past day or so.

When Lollita tossed Bholi Punjabban some titbits, she didn't even crane her neck.

She went back to the Future. The Bifocals of Bholi Punjabban's being stared yonder, through the contact lenses of the window.

Bholi Punjabban had lost not only her joie de vivre, but also her appetite.

Lollita and Ruhaan, contrarily, gorged gluttonously on the hearty breakfast, rather brunch that Ruhaan had prepared, since it was close to noon by the time they tucked into the meal like ravenous schoolkids who're past tiffin time.

Her smartphone squirmed soon after. The screen flashed to reveal it was Meeraya Di, giving her customary noon call, just before her online bridge session got underway.

"Guess what, sweetie?" Meeraya Di gushed. "Just finished watching such a sweet, sad flick on Netflix. About an adorable dog..."

"Di, since when are you into pet flicks?" Lollita sounded a bit surprised.

"How that poor dog saves his master from impending danger... The master was meant to die of a terminal disease, instead the dog is the one who meets that fate...," Meeraya Di almost choked.

"Di, this is such a sad tale...," Lollita almost felt goose-bumpy. "Watch something to cheer you, Di...like *Tom and Jerry*!"

Later that evening, Lollita skimmed through the news notifications landing this morning as her smartphone squiggled to announce them.

"Gosh," she gasped as she read the latest Twitter alert which showed the trending hashtag #RIP.

"Now what?" Ruhaan looked up from his iPad.

"Can you believe this, so many of those quaint book cafés, such as that Café Tortoise, where we went for our first date, they've closed down post-lockdown. A casualty of the economic closedown!" Lollita's voice almost choked.

Strange, isn't it, how an innocuous looking place becomes a repository of life's memories and milestones, like a mental museum we visit and revisit for the moments showcased on memory's walls.

Sid's first Enid Blyton and *Harry Potter* had been bought and read there, on its funky furniture, which exuded a European feel, as their very styling bespoke contemporary meets chic.

It was where, post-PTMs or post-Board results, Sid and Lollita headed for their celebratory carrot and date cake.

It was where, on obscure back shelves, that Lollita had perchance found that relic of a PGW—tattered cover and dog-eared pages, that was among the titles up for throwaway sale—for a mere Rs 50!

It was where, in sometimes clumsily stacked piles, that Lollita had had her first tryst with Rumi. By sheer chance. She'd barely stretched out her arm one day to grab at a Jane Austen staring at her from a haphazard heap on a shelf when another hand had snatched at that same title at the same moment, and the awkwardness of the two tugging hands had unsettled the entire pile that had flown off the shelf, like a ton of plaster dismantling from an ancient CPWD guest house wall whilst one is merely chasing a spider that's established permanent residence on its sooty niches. And, atop the heap that landed on the floor, lay that undiscovered treasure, *The Essential Rumi*, which was to become a jewel in Lollita's book collection and her initiation into the world of Sufism's velvety verse.

"Awww, so so sad...it spells the end of an era," is all she could muster, as she hungrily lapped all the titbits of tweets spilling sentimentality from all those bibliophiles for whom it was more than a bookstore—a Lifeline.

Ruhaan couldn't help but feel the sense of lament rubbing off on him, too, for he had fond memories of his first date with her there.

"These are dark times indeed!" He squeezed her hand to comfort her. "I had been thinking of telling you... But, I don't know if this is the right time?"

Lollita looked up a tad alarmed. "Tell *naa*...what is it?"

"I just heard two of your neighbours talk at the gate when I went to collect deliveries yesterday," Ruhaan said. "It seems that next-door neighbour of yours..." Ruhaan nodded to the terrace across.

'You mean Gupta ji?" Lollita was all agog.

"Nah, the one with that stunning scarlet car," Ruhaan went on, "Well, I heard he's lost his job, too..."

"Oh no!" Lollita exclaimed.

"He was the Managing Director of the franchise of that fabled book cafe, Café Turtlez, that's also been shut down for good!" Ruhaan dropped the tidings like a bombshell.

Lollita was at a loss of words as her eyes wandered to their courtyard, "Remember how Ganguly ji would be washing his red car so religiously every morning in lockdown even though it went nowhere?" Lollita rambled. "And, guess what, though Ganguly ji is very much seen around, I've been wondering—it's been days, I haven't seen his Lamborghini!"

"And, I'd been wondering why we haven't seen Gupta ji much in his kitchen garden these past few weeks?" Lollita dropped her bit of 'breaking news'.

"Yeah. He had been plodding away at his *laukis* which were all set to make it to the Limca book." Ruhaan reminisced about the cross-talk between Gupta ji and Ganguly ji that the neighbours had so much been privy to.

"Well, the garbage woman, who had to clear up their garden junk, told me...Gupta ji's garden was attacked by, guess what?

"What?"

"Locusts!"

Just then, Sid, who had just got back from his internship stint for the day, barged into the room.

He looked at Lollita thoughtfully, as if gauging her mood. Then, he dropped the tidings.

"Mom, this is not going to be easy," he dropped his voice to a gentleness.

"What?" Lollita looked up, alarmed.

"Come and have a look in the corridor. The ginger cat is...*dead*."

POST PANDEMIC

"Don't grieve. Anything you lose

comes round

in another form."

—RUMI

40

The Curious Case of the Yellow Ferrari

Somewhere on the outskirts of 'City Beautiful'

"Hey sweetie, will you prefer our traditional Rajput cuisine or Continental for luncheon? I'll instruct the khansaama accordingly."

Raagini Singh had popped this question without much preamble on the phone, within seconds of Lollita telling her that she would soon be landing at her palatial residence for their first post-Pandemic tête-à-tête.

It was almost an hour's drive out of town to Raagini's royal haveli on the outskirts of their 'City Beautiful', nestling in the foothills of the Morni mountainside of the Himalayas.

The long, dusty road along the way looked a barren, brown landscape depleted of its forest cover by the rash of banquet halls and marriage palaces coming up in that part. But, just as the eyes begin to tire of the endless barrenness of the stretch, looming large before the unsuspecting eyes is that breath-taking jewel in this countryside. Perhaps, the best kept secret of a contemporary cityscape that is so cosmopolitan in attitude and architecture—Fort Ramgarh.

A Rajput haveli built by the scions of the Chandel Dynasty, it is an architectural wonder studded in a barren hillside in more ways than one. For one, its crowning glory is the majestic and mammoth gateway into the haveli that has made it into the *Limca Book of Records* as the tallest wooden doorway of India.

As Lollita had rolled into this barren landscape in the Himalayan foothills, she was struck by how much was unchanged, yet how much stood changed.

The tallest doorway.

The towering doorway that had fortified its relics of erstwhile royalty against the unforeseen infiltrator called Corona.

The ancient archway that was the grilled armour behind which had crouched an ebbing Past panting to survive not only the Present, but also the other 'P'—Pandemic.

The looming landmark on a landscape of barrenness through the jaalis and jharokhas of which had seeped in the side-effects—Dwarfing by Downsizing.

Raagini's maternal family, headed now by her cousin Ameyaa Singh Chandel, were scions of the fabled Chandel Rajputs from the *Mahabharata* and *Ramayana* era.

When Ameyaa's ancestors from the family of the Raja of Bilaspur had landed in Ramgarh nearly 360 years ago, this Fort came into being, where Lollita arrived, after turns and twists, of terrain and a timeline.

It was through its imposing facade flanked on both sides by lion sculptures, that Lollita, after parking her Maruti next to a quaint Ferrari in the sandy driveway, had strolled in that weekend morning many months post her book, *Wannabe Bestseller*, was published. The 'Durban' at the reception had accompanied her to Raagini's part of the haveli on the farther east side, first floor.

Every time Lollita came here, she never failed to gasp afresh at the vintage car parked in the driveway of the east wing, which was still used for ferrying 'Kunwar Saheb'. A bewitching beauty in Burnt Sienna, its vintage orange-ness was a repository of many royal visits to and fro from this seat of erstwhile royalty. As she threaded her way up the winding stairway to the first floor, Lollita briefly stopped to peer into the arms and ammunition showcased on the ground floor living area—daggers, guns, arrows, and all that the Chandel rulers had used for the battles of yore.

Maintaining all this legacy was not easy, in fact a huge dent in the earnings that now came to the family from having converted the heritage haveli into a part hotel.

"Hey, so good to see you after all these months," Raagini had outstretched her arms as a restrained gesture of welcome but hadn't rushed forward for that 'Jaadu ji Japphi' as they were wont to exchanging.

Lollita, too, gesticulated flying kisses at Raagini as she placed a beautifully wrapped basket of goodies on the centre-table as a token of their reunion after a season of Pandemic-induced separation.

"You look so chilled and charming as ever...being home bound all these months has done you a world of good," Lollita gushed as she admiringly glanced at the black, Kutch-embroidery kurti Raagini was sporting over a glitzy mirror-work-and-sequins skirt with a lehariya stole camouflaging the slight double chin that would peep out every now and then.

"Haha, as good as a butterfly with its wings clipped can look!" laughed Raagini.

A poet, writer, and happiness coach all rolled into one, Raagini was one feisty single mom who wore her flamboyance on her sleeves with as much elan as her royal roots and literary profile.

"Gosh, how did the city's social life survive the pandemic without our Page Three socialite popping out of its pages and parties?" Lollita teased her for the social butterfly tag she had earned from being the fashionista face at every happening social-do about town.

Though like the cookies in a cookie jar came in all shapes and sizes, the social butterflies in a cosmopolitan new-age city too came with all sorts of frills and frothiness. The only thing different was that the Pandemic had made socialites look like cookies wrapped in cling films or butter paper—the mask being their New Burqa or, for Rajput royalty, Reverse Ghunghat.

You may have noticed, dear discerning reader, this breed of sarkari socialite or the crème de la crème of cosmopolitan India that is made up of women bureaucrats, wives of bureaucrats, and the better halves of the Who's Who of the sarkari machinery—defence officers to diplomats—whose chiffons or conversations drip an elitism that comes from residing in sprawling sarkari kothis with bahadurs and chaprasis at their beck and call at home as much as in office; from wining 'n' dining with the Governors at the 'At Homes' or with visiting dignitaries. These are the pearls-and-chiffon socialites with substance who unravel conversational pearls like the pallus of their prized Chanderis and Chikankaaris with as much aplomb as they unfurl inaugural ribbons with their bureaucrat other halves at official galas. That is the pre-Pandemic picture.

The Pandemic picture of the sarkari socialite has its masked face, obviously. Peeping out from (where else) haute monde Zoom screens or FB Lives, spouting 'Green in Lockdown' messages on Environment Day to spilling status updates of lolling in luxuriantly lush, sarkari bungalows with their Labs and Lal Bahadurs in tow (remember, the Bahadurs in bureaucratic bastions didn't really migrate since it was not just about buttering up to memsahibs, it's about knowing which side of the bread was better buttered—Dhulia versus Sahib-dom's regalia).

Then, there is the Pandemic's Page Three Socialite—game changers to noveau riche to fashionistas with frills as much as frivolity—who have embedded in their DNA the knack of making it to glossies and Page Three columns even in a world plagued by virus. You might have spotted, dear discerning reader, peering at you from Page Three pictures propelling #couplegoals to new highs by hoeing or gardening in Lockdown's gardens; flaunting their fashionista masks;

playing the perfect Pandemic parent by presiding over kids' painting or sculpture sessions; and all that. The virus may rein them in from stepping out for Page Three parties, but it can't take the Page Three out of them.

But, what set apart Raagini and her ilk of royal socialites was that they were torchbearers of the tag of erstwhile royalty caught in the cusp between the contemporary and a glorious past that rested on their Chanderi sarees and Bandhini stoles like a legacy that was hard to maintain yet harder to relinquish. So much like this heritage haveli itself, the walls of which were steeped in centuries of Rajput tradition that was its signature stamp yet it was a façade hard to sustain in a post-Independence world, and thus had propelled the scions towards reinventing the past for the present—as a heritage resort.

The Pandemic had made the royal socialites' palatial mansions with their fleet of liveried retainers and an even longer fleet of vintage or new-age cars a drain on their resources; and mandated a mirror introspection.

Nobody mirrored this better than Raagini who, with her socialite life snuffed out like the Benson & Hedges cigarettes that quarantine had denied her, had during Lockdown looked at newer ways of engagement—consolidating her role as stress columnist-cum-consultant by content writing for more and more portals and blogs, holding webinars in her role as happiness coach; and all that.

It was thus this subdued socialite that Raagini now was who greeted Lollita from those leopard-print, walnut wood recliner propped by fuchsia pink cushions reflecting the curtain-scape that made her backdrop.

"Hey, but how's your book been doing?" Raagini steered the conversation to more literary pursuits.

"Doing?" Lollita said in a self-mocking tone, "It hasn't even taken off!"

"Awww...what a pity your book got caught in this whole cusp of the Pandemic!" Raagini clicked her tongue.

"It's like being caught between the Pen's Ageism and the Plague...a devil-and-the dead-sea dilemma," Lollita summed up the irony of her situation.

"Things are returning to normal...or New Normal now... So, maybe you'll get a chance to take your book out there into the new literary universe," Raagini's mind was exploring possibilities of pushing Lollita's book in a post-Pandemic world.

"Ah, that seems a remote possibility yet... Most big litfests aren't having Season 2021 or 22...even if they were, why would the biggie shows invite small fish like us?"

"Ya, I heard that most litfests had been called off...no sponsors, no funds... Imagine even big names like JLF and others have had to do a relook," Raagini said. "But thank God, some litfests have announced a comeback..." Raagini winked at her.

"Really...?" Lollita was all ears since she knew Raagini was wired into literary circles. "Which ones are happening now?"

Raagini gave her a mysterious smile. "Come, let's move to the Dastarkhawan for lunch...Ameyaa Bhaisaheb is waiting for us there," she propelled Lollita towards the West Wing where the ethnic Rajput *rasoi* and restaurant were.

Raagini's Maybelline 'Colossal'-smeared brown eyes bubbled with a glint of mischief and mysteriousness.

"You couldn't have come on a better day...Bhaisaheb has a special guest dining with him today...!"

41

The Curious Case of Currying Favours

"Yuuuum...having this Gatte ki Curry after ages," Lollita ravenously tucked into the savoury Rajasthani cuisine being dished out. Raagini and she had moved to the Dastarkhawan, the Fort's ethnic restaurant done up in subtle yet tasteful royal décor, with the waiters liveried in traditional Rajasthani regalia.

The décor reflected the philosophy behind this heritage property, as much as elsewhere, of being a confluence between the past and present. The niches carved in the pillars of the Dastarkhawan were imitations of miniature jharokhas, giving a feel of ethnic architecture while the plush upholstery and furnishings bespoke a contemporary taste for the modern heritage traveller looking out for a mélange.

Over a sumptuous spread of Tomato Jaipuri, Papad ki Subzi, and Gatte ki Curry, the two friends were catching up over luncheon with Ameyaa Bhaisaheb and Pranyaa Bhabhi.

The dapper and debonair face of erstwhile royalty. The pedigreed shoulders sagging under trappings of a sepia-wrapped past and an uncertain future. A weathered and wise profile that was refashioning itself, from a scion into a raconteur of the rich Rajput legacy. By penning a coffeetable book chronicling the culinary secrets of Ramgarh's royal kitchens. By returning to the roots as a practitioner of Naturopathy.

Accompanying Ameyaa Bhaisaheb was his old family friend, sporting a salt-and-pepper beard with the luxuriant silver on the scalp swept into a ponytail at the back. Gucci glares stood perched nonchalantly atop a wrinkled brow boasting eyebrows as bushy as the Sundarbans mangrove forests, those that seemed to be Siamese twins joined at the buttocks, since there was not much terrain separating the two eyebrows.

"Meet my friend, Rakul Singh," Ameyaa Bhaisaheb initiated the introductions. "This is Lollita, a leading columnist and now a budding writer."

"Hi," Rakul greeted her. "Interesting, so what is it that you're writing about?" he asked out of politeness.

Raagini spoke on her behalf, "She's a wonderful writer and has penned this funny book. The only thing is the timing..."

"Timing?" Rakul's silvery eyebrows hopped northwards, almost saying a quick hello to the Gucci glares peeping down from the head, mirroring the cuisine piled on his platter every time he chomped into the poppadams and soya *chaamps* with molars that were fast disappearing like Pandemic's litfests.

"Oh, the book couldn't have had worse timing...caught on the cusp of these cataclysmic times! No proper launch, no promos, and other problems that came with the Pandemic," Lollita said.

"Yes, yes, it's been a bad season for all," Rakul remarked. "It's spelt a death blow to litfests, too...," he added.

"Try this Papad ki Subzi, dear," Pranyaa Bhabhi fussed over Lollita. "You're hardly eating anything."

"By the way, do you know who Rakul is?" Raagini looked at Lollita as if she was supposed to know the Who's Who directory by heart.

"Well, he is the former Editor of the *India News Express*, that's how Ameyaa Bhaisaheb and he are friends and colleagues from those media days," Raagini was in her inimitable style lifting the veil of mystery surrounding the bearded man sitting across Lollita.

Rakul was nodding his head in affirmation, "Those were golden times for us journos, isn't it Ameyaa?" The latter smiled his reticent smile.

Raagini butted in, refusing to let the conversation be derailed in another direction, and carried on with her unveiling, "But, all that's in the past. The important thing is that now Rakul is the man behind that beautifully curated Kussowlie Writers' Fest!" she dropped her bombshell.

Lollita nearly choked on the *chaamps* she was chomping, much in the manner that a Siamese cat, who was thus far engrossed in sighting sundry sparrows far in the sky but suddenly finds a pot-bellied pigeon perambulating onto the patio itself, may gasp in glee.

"Haha... The man behind a festival that's struggling to survive," Rakul retorted.

"Yes, things must be tough for you all, too," Lollita nodded in understanding.

"Tough is an understatement," Rakul said on a serious note. "No sponsors, no funds, safety concerns and a scare still."

"So, are you planning to do the next season?" Lollita asked.

"Our fest happens in the early part of the year—which is three months from now—and we still don't know where we stand," he said.

"But, you were saying you'll host a reformatted version?" Raagini butted in.

"Yeah, we're hoping to host a downsized version, cutting it down from three days to a one-day affair," Rakul responded.

"That sounds sensible," Raagini said. "Not too many authors may be willing to come, anyway."

"Yes, we want to keep the spirit alive but also factor in social distancing and safety concerns, so a one-day format it shall be!" Rakul announced decidedly.

Lollita's heart was doing a hop skip jump. Aloud she only said, "That's a step forward…New Normal's new format."

"Hey Rakul, hope you'll have me on board like always," Raagini was trying to secure her berth.

"Haha, how dare I not star you on board!" he looked teasingly at Ameyaa Bhaisaheb. "Don't I want to be treated to this Gatta Curry again?"

"Haha, yes yes you dare not forget to feature me!" Raagini sounded placated. She had been a regular feature at most previous editions of the KWF, either as a moderator or as a poet-panellist.

"Is it possible to give Lollita a slot, too, Rakul?" she asked a tad tentatively.

Rakul munched on his *gattas* a bit thoughtfully, taking his time to reply.

"Hmmm…*ek ke saath ek free*?" he teased. "Seriously speaking, would love to give her a chance but…"

Lollita had nearly stopped crunching on her crisp papad subzi. Raagini was winking away at her like a partner in crime.

"In a post-Pandemic world, it's hard to make promises!" Rakul slowly dished out his reply as he wiped off the last relics of the Tomato Jaipuri on his platter.

"Litfests will now look like these baby tomatoes…there's only that much you can stuff into them!"

42

The Curious Case of Breakfast At Tanny's

Somewhere in the heart of the hills

It came like an affectionate peck caressing the cheeks. A friendly slap on the face.

Oxygen, oxygen, and more oxygen all around.

After a season of begging, grovelling, and gasping for air, a full blast, at last.

The car carrying the four friends—Lollita, Rehmat, Ibaadat, and Krrish—meandered up the serpentine landscape, while below them meandered the famous Kalka-Shimla rail line, that bestirred in Lollita bouts of nostalgia. It was her great-grandfathers who had built a vast stretch of this Himalayan lifeline!

The hillside unfurled its emerald umbrella of pine trees. Standing as sentinels over signposts dotting quaint Kasauli. The colonial, cantonment town where the four friends had been driven up by Rehmat's driver, Gurmukh, two days ahead of the Kussowlie Writers' Fest.

The landscape was the same, yet not the same.

The one thing that conspicuously seemed to have survived in the post-Pandemic hill-scape was flora's humungous herds.

The huddled herds of Hydrangeas. Their powder pink prettiness or lilac-hued loveliness peeping from behind pine promenades like rosy-cheeked, cherubic children gazing shyly from behind sheer curtains after surviving a storm.

Was this that had seen them through? Herd immunity?

Hydrangeas.

The hillside's harbingers of Hope bursting out of the warp 'n' weft of wooded wilderness that had weathered a Pandemic season.

Mother Nature's paint-brushed petals proclaiming the pink palette of the pine-studded mountainside.

Signposts of shrubbery on the sloping terrain signalling a subtle shift in the landscape. Enchanting emblems of its local flora and fauna.

Punctuating the huddled population of the hillside was another palette of pinkness.

Gulaal.

The wildflower that wove a tapestry of flaming pinkness across the forested fabric of cedars and conifers.

The spell of silence was broken by Rehmat, as she looked at Lollita and the poet in her gushed. "Gulaal on your mouth!"

Rehmat had noticed. Rehmat would notice. The pupils of her poet's heart saw things other's eyes didn't.

Rehmat had noticed the Flaming Fuchsia that Lollita was experimenting with, on her lips.

As they rolled along, all looked much the same... the clouds still came out of nowhere as an ensemble of cumulonimbus couture caught one in its misty magic folds like a long-lost friend comes and hugs you unannounced from behind. The hill flora and fauna still smiled their scent-bathed brightness from behind veils of vegetation well-entrenched in its denseness in this relatively unspoilt, un-plundered majestic mountainside that was Kasauli.

But, it was not its flora and fauna that wore a look of sparseness. It was the human-scape that stood clothed in bits of barrenness.

Looming over the landscape was the virtually empty concrete monstrosity that was the new, neon green car and bus parking stand, that wore its loud makeover like a gatecrasher in parakeet green Hawaiian couture cloaking the colonial façade of the hill-scape. An eyesore eclipsing the landmarks that made up The Mall—the Jukki Mull building studded with ancient billboards and nameplates, like the Sharma & Bros photography studio, showcasing its sepia photo gallery of famous stars to Sanawarians that the hill town had hosted, from a scrawny Sanjay Dutt to gorgeous Maneka Gandhi and *Maya Memsaab*'s Deepa Sahi, to frames of actors Pankaj Kapur or Pooja Bedi.

Was this new concrete eyesore emblematic of a bridge between Kasauli's Before Corona and Post Pandemic era?

Before Corona, the miniscule open bus stand in its place had greeted touristy throngs with the cranky and cantankerous chorus of blaring horns, beckoning coolies, and bystanders. Post Lockdown, it had much the mien of a noisy school-kid that's been ticked off and subdued by the headmaster into sobriety.

They rolled past this concrete encroacher, that had now come to obscure the quaint face of the Mall Road, and meandered towards their guest house. Ros Common and its new twin resort towered on the horizon.

An epitome of colonial architecture, resembling those relics of the Raj that had been taken over by the tourism department and converted into tourist resorts—the Dak Bungalow.

Where old-world charm meets a contemporariness trying to cash in upon tourism's Incredible India narrative.

Where a faded colonial past still steals up to wrap its arms, like the molten mists, around a refashioned present treading gingerly on the Kullu-sourced 'Khaasru' wood flooring.

Where antiquities from another age—poster beds, deodar dressers, teakwood writing desks or lantern-like candelabra—still crawl out of the chest-drawers of Time Warp to echo with the impersonal clink of ceramic crockery or cutlery culled from the warehouses of a tourism-driven hill economy.

Oozing old-world feel at its best, Ros Common not only stood strategically positioned on the road snaking up to

Monkey Point and the Hanuman Mandir, but also offered breath-taking views of Himalayan hillsides.

The four friends alighted and ambled for selfies along its pine-hemmed slopes and hydrangea-dotted patio crowned by an emerald gabled roof.

They were greeted by Bhoopesh Singh, the quintessential old, Dak Bungalow caretaker brandishing the black umbrella. A breed catapulted to cult status by yesteryear Bollywood classics such as a *Bees Saal Baad* or *Woh Kaun Thhi*.

The only contemporary twist in the reel and real being that while those cinematic caretakers crept about crumbling or creepy edifices with 'laltains', the real-life equivalents like the Bhoopesh Singhs now went pottering about boasting new-age LED flashlights. Laltains meet LEDs.

Meeting them on the patio was Manager Sharma ji, who happily played Wikipedia, showcasing with pride the panoramic jewels. He pointed out the crowning glory of the Sirmaur range in the distance, "That's the Choor Chandini peak."

Choor Chandini, so named for its snow-studded crown that shone like a silver bangle in moonlight.

"And, can you see those twin peaks beyond Choor Chandini?" he said with an air of suspense, like a magician about to unveil the most prized gem in his repository.

Four pairs of pupils strained to peer yonder, all agog.

"Kedarnath and Badrinath!" Sharma ji pointed with pride towards the piece de resistance of this live panoramic picture gallery of peaks.

As four smartphones squiggled to mount a thousand selfies against this bewitching backdrop, the second in command, Karan ji, too, stepped in, like a live Google map.

"Madam ji, don't forget to click selfies on the other side." Karan ji shepherded them thither, "There, that's the Dhauladhar range!"

Selfies against the snow-capped peaks done, they were turning away, when Lollita squealed.

"OMG...look!" she raved in raptures, pointing down at the pathway.

Snow-like flakes at their feet.

Clouds of whiteness enveloping a million micro suns on the ground.

Choor Chandini upon their cobbled courtyard.

William Wordsworth 'blooming' in the woods of Kasauli.

White Daffodils!

What this sparked was Selfie-ism's date with daffodils. Post this feast for the eyes, the four feasted on the Pahadi platter rustled up by Pyare Lal ji, Harvinder Bhaiya, and Jai Kishen ji. Kheru with Himachali Pulao and Patteer from Arbi leaves.

Refreshed and refuelled, the four friends trooped into the tiny hill town's Mall Road. The staple sight for most hill stations from the British Raj days, forming the lifeline along which the touristy throngs navigated its confluence of the past and present. The Mall Road was, perhaps, the biggest testimony to a human-scape altered by a Pandemic.

Its Tibetan bazaar, a medley of makeshift stalls peddling anything and everything—from Chinese phones, headphones, watches to name any gizmo to cheap casual wear plucked from the wholesale bazaars of Sarojini or Sadar in the national Capital—manifested the maximum changes. The Pandemic and the anti-China #BoycottChineseGoods sentiments post the India-China border skirmishes had combined to spell a death blow of this mini market, which only had one or two stray stalls open now.

"Gosh, can't believe the Tibetan bazaar has shrunk so much!" Ibaadat gasped.

"Ya, what a pity!" Lollita lamented. "I picked some snazzy shrugs and shawls from here last time," she sighed.

'Last time' now denoted a whole new time-scape called Before Corona (BC).

"I'm ravenous again," Ibaadat said, stepping out of the car to catch a bit of fresh mountain air on the Mall Road. "Do you want to snatch a snack somewhere here?"

"Hah, I won't survive without a bite till reaching the room," Lollita stretched her legs, cramped from the over two-hour drive uphill and stepped out in her snazzy black and white striped woollen shrug worn over palazzos with sturdy but stylish Bata sneakers. "Let's just stroll a bit and snatch something light right here."

"I need to walk my limbs badly, look at where my waist is going with all this zero-gymming during the long Lockdown!" Ibaadat wrapped the light pashmina stole around her neck as the mountain breeze naughtily poked its nippy fingers into the sweater-and-slacks-clad frame of the foodie that Ibaadat was.

Lockdown had left its tell-tale signs everywhere and on everybody, but most visibly on the middle regions of the middle aged making up much of middle-class India.

It was thus with some breathlessness that Lollita, along with Ibaadat, Rehmat, and Krrish, heaved up the slopes stretching further along the Mall Road, on one side, and the Church Road, on the other side, like a puffing and panting bunch of chihuahuas who have to clamber up a tree to fetch their bones.

Ibaadat gave instructions to the driver to find place in a parking zone and get himself some lunch, too. But, before letting him go, how could they not have their customary selfie in front of the Kasauli Church!

The most conspicuous emblem of its colonial and Christian past that greets tourists is the Christ Church, established in 1853, and now run under the auspices of the CNI. Its antiquity and colonial historicity make for a perfect backdrop for many a selfie moment and its Spanish and Italian stained-glass windows with carvings of Jesus Christ, Mother Mary, Saint Barnabas, and St Francis make for a stunning photo-op.

In this post-Pandemic landscape, there were fewer visitors straying in and out of the famous Kasauli Church for a selfie moment. The four, too, had the driver click them at its stunning façade, with the tower and gate making the backdrop, and later did some snapshots before the stained glass ornate entrance into the chapel.

They mapped the twists and turns up the Mall Road, halting here and there to survey the scenario, digging deeper into the nostalgia of the Before Corona era.

Steeped in colonial history, Kasauli was so named by the Rajput kings of Rewari, who sold this hillside to the British. The latter developed it into a cantonment town for garrisoning troops for the first Anglo-Sikh war. But, the historicity of the hill town goes deeper and it is as much steeped in Hindu mythology as in a colonial past. For, legend has it that when Lord Hanuman was going in search of the Sanjeevani hill, he set foot here. Hence, it's believed the mountain top is in the shape of Hanumanji's footprint.

While many British-era hill stations have fallen prey to crass commercialisation and unbridled crowding, Kasauli's status as a cantonment town with restricted entry and near-zero urbanisation, has served as an armour against its turning into a jungle of concrete. It is this old-world charm, unspoilt by a concrete jungle, and unsullied by a human jungle, that made Kasauli the summer haunt and home of creative minds. What Mussoorie is to Ruskin Bond, Kasauli was to legendary writer Khushwant Singh.

"Hello, ladies! Seeing you after ages," it was retired Maj-General Grewal, one of The Mall's distinguished and dapper tribe of evening walkers from the Forces who had made this cantonment hill station their second home. A species of silver-haired strollers whose numbers seemed to have become sparse in the Pandemic.

Some chitchat with him later, they moved up The Mall, bumping into more of the mountain strollers, chronicler Rajaa ji, bureaucrat Kavita ji, physician Shivani ji, tourism head honcho Soni ji, Mohan Sharma ji, Pammi ji, and others.

The four strolled past Bunty ji's Luxmi Daily Needs, Gupta Ji's general store, and Sanju subziwallah to slacken at the spot where their favourite Chacha Chai Wala and Ballu Momos Wala used to be. They looked hither-thither in the hope that they may have relocated their stall. Then, they asked some locals passing by, to learn that the two had shut shop.

"They went away to the village, Didi," told the wizened Pahadi selling subzi at a nearby stall. *"Kaam dhanda toh thha nahin kitne din. Woh gaon se wapas hii nahin aaya."*

His *kadak* chai with bread pakoras was a must in the cool climes and an absolute heart-warmer in times it rained.

Hunger was now gnawing at the innards of the four friends and there didn't seem much respite in sight.

"Let's go higher up the road to that shop where we always snacked," Lollita suggested, craving for her evening cup of 'cutting chai', as the dhabawallahs call it, and savouries.

They turned to the steeper path leading right towards the Lower Bazaar. The Heritage Bazaar. The landscape looked like a deserted Marriage Banquet Hall, bereft of guests where once had echoed the hustle bustle of camaraderie and celebration.

The four reached the block where once had stood the shop which served snacks so fabled that be it the biggies from Bollywood or beyond, nobody ever thought a trip to Kasauli complete without tucking into the vendor's lip-smacking stuff.

His specialty was that he served the humble samosa sandwiched between butter-fried bread and served it with chhole or tangy green chutney and tamarind chutney. A variation of this was his other specialty—the Gulab Jamun Burger. Half the fun had been not so much in the ingredients but the way he tossed the bread and the flourish with which he stuffed in it the crisp-off-the-kadai samosas.

Simply the sheer memory of it made their mouths water as the four stood where the shop was supposed to be, only to see the shutters down. They asked the driver Gurmukh to enquire at the neighbouring shops, just in case it was closed only for that day.

As they waited for the driver, they sauntered up and down the Heritage Bazaar, peeping out even for other familiar signposts, like the quilt shop where Lollita loved to pick those locally crafted quilted bedcovers. Alas, its shutters were down, too.

Just then, Lollita felt a tug at the flowing end of her ankle-length woollen shrug. She thought it had gotten stuck on a protruding pebble on the cobbled path. She turned to look. Only to see a pair of molten pools peering from behind a furry coat. Piercing the mists, of Time.

A beautiful ginger cat staring back at her from a shaggy fur soiled from stray living. As scrawny as the iconic Cat 'Orangey' from the Audrey Hepburn classic, *Breakfast At Tiffany's*.

Lollita's heart missed a beat. Another uncanny resemblance tugged at her heartstrings. She bent down to pet the furry feline bundle and scoop it up in her arms.

"Shakira...Shakira...aren't you Shakira!" Lollita whispered. A pair of pupils as grey as slate peered into hers, eyes from another lifetime, bulbs from yesterday's shadows.

Just then, Gurmukh returned shaking his head vigorously.

The four friends were crestfallen as he brought them the tidings.

The Lockdown had forced the Mall Road's iconic savoury shop, presided over by Tanny, to shut—the Bun Samosa Wala!

43

The Curious Case of a Red Alert

The next morning, Rehmat chose to laze around and give her bad back a rest, while the other three set out for a day out in the higher hills of Himachal.

As their car rolled up the steeper slopes, Lollita rolled down the window. The car turned a steep, sharp bend towards Kali Ka Tibba, a turn that took Lollita's breath away.

The sight of a scarlet shamiana swathing the valley cast its spell. As much for its suddenness as its splendour.

A canvas of crimson coloured the warp and weft of the wooded wilderness.

As if laal gulaal sprayed upon hara gulaal.

The ravishing Rhododendrons.

The state flower of Himachal Pradesh. 'Flame of the Forest'. 'Buransh ka Phool', in popular parlance.

What the crimson canopy of Gulmohars is to Le Corbusier's landscape, the humongous herds of Rhododendrons are to Himachal's hillscape.

The fabled flower which, going by folklore, was a favourite of Mughal emperor Shah Jahan's beloved queen, Mumtaz Mahal. Such was her fascination for this red enchantment of mountain flora that a fresh bunch was ferried every Friday for her from Shimla and the surrounding hills.

"Selfie toh banti hai," Lollita tugged at Krrish and Ibaadat. The three legged it out and wound their way up a small hamlet tucked in the lap of this open-air museum of Mother Nature's masterpieces.

Selfies thus bloomed among the boulevards of blood red that had unlocked their canvas before time.

As if in a hurry to bid adieu to the harshest of winter. As if in haste to herald the hopefulness of Spring.

The locals saw in it a different signal. They shook their weather-beaten faces. They clicked their Pandemic-starved tongues.

The tongues of the trio were, at the same time, being treated to sumptuous Pahadi cuisine by the hospitable hill folk. 'Nuskhey' (fluffy wheat flour flat breads) and 'Patandey' (rice flour versions of rumaalis cooked on hot stone) served with Chana Madira.

Natives of a village around Chail, Seema Didi and Bunty ji, who ran a provision store near the Kasauli church, were a picture of Pahadi hospitality and repository of recipes rooted in folk cuisine as they dished out a garnet red delectable delicacy. Serving out this surprise, Bunty ji gushed, *"Aap sab ne yeh pehle kabhi nahin khayi hogi!"*

The voices of village elders, though, struck a sombre note about the early coming of the Rhododendrons.

"Yeh shubh nahin hai, madam ji," was the refrain from the mountainside's wise men that echoed in the ears of the three friends as, post the repast, they lost themselves in Mother Nature's banquet hall of breath-taking scarlet.

"This is *my* Valley of Flowers!" Lollita thought mesmerised.

Plucking here and there, the three were a picture of enchantment as they fingered flora's red royalty. Popping out of the pine-hemmed hillside were villagers Jassi Bhaiya, Sarika, and Trishaa, who, with their nimble-footedness, helped Lollita and her friends gather the rhododendrons. Soon the stoles and mufflers of the three friends were like a velvety veil studded with red rubies.

When dusk began to cast its shadow, the trio ambled out of the woods. As they meandered along the valley to head to the Kali temple close to Chail to pay obeisance, Lollita's awestruck gaze spotted a small pond cloaked with circular greenness.

"OMG...OMG... See this!" Lollita gushed.

A powder pink pearl peeping like a brooch out of a mud brown overcoat. A Pink Sapphire being born out of the womb of murkiness and mossy sliminess.

"Lotus!" Ibaadat gushed.

"'Lotus is the only flower that teaches us where we reach is important, not where we come from.' That's the pearl of wisdom, isn't it?" Lollita was mesmerised into mouthing this proverb.

The Lotus lips parted layer by layer like a devout smiling up at the Vaishno Devi or Amarnath shrine. A spellbound silence is what accompanied the girls as they meandered up the valley, their own heads poised up in prayer.

Atop the valley of scarlet stood studded the Kali Ka Tibba, resplendent as a ruby and diamond crown.

Selfies done on the sprawling ramparts of the Tibba, the trio legged it out of the valley. Krrish and Ibaadat headed ahead towards the car as Lollita brought up the rear.

Ouch!

Lollita felt something graze her leg that pricked like a million needles. She bent down to see a red rashness breaking out on her epidermis.

Bichhoo Booti.

As she cried out in pain, Ibaadat and Krrish rushed back. Bunty ji, his better half Seema ji, Raj Didi and Jaspal ji, elders of the village, were by her side before she knew, with a remedy in hand. Raj Didi and Jaspal ji rubbed over her red patchwork crushed green leaves, plucked from right under the nose of the Stinging Nettle.

Interestingly, in shooing away the venom from Lollita's skin, the two rival village women, Raj Didi and Jaspal ji, rubbed away their own poison. The bitter rivalry between them.

A rivalry born of believing in different Gods. A rivalry bred from being born in different castes. A festering poison being dissolved at the feet of a shrine.

"Zehar ka tod bhi zehar ke paas hi hota hai," pearls of Pahadi wisdom were mouthed by Raj Didi.

A wisdom rooted in the Himalayan hillside that echoed through the pores of the post-Pandemic valley, resonating the richness of Rumi's gems, "The cure for pain is in the pain."

As their car rolled away, Lollita craned her neck out of the window to soak in that one last look.

A red carpet rolling out before time.

The rhododendrons' earlier than usual blooming was furrowing the brows of folk wisdom, creased in concern, as it cast a cloud over crop cycles. The hurried arrival of these harbingers of Spring sounded for scientists a red alert, about the other 'C' that threatened a planet plagued by Corona—Climate Change.

44

The Curious Case of Colonial Meets Queens of Prose

Strains of soft music wafted over the deodar-scented canopies shrouding the sprawling lush lawns as Lollita, Rehmat, Ibaadat, and Krrish landed at the Kasauli Club.

Lollita was the last to step out of the car, resplendent in her black Phulkari silk saree teamed with a Kalamkari blouse depicting Ardhanareshwar. Her customised pallu, emblazoned with an exotic embroidery of Mevlana Rumi, the Whirling Dervish, kissed the Kasauli-scape like a devout meandering a mountainside to offer obeisance at a Kedarnath or Bhimashankar. Poetry in motion.

The four friends made entries at the reception podium near its cobbled gateway for the Kussowlie Writers' Fest.

What this quaint hill town lacked in terms of famous book nooks and ancient bookstores passed on as family establishments, unlike its other country cousins such as Mussoorie and Shimla, Kasauli made up for by playing host to the other kind of literary action. By emerging as an enchanting litfest stage.

Where, under canopies of cloudscapes and across cobbled pathways, the well-heeled collided with the well-read, well-versed or well marketed (more often than not, the last).

Greeting them and waving out animatedly near the Kasauli Club gate were Kishwar Singh and better half Naini—bulwarks of the enterprising team that gave shape to the festival season after season—as the foursome passed through the screening for sanitisers and masks. Lollita and her Lit gang sallied forth into the pine-hemmed precincts of this colonial era club nestling in the Himalayas that came into being essentially as a reading room and assembly room for the officers of the British Raj.

Fabled for its Queen's Ball, a ritual of the Raj, the club was a congregation hub for army officers of the British Raj, serving from Subathu to Solan to Shimla, becoming a picture postcard setting for wine 'n' dine and dance galas in the pristine pine-fresh cool climes of the Kasauli hills.

A club steeped in colonialism, a hub dressed in elitism gasping for breath in the arms of dying exclusivity.

As the four ambled in leisurely, they saw a motley bunch of spectators preening and primping for selfies in the left corner just beyond the gate.

Curious, they craned their necks to see what all the commotion was about, almost as if egged on by that social media-driven FOMO (fear of missing out).

There, perched on a puny pebbled pedestal stood another kind of 'Show Stopper'—an antique Letter Box from the British era. Resplendent in its redness, its crowning glory was its head that was reminiscent of the Coat of Arms. This signpost of the colonial times was a sure-shot photo op or selfie prop for all visitors to this elite club.

Lollita and Ibaadat exchanged knowing glances and chorused, "How can we not have our selfie moment, too… with this relic of the Raj!"

"C'mon, Rehmat…Krrish, a slice of the Raj!" they both chorused again.

Selfies done, Krrish and Rehmat propelled them both towards the sprawling lawns leading to the lounge.

"Hurry up… Selfies can wait, sessions can't. You'll be late," Krrish chidingly glanced at Lollita.

A sea of cotton-wool cloudiness greeted their eyes. A sea of strayed nimbus waltzing over the colonial club's crown.

The seasons gone by, the Before Corona era, had seen another sea, a sea of silvery moustaches and salt 'n' pepper coiffured craniums. A sea of silver belonging to the gentry from the defence forces who had made Kasauli their first or second home. A sea of silvery scalps that stood depleted or distanced now in this post-Pandemic social hillscape.

Lollita was tickled back to reality, from a kind of reverie induced by the surreal old-world colonial charm of the Club.

Rakul had made it clear that since the Litfest was being downsized from a three-day affair to one day of back-to-back action, there was no chance of Lollita making it to the sessions as a panellist. Only select star names would be making it to the literary red carpet to draw in the footfalls and eyeballs.

Out of regard for Raagini, he had proffered Lollita a consolation prize. It came with a rider—in case a panellist played truant at the eleventh hour, with a cancellation. To play a panellist on Waiting List, not A-List.

Even being invited to be standby participant for a session at the prestigious Kussowlie Writers' Fest was nothing less than a prize catch. It was as good as a player, who can't be out in the stadium to play an IPL, getting a chance to be in the commentary box instead.

It was riding this hope and its attendant jitters that Lollita had landed at Kasauli.

"Ah, at last, looks Dame Luck is beginning to smile at me!" Lollita's gait, as she sallied into the lobby, was of a cat striding out of the shadows into a patch of sunshine.

A sentiment that was sort of reinforced when they saw a beaming Rakul waving at them in the lounge. Tugging at his arms, calling him to the stage to get the sessions rolling, was his Parsi girlfriend, Naseem Mistry.

Hers was the petite prettiness that harboured nerves of steel which prodded the fest to fruition season after season.

Hers was the fragile frame that housed a powerhouse of networking presiding over the fortunes of many a Wannabe Bestselling Author. A mere text typed from the carpal tendons of whose artistic fingers determined who would or would not get an outing on the high podiums playing host to heavyweights like the Dalrymples and Devakarunis.

As they trooped into the back lawns where the action was meant to be, Lollita noticed some bookstalls studding the lush landscape. One stall caught her eye, the one by Harinder Chadha, aka Harry.

All his new titles were laid out neatly. Mythology's new releases jostled with biographies in the front rows. Romances rubbed shoulders with thrillers in the middle regions. Among them was a fellow author's spy story that had pitchforked to the Top 100 riding her aggressive marketing strategies on Instagram and other social media.

A pang stabbed through Lollita's bosom as her gaze did not behold her book at the bookstall's display section.

"Hey, where be my book?" she hesitatingly ventured to ask.

Harry grinned sheepishly, pretending to finger and fumble through some shelves at the back. "Must be somewhere here…," he mumbled. "Actually, on the display table we showcase only titles that are top of the charts," his tone smacked more of smugness now.

Lollita lingered at Harry's stall to soak in the sundry titles he had been dabbling in lately, publishing mostly the Who's Who making up Punjab's corridors of power, whose aspiration it was to achieve overnight celebrity author-hood and who found in Harry a pliant publisher. From an IPS officer who turned raconteur riding on his field anecdotes to a landlord fashioned into farm entrepreneur who hoped to gain a toehold in the corridors of power by penning a biography of the state Governor, Harry boasted all such state bureaucracy and aristocracy heavyweights on his publishing list.

Just as Lollita was hoping to hobnob with Harry about showcasing her book at the stall, an A-lister from his publishing list called out to Harry. An Arrived Author in Khaki. Call of the Constabulary. Off hastened Harry.

Harry in a Hurry.

Lollita had just begun browsing through the biography of the Governor, from the frills of it looking very much a PR exercise by its tycoon-turned-author, when she looked up to find a familiar face among the few people dotting the stall.

Where had she seen that face? She tried to rack her brain but full recognition eluded her just then.

But the person had recognised her and gave a friendly wave. She returned it with a half wave.

Ibaadat had come looking for them and shepherded them away to the lobby and authors lounge for some selfie hopping with celebrity authors.

Rehmat spotted her long-time writer-friend and threaded her way towards him. Lollita and Ibaadat came close on her heels as Rehmat rushed forward.

"Just the person I was looking for, for my next book!" Rehmat gushed to publisher friend Raazi Singh.

"Just the person you need to meet," the friend said, his eyes twinkling teasingly at Rehmat, as he introduced her to the man standing next to him. "Meet the man behind a new publishing portal dedicated to poetry...Mr Kavi Singh."

Rehmat erupted into a rash of exclamatory delight.

Ibaadat and she then moved to do some more selfie hopping with the other Who's Who of writing—the 'Twin' Maharajas of Mythological fiction, Ashwamedh Sanghi and Amodh Tripathi, columnist Bachi Karkaria, debonair diplomat-author Navtej Sarna, and the poster girls of diva-hood, Shobhaa De, Sharmila Tagore, and Shabana Azmi.

In the crammed orbit of famous bobbing heads, Lollita spotted the face who had oftentimes sent her diving for the dictionary.

"OMG, His Highness himself!" Lollita gushed, tugging at Ibaadat's selfie-engaged arm.

Ibaadat turned to look why Lollita was plucking at her so frantically.

"OMG!" she chirruped excitedly, her hand gravitating to pat into place her pashmina and pearls for this prized selfie moment.

"Shashi *ke saath selfie toh banti hai,*" Ibaadat spouted his first name with such familiarity as though he were her buddy author.

At his suave best, Shashi Tharoor obliged them easily with a selfie. He then sallied out from the authors' lounge with his fellow panellists for the next session.

Krrish, too, angled out of the authors' lounge, heading towards the front lawns, where he was hoping to hobnob with some publishers for switching to more saleable self-help genres.

Just then, a sweet voice fell upon his ears.

"Autograph, please!"

Krrish stopped in his tracks, seeing the outstretched hand that was plucking him out of anonymity.

"Hi...err...were you speaking to me?" is all that he could mumble in puzzlement.

"Aren't you Prof Krrish who taught us...the one who has written that book on true tales of Rebirth?" the pretty young thing asked, all eyes.

A moment of Rebirth.

Tutor and taught gravitated towards the front lawns. Rebirth offering fresh food for thought and conversation.

"Let's grab some coffee. I need to refuel," Rehmat tugged at Lollita and Ibaadat's arms.

They headed towards the food stalls passing through the main lawns, where a session was just about to begin.

As they queued up for the coffee, what caught Lollita's eye in the melee was the fingers of the man in front of her as he stretched his hand to grab his coffee in the push and shove.

How well she knew those ring-laden fingers!

"Gosh, it's you," she did coo to the familiar man ahead of her in the queue.

He turned around, coffee in hand.

"Hello...hello...," he greeted in his gregarious manner.

"How come you're here?" Lollita sounded surprised. "Aren't you supposed to be at the Kochi Lit Fest?"

"Yes yes, I had to come here to promote one of my last books..."

"Last book?" Lollita was befuddled.

"You see, dear...I'm going away to Kochi after this," he elaborated.

Lollita still couldn't put two and two together. What did Kochi have to do with his so-called last book?

"You see...I'm going away to Kochi for good," he dropped the bombshell.

"For good?" Lollita sounded concerned.

"You see, dear, I'm shutting shop. The book business isn't the same since the Pandemic...," his voice trailed off as Lollita noticed a lump in his throat.

"OMG...this is terrible news," Lollita felt saddened for the man who had given her a break into authorhood.

The light Kasauli breeze suddenly seemed pregnant with mists of melancholy. Lasith ji chattered to change the topic.

"This is no match for filter coffee," he grimaced as he receded into the milling crowds with the takeaway glass of espresso in his hand. "Catch you later!"

Recharged with piping hot coffee, just as Lollita and Ibaadat were ambling down the lush sidewalk, they almost bumped into someone. It was the same familiar-looking person from the book stall whom Lollita had failed to recognise.

"Hello," the voice called out pleasantly.

"Hi...er," Lollita's voice sounded uncertain.

"You haven't recognised me, ma'am," the voice dripped civility.

Before Lollita could shake her head, pat came the introduction.

"Commander Ganguly. Your neighbour in Gurugram!" he said with a flourish.

"OMG," is all that escaped Lollita's lips in that moment of revelation.

She had always seen her neighbours from a distance, a distance only amplified by Lockdown, wherein they had been like remote figures filtered through the lens of her Lockdown window, much in the manner of miniaturised filmi characters screened through the Bioscope at Dilli Haat. Like a multiplex ensemble cast come alive through 3-D spectacles.

Through her Lockdown window, she had always seen Ganguly ji in semi-casuals, boxers teamed with a T-shirt or sometimes, just a vest. But, this dapper vision in front of her now stood fully suited-booted and wearing the smile of a suave Ladies Man.

Up close and personal, Lollita now got a full view of his toothy smile, the smile that had cost Ganguly ji nearly a fortune. The faux smile that had cemented his bond with a fellow Bong. Such that it had made his Banerjee orthodontist richer by a few months of Ganguly ji's full pension in exchange for excavating relics of chipped enamel in his mouth and, much oral architectural operations later, cementing it with that boon for a Middle Class India and Middle Aged India low on oral hygiene—ceramic.

Ceramic and more ceramic, studded in every nook and cranny. Such that when Ganguly ji smiled, what glistened even more than the car-waxed epidermis of his Lamborghini, was none other than a mouthful of polished ceramic crowns.

"Gupta ji's neighbour?" it was falling into place in Lolita's mind. "Ganguly ji!" Lollita managed to find her voice.

"Yes, yes, so you recognised finally," he smiled.

"Sad how Gupta ji lost his precious crop in that locust attack," Lollita tried to commiserate.

"Sadly yes, it took him time to get over it, obviously his veggies couldn't make it to the *Limca Book*. But, he has started from scratch again," Ganguly ji said.

"Wow, what a way to bounce back," Lollita lauded the spirit.

"Gupta ji has now launched a localised delivery of home-fresh greens," Ganguly ji filled her in on the latest Unlock neighbourhood developments. "You see, we have joined hands for this new start-up."

"Start-up?" Lollita was impressed. But what intrigued her more was the neighbours at loggerheads joining hands.

"Purple Chilli," Ganguly ji rambled on.

"Gupta ji cultivates the greens, and I look after the logistics and marketing gyaan," Ganguly ji spelt out their start-up model. "You, too, can order daily greens from us."

"Wow, truly a case of Bengal meets Bareilly!" Lollita lauded the cultural confluence.

"But, the best part is that Gupta ji has been supplying some of his greens free of cost to our nearby gurdwara," Ganguly ji added.

"Really!" Lollita sounded surprised at this change of heart on the part of the penny-pinching Gupta ji.

"Yes, for the Covid langar," Ganguly ji dropped another surprise.

Lollita found this bit of news truly heartwarming. But she was even more intrigued at finding Ganguly ji at the Litfest.

"Well, ma'am, I was invited here. For..." his voice trailed off just as the microphone on stage began booming back to life with an announcement.

"To get our next session rolling...," the emcee's voice sailed through the salubrious surroundings. "...we invite on stage..."

Ganguly ji interrupted into her thoughts, 'Ma'am, I have to leave now...will catch up soon."

Lollita goggled at his receding back as the anchor continued calling out, "We invite on stage bestselling author Shiv Khera, motivational author Vivaan Agarkar, and..."

Amid all the shuffle of a new session, Lollita could now see a glistening balding pate clamber atop the stage.

The emcee continued to call out in her exaggerated staccato manner, like a filmi awards night presenter, "And the newest sensation in the Self-Help genre...Commander Ganguly..."

Lollita stood rooted awestruck to the spot when the announcer delivered her punchline.

"...Author of the new, million-copy bestseller, *The Rallyist Who Sold His Lamborghini.*"

A parallel session by big names was on in the front lawns and Lollita, Ibaadat, and Rehmat found themselves being drawn to that, rather than lingering to hear these self-help authors.

Ketan Bhagwat, Upnendu Mukherjee & Co were debating the future of books in a post-Pandemic litscape.

Lollita's heart missed a beat as she took a seat, on the other side of the stage. Yes, this was the same session for which Rakul Singh had promised her the fourth berth on the stage, as a stand-by, in case the fourth celebrity author they had invited did a last-minute cancellation.

Alas, Lollita's one little dream of a chance to make it to the prestigious Litfest stage was dashed, as the fourth celebrity turned up. There she was, pouting at the Paps her mega-watt Bobbi Brown smile. Blow-dried Bibliophile Diva-hood.

The anointed Queen of Quirky Lit who sold more than a mega million copies—Taarika Khambatta.

The session had almost neared its close by the time Lollita, Ibaadat, and Rehmat had legged it to the seats at the far end. As the house was thrown open for Q&A, many a concern of budding writers and writers-in-the-making were voiced, some whose launches had been shelved, some whose scripts.

In all the cacophonous melee of mic grabbing, to snatch few moments of fame or to address serious concerns, one of the usherers in the aisles was passing the mic to a raised hand in the row the trio was seated. A bit of mix-up made him think it was Lollita who had raised her hand. Sure enough, in a jiffy, Lollita found the mic thrust in her hand.

She stared at it like a chihuahua who lands a bone he hadn't been groping and grabbing at.

"I...err...I," she stuttered and staccato-ed, racking her grey cells for a smart question to ask.

"To whom is your question addressed?" the moderator butted into her reverie.

"Err...My question is...to...Taarika," Lollita let her gaze sweep over the panellists, trying to gain time, whilst the panellists goggled at each other like a bunch of fielders, hoping the other was going to get the catch.

"And, what is your question?" the moderator's voice betrayed a bit of impatience.

"My question is...," Lollita rambled like a Metro rolling off to a start. "Will small-town authors ever get a chance to be on the big stage?"

The panellists appeared to confer among themselves on how to field the awkward question. Ketan and Taarika glanced at each other, hoping the other would field this poser.

The mic landed in the beach-tanned, ringed hand boasting the king-sized solitaire.

"Well, lady, I have only one thing to say to that—if they can't have the big stage...why not small-town writers start their own Litfest!" Taarika cooed with calm confidence from a rarefied stratosphere.

A composure born of Advantaged Authorhood. Born of Advanced Authorhood. The kind that pockets astronomical advances.

A curated confidence that comes from being on the other side of the stage. A cool that comes from being Authorhood's A-Listers.

The mic squirmed in the stillness sparked by the hand with the solitaire ring. Was there a Marie Antoinette ring to it all?

The sound bytes were greeted by a pregnant silence.

A telling silence. That bespoke of the chasms of a caste system governing the literary landscape. The Bestselling Big League on the stage versus the Back Benchers, the Wannabes.

A silence that was all too suddenly pierced by the shrillness of the moderator's swagger, as she again prattled to propel the session to a close with a vote of thanks.

As the audience dispersed, Lollita and Ibaadat wondered where to head next.

It was hunger for food of the real kind that was gnawing at Lollita and Ibaadat. They were famished, hardly having had a proper breakfast, having barely grabbed a couple of sandwiches with the morning cuppa. Thus, it was the food counters where they headed to line up for buying coupons.

The spread was the staple but with a dash of hill cuisine tossed in—the usual non-veg spread of Chicken Anaardana rubbing shoulders with the veg version made up of Himachali 'Rajma Madira', Lingdu ki Subzi, and all that.

The three piled on hearty helpings on their plates and were proceeding past the veg corner, when a face behind the counter arrested Lollita's attention.

She cast a second glance, hoping the vague familiarity of face could crystallise into clarity of recognition. She was about to sally forth when it clicked.

And she found herself asking, "Aren't you the Bun Samosa Wale uncleji?"

The Himachali sun-tanned fair face lit up with delight at being recognised.

"Yes, madam ji. *Aap*...?" his voice trailed off.

"Have you shut shop?" Lollita pressed on with the question niggling at the back of her mind.

"What to do, madam ji? *Lockdown mein dhanda bund ho gaya thha*!"

"Ohh...yes, tough times. So, how are you here?" Lollita asked.

"Rakul ji was kind enough to include our famous Bun Tikki in the snacks menu... His kind gesture that holds big hope for reviving our local economy," the Bun Samosa Wala said in gratitude, pointing towards the chaat-papri section at the far end.

As they moved towards that side, Lollita couldn't help asking, "So, would you be reopening the shop?"

A frown furrowed deeper on the wrinkled forehead, "I'm afraid not, madam ji. No money to pay the shop rent and the workers." He shook his head, then added on a note of optimism, "But, we're restarting...with something different."

"Rebooting, you mean? And, how is that?" Lollita was curious as much as concerned.

"Since my sons lost their jobs in the big cities, they've come back to the villages," he went on. "So, near our orchards, we've started making fruit wines and jams on a small scale."

"Fruit wine! Start-up!" Lollita exclaimed with expectation. "Any brand name?"

Memory of a delectable, garnet-hued chutney partaken lately bestirred in her mindscape.

His reply flavoured her empathy with excitement. Delight undistilled.

"Rhodoz."

Lollita piled on some Bun Samosa on her plate to relive the good old pre-Pandemic times.

Looking for empty chairs, she settled down on some. She couldn't spot Rehmat, Ibaadat, and Krrish now, so she presumed they were in the front lawns hobnobbing with the famous literary figures.

She looked at her phone to find a string of messages and missed calls from Ruhaan. Her phone had been on silent during the session.

"Sweetie, need to speak to you right now."

"Hey honey, call the moment you see my text."

Lollita was concerned as much as curious as a cat.

"Darling, sorry I was at a session. Is all good?" Lollita said.

"Yup. Remember that mail I'd received about my Dalai Lama pics being shortlisted…?" Ruhaan sounded as chirrupy as a child who's entered for a NASA student championship.

"Yes, those incredible pics you'd shot of His Highness in his blooming boulevard… What about them?"

"I'd clean forgotten about them…," Ruhaan rambled.

The suspense was getting bigger.

"How I love the surrealism of those shots!" she gushed.

"The thing is, honey…they added so much weight to my portfolio…"

"And?" Lollita's heart was racing.

"Well, well… You're now speaking to an awardee of the Academie Des Beaux-Arts, France!" Ruhaan dropped the bombshell. Just like that.

"OMG! OMG!" Lollita let out squeals of delight, loud enough to make passers-by stare at her.

"Rooh, this is not like a dream come true…," Lollita gurgled on with her gushing.

"Not a dream come true?" Ruhaan asked, trying to get the drift of her words.

"Darling, this is MORE than you ever dreamt of!" Lollita spelt out the big picture.

In all the jiving with jollification she erupted into, she ended up toppling the plate of Bun Samosa that she had had the joy of tucking into after ages.

"Also, I had to tell you... This means...," Ruhaan's voice pierced into her reverie.

"Means what?" Lollita found the jubilation being put on pause mode, as she sensed Ruhaan's voice sounded serious now.

"This means that I'll have to be flying away to Paris sometime soon, my love," he tried to keep his voice steady. "We'll discuss all that when you return," he signed off.

Lollita was engulfed by a tsunami of tugs. Like fruit cream being whipped with both the sweetness of strawberry chunks and the slight sourness of kiwi.

A sense of pride collided with a sense of uncertainty in every pore of her pulsating breath. A breath gasping for emotional oxygen.

Ruhaan would be going away....

"Going away forever? Or going away together?"

Beginning of a new beginning? Or beginning of the end?

Life and Death. Hand in hand? Or a rebirth?

The echo of Ruhaan's velvety voice collided on the corrugated cliffs of her heartbeat. Rumi resonated on her retinas.

"A mountain keeps an echo deep inside itself. That's how I hold your voice."

45

The Curious Case of Red Wines and Red Carpets

The After Party at the colonial hill town's famous landmark was not really looking like Lollita's cup of tea.

Raj Villa.

The Villa huddled in the hill-scape which had been home to late writer Khushwant Singh and which sprang to life on being thrown open for literary galas every season. Corona's closedowns comprising the only aberrations clouding its literary calendar.

A mountain-tucked museum. To the literary legend's later life journey.

A gate-less getaway that had not been gatecrashed into by the plundering Pandemic. A relic from the Raj days cocooned from the Corona-scape by the cotton-wool cloudy couture cloaking it.

A Villa whose windows had tonight un-shuttered their eyelids to stare at the uncertainty of a post-Pandemic landscape. To stare out at its own uncertain future.

Lollita's mind was in a whirr with Ruhaan's tidings, and she was not much in the mood to socialise and make small talk.

"Will he...won't he?" was the dilemma throbbing in the threadwork of her thoughts, like a pestilent housefly that stubbornly refuses to be shooed away.

She ambled indoors instead to soak in the atmosphere of this landmark literary haven. A haven with a shroud of history behind which, perhaps, she could hide, take refuge from the sense of uncertainty clouding her own mindscape.

The library and living room studded with shelves and shelves of books and old-world furniture and fireplace cast an instant spell that intrigued her.

A library in the lap of Mother Nature. A treasure trove of tomes, where time stands still, yet throbs with the timeless echoes of colonial charm, chatter around its fireplace, clink of cocktail glasses and curios cramming its teak 'n' time-weathered tapestry.

Where the past dwells in the musty smells of the paperbacks and hard-bounds huddled on the shelves that stand like sentinels around quaint carved fireplaces that have basked in better days. Of glowing warmth as much as glowing conversations.

Majestic mantlepieces rubbing shoulders with Deodar-crafted shelves. That had once been encased with the fabric of familiarity, the patchwork of personal touch—the Sardar plucking out a forgotten book to look up a quote or passage, or fingering pages from a crisp copy presented to him by a debut writer for the Sardar's scholarly perusal or autograph, before it was casually consigned to some back shelf of this laden library, to live a life of obscurity in the back benches of author-hood, or to breathe its last from visitations less from a reading eye, more from silver fish.

The Fabled Fireplace. That had seen Scotch meet Satire, so synonymous with the Sardar. That had played host to and stoked conversations he hosted, be it with the intelligentsia or inquisitive walk-in admirers. Where his famous pen had perhaps scripted his popular column *Malice Towards One and All* or his novels.

The Fading Fireside. That had now been cold shouldered in favour of contraptions of contemporary living. Having to be content with an electric heater shoved into its lap.

Lollita gazed awestruck at the mantlepiece lined with a parade of paraphernalia that clocked KS's milestones as much as maverick manifestations. She fascinatedly clicked his caricatures crafted by cartoonists, for whom the Sardar satirist was an abiding muse.

Lollita was lost in the ambience of this relic of a home from the Raj days when a soft voice infiltrated into her ears.

"Hey, aren't you the lady who grilled the poor panellists about small-time authors not making it to the big Lit stage?" asked the silken voice.

Lollita looked up from her phone at which she had been staring rather absent-mindedly. The face looked so familiar that Lollita started racking her brains at which famous author the person was.

"So, you're an author wanting to break into the big league," the guest teased her. "And, this cruel book biz won't let you?"

"Ahhh...how did you know that?" Lollita couldn't find anything better to say.

"Well, I was there listening to you at the fag end of the session."

"You know how it is," Lollita made small talk, still trying to figure where she had seen the face.

"What if I give you a break?"

"OMG, are you a publisher?" Lollita asked, beginning to get excited.

"No..." the eyes twinkled in amusement at Lollita's puckered brow.

"Break...as a writer?" she asked, intrigued as to why anybody want to give her a break.

"Kind of...but, better than that...," the articulate and amiable voice answered.

"OMG! Better...what?"

"Your book strikes a chord!" the voice dripped silkiness as it dropped the bombshell. "I happened to read bits of it on a flight..."

Lollita's mouth gaped open wider. And, as her nostrils wiggled in anticipation, her 'Trishul' signature nosestud started to stage its 'Chaali'.

Just then, Lamba ji landed on the scene, with his loud baritone and louder wardrobe—a tomato red Hawaii kurta over his pencil pants. The moment he set sight on the stylish and suave person engaged in a tête-à-tête with Lollita, his eyes bulged as bulbously as a frog's.

"OMG!" he gawked and gasped. "*Cha...Cha...*," he was about to gasp in recognition.

Ah, trust his cellphone to have trilled just then, with his broker bloke at the other end. His visage, which till a few milliseconds back looked like a million rainbows breaking out, now suddenly looked clouded by a cumulonimbus cover on the verge of copious condensation.

"*Cha...Cha...Cha*?" Lamba ji stuttered. "*Chala gaya sara cash in stock crash*?" Lamba ji crashed out of the hall and retreated towards the rear ramparts of Raj Villa like a receding caterpillar that has been bitten badly.

"The choice is yours... It could mean a chance to come to a shoot at an exotic foreign locale," the soft voice broke into Lollita's distractedness.

"Foreign locale...?" Lollita almost choked on a mouthful of wine.

"Yup," the voice sounded nonchalant as it sipped its sparkling wine.

"Err...I...where...?" Lollita stumbled on speechlessly.

"Ah, well the destination will be a surprise! That is, if you agree...," the voice sounded more mysterious.

"Agree to what?" By now Lollita's eyes had enlarged into browned molten pools as big and liquidy as her favourite 'Death by Chocolate Donut'.

"Well, if you give me the rights, I can make an offer about your brilliant book...," the nonchalance in the person's voice was killing.

"OMG! OMG!" Lollita shrieked with excitement loud enough for the wining 'n' dining guests to swivel their cervicals 180 degrees in her direction.

"...Of making your book into a film," the assured voice was quite enjoying the effect it was having on Lollita,

"Film...film? You mean...you mean...*HOLLYWOOD*?" Lollita's voice ululated on the last word so loudly that the circumnavigating cervicals of the wining 'n' dining Who's Who in the lounge could be heard cracking from many a crick.

By then, in Lollita's head it had all started to click.

"*Cha...Cha...Cha*?" it was now Lollita's turn to stutter on the same syllables. On the letters that made up the famous last name.

The ebbing embers in the fireplace, that were comatose for want of ventilators, bestirred to consciousness. Blinking back to breath on the oximeter of opalescence.

The person before Lollita, a pretty picture in the scarlet ensemble and solitaires, was indeed a famous face. But, not of a bestselling author.

The fireplace was awaking from its darkest winter.

Rebirth. Rebirth in its rawest fleshiness.

An invigorated iridescence that comes from being reborn. A leaping luminescence that comes from being able to breathe again.

Incredible! She was being dished out a dream Bollywood-esque ride down bestseller-hood. To rescript her life narrative. To be Reborn. A big ticket to the B-List by none other than a global A-Lister.

Was this a global Raani of the Red Carpet?

Was this the LIGHT at the end of the darkest tunnel of the Tandav that was the Pandemic?

Was life dishing out to Lollita *HOPE* as shimmering red as her Rhodo wine?

The red hot Hope shimmying before her was none other than *End it Like Beckham*-fame, Indian-origin, global filmmaker Gurmehar Chadha!

Lollita leapt forward for a *jaadu ki japphi*.

Rumi leapt out of Lollita's saree pallu into the fireplace.

To fashion the flames into doing the dance of the Dervish.

The fieriness from the Ardhanareshwar on her blouse flowed to the fireplace to breathe oxygen into its ashen bosom. To exhale new life into the womb of the log embers in the throes of Rebirth.

The flames leapt up into a life-giving Laasya.

HOPE held out the hands that were daintily clasping the slim-stemmed goblet harbouring the red plum wine.

The reborn flames raised their arms higher and higher for a bowing, as if in an 'Angahara' at the altar.

Rumi meets Rameshwaram. Laasya meets Giddha.

"The soul sometimes leaves the body,

Then returns.

When someone doesn't believe this,

Walk back into my house

Like This."

Acknowledgments

Special remembrance of late Principal Bhupinder, for being my Chief Cheerleading Officer (CCO) at Tricity book events. Heart-wrenching that our litscape's 'Rainbow' bowed out in the Coronascape before my third book's curtains up.

My everlasting gratitude to...

Maa, for being the eternal pearls of poetry in my prose, for being the nazaakat in the way my saree flows.

Paa, for having schooled us in living Life funny side up.

Dipankar Mukherjee, Priyanka Sarkar, and Indrani Ganguly, for believing my humble script to be 'world-class' writing in Pandemic's darkest of times, when it was difficult to make head or tail of Life itself, leave alone a satirical tale.

The Sisterhood of the Travelling 'Pats'—*Meri gur naalo mithhi* Meenakshi Duggal and Inderdeep Thapar, to Nirupama Dutt, Reema Anand, Sumita Misra, Aparna, Una, Puja, Sabrina, Sunita Di, Gita, Guneet, Jyotin and Kaavya, to Narinderjit ji, Ritika, Renee, Ritu, Alka, Mandeep, Yojana, Nisha Luthra, Ayesha Banerjee, Livleen, Lippi & Co—million hugs for that much-needed Vaccine in the Coronascape, morale booster.

The 3 am Go-To Gang—Sangeet, Tulika, Nutan, Nikki, Reena, Rita, Simran, Madhu Popli, Geeta, Shivshakti, Anju, Archana, Avantika, Jagdish Arora ji & Co—for those never-ending midnight 'convos' and satsangs that enriched my book writing and that sometimes made us look less the practitioners of Amritvela, more a bunch of many a Vela.

Shaurya and Ajay, for being the Back-End Boys so that yours truly could be left at peace to potter with pen as the Back-of-Beyond Girl.

Team Ros Common of HPTDC, Kasauli—Ashwani Soni, U.D. Sharma, Karan Shandil & Co—for the warm hospitality.

Thanks to Hari ji, Pyarelal ji, Bhoop Singh ji, Harvinder, Jaikishen, Jaggu, Gopal, Jassi, Mahinder, Titu, Manku, and Naresh bhaiyas for refuelling the last leg of my book, not with butter chicken legs but with lean-legged Lingdu and folksy 'food for thought', Kheru to Baathu ki Kheer. Also, ever indebted to the entire team for saving yours truly from imminent attacks by Lockdown-famished langurs and monkeys in the middle of penning the book, so that my intellectual property rights didn't go intestate. And, I survived the tailed threats to tell my tale, hopefully in fine taste.

Aman Kashyap, Anil Dayal, Kuldip Dhiman, Viney Sharma, Dhavneet Dheer, Saurabh Duggal & Co, for support in navigating digital, legal, infrastructural or structural speed-breakers.

All my teachers, mentors, and gurus, for shaping me to walk the write path. Commander Sharma uncle, for resonating the reassuring ring of my dearest Guruji Maharaj that calmed my last-minute butterflies in the belly and birthing pangs of the book.

Last but not the least, a huge shout-out to my Humourista twin Indu Balachandran. At a time whilst she was neck-deep in shattering glass ceilings at *NYT*, when I needed her to fish out some documents for my reference, she pronto ran the risk of shattering glass in the process of scaling that other ceiling—The Attic!

Chetna Keer
Chandigarh, 2022

About the Author

Chetna Keer is a humourista at *LIFE*, columnist at *Hindustan Times*, satirist at Khushwant Singh HumourFest 2020; and conversationist at TED Circles.

Author of two books, *Veggies Go On A Beauty Parade* (Rupa) and *Trollitically Incorrect*, and humour column *Witerati* (*HT*), she has also penned Pandemic poetry that was broadcast on AIR ESD and podcast *Subtle Lyrics*.

Chandigarh-bred Chetna navigated Planet Print Media for nearly quarter of a century, as Features Writer to Lifestyle Editor, with *The Tribune*, 'Simply Punjabi' of *India Today*, *HT*, *Deccan Herald*, *Femina*, etc.

Twenty-five years later (or late!), this aborted economist trotted off to turn Travelista, becoming part of shows like *Destination India* and *Tasveer* on AIR, FM Gold etc. The economy's gain was travelogue writings' S-pain.

When not juggling brats and cats, Chetna dons other hats. When there looked little signs of her making it to certain dream B-Lists, she refashioned herself to join that other B-List—bloggers' list. Enter, Saree Revivalist@Blogging.

Realising she wields zero influence with Brats to Bais, she next dreams of inflicting herself on the world as the newest 'IN' thing—INFLUENCER.

She can be contacted at:

Twitter: @chetna_keer

Instagram: @witerati_chetna.keer; @chicerati_chetna.keer

LinkedIn: @Chetna Keer

Readomania

Readomania exists to nurture, curate, and bring to you content you love. We are a publishing house that takes pride in encouraging talent, new or old, and provide a wonderful platform for awesome stories.

We make this possible in multiple ways.

First, as an independent publishing house. Readomania boasts of multiple imprints across various categories—fiction, nonfiction, children, to name a few. An eclectic mix of content for its readers, when you read a Readomania title, you enter a world that's yours, supported by unique and quality narratives.

Second, as an online publishing platform for writers—a place to share stories, poems, opinions, travelogues, a way to explore your creative talent. Available as premium, as well as free-to-read content across multiple genres, the reader is spoilt for choice.

Join us in this journey, as we explore, develop, and present stories to our readers and audiences. Welcome to the world of Readomania, get ready to craft stories that enrich lives.

You can visit us at: www.readomania.com